MANY DEADLY RETURNS

One word was all Rider said. "Bodine." Without hesitation, the bartender pointed to a big man seated at a table, relieved that it was not his name this messenger of death had called out.

Bodine, having heard his name in the silent barroom, instinctively reached under the table when he recognized the tall scout. He brought his pistol up, aimed and cocked, ready to shoot. Ignoring the weapon threatening him, Rider walked up to stand over the table. Bodine grinned. "Well, look who's here. What the hell do you want?"

"Johnny Hawk says hello," Rider pronounced, his voice low and lethal. He grabbed the edge of the table and turned it upside down on Bodine, sending him and his chair crashing to the floor. By the time Bodine pulled the trigger, his pistol was aimed straight up at the ceiling. Before he could pull it again, his wrist was pinned against the floor by Rider's foot. Desperate to free his gun hand, he clawed at Rider's leg with his other hand. His eyes wild with fright, he looked into the cold dark eyes of his executioner. . . .

RIDE THE HIGH RANGE

Charles G. West

A SIGNET BOOK

SIGNET
Published by New American Library, a division of
Penguin Group (USA) Inc., 375 Hudson Street,
New York, New York 10014, USA
Penguin Group (Canada), 90 Eglinton Avenue East, Suite 700, Toronto,
Ontario M4P 2Y3, Canada (a division of Pearson Penguin Canada Inc.)
Penguin Books Ltd., 80 Strand, London WC2R 0RL, England
Penguin Ireland, 25 St. Stephen's Green, Dublin 2,
Ireland (a division of Penguin Books Ltd.)
Penguin Group (Australia), 250 Camberwell Road, Camberwell, Victoria 3124,
Australia (a division of Pearson Australia Group Pty. Ltd.)
Penguin Books India Pvt. Ltd., 11 Community Centre, Panchsheel Park,
New Delhi - 110 017, India
Penguin Group (NZ), 67 Apollo Drive, Rosedale, North Shore 0632,
New Zealand (a division of Pearson New Zealand Ltd.)
Penguin Books (South Africa) (Pty.) Ltd., 24 Sturdee Avenue,
Rosebank, Johannesburg 2196, South Africa

Penguin Books Ltd., Registered Offices:
80 Strand, London WC2R 0RL, England

First published by Signet, an imprint of New American Library,
a division of Penguin Group (USA) Inc.

First Printing, December 2010
10   9   8   7   6   5   4   3   2   1

For Ronda

Chapter 1

"Moran!" Henry Butcher called out, then waited for the boy to pull his horse up even with his.

Jim Moran nudged his horse into a gentle lope and passed the other riders in the twelve-man raiding party plodding a dusty road that followed the Solomon River. When he reached the head of the column he pulled in and looked expectantly at Butcher. "You call me, Captain?" As leader of the gang of raiders, Henry Butcher liked to be called captain, although he had no rank, and in reality, no military standing in the Confederate army.

"Yeah," Butcher replied. "Ride on up ahead and see what's farther up this river. Me and the rest of the boys will stop here for a spell to water the horses." This was not the first time he had sent Jim ahead as a scout since leaving the remnants of Quantrill's Raiders behind in Missouri. The young boy, barely fourteen years of age when he had joined Quantrill's band a year and a half ago, was a perfect choice to reconnoiter the countryside ahead when approaching a town or crossroads. Jim had a sharp eye, and with his smooth cheeks and dark hair, he displayed a picture of innocence that gave no cause for suspicion in the event he ran into the local law or a Union patrol. Adding to that, the boy appeared to be fearless. Judging by the wheat fields on either side of the road, Butcher knew they were approaching civilization of some kind, hopefully a community ripe for the picking.

"Yes, sir," Jim replied, and pushed on ahead. It had been six months since they had received word that Lee had surrendered and the war was over. Butcher had insisted that General Lee might have surrendered the Army of Northern Virginia, but the war was still going on in Missouri. So they had continued their particular brand of guerrilla warfare—bushwhacking small Union patrols, attacking stage coaches and robbing trains—all of which helped cripple the Union forces according to Butcher. Their activities, though small in perspective, had attracted the Union army's attention, resulting in a concentrated effort to run them to ground. As a result, Missouri had become too hot for them and was the reason Jim Moran found himself on this late fall afternoon astride a weary sorrel gelding on a dusty road north of Salina, Kansas.

Butcher had sworn that he would keep raiding if he had to ride to Montana to stay ahead of the troops hunting them. Some of the men were talking about calling it off and going back to whatever was left of their homes. Butcher, a flint-hard brute of a man, had suggested that such talk was treason and would be dealt with accordingly. In spite of this, three of their original fifteen had slipped away in the night, leaving them to be a force of a dozen men. Butcher was furious, but because of an increase in Union patrols chasing the raiders, he was reluctant to turn back to search for the deserters.

Jim gave this a lot of thought as he rode along the river road. He was thinking that maybe he should have gone with the three who took off. One of them, Amos Barfield, had told Jim that the real war was over, and they were now no more than a gang of common outlaws, and Butcher knew it. Jim had a lot of respect for Amos. He was a little older than the others and not half so wild when it came to killing and burning. Amos had shown a special interest in the naive young man who had shown up one day near the Marais des Cygnes River in Linn County, Missouri, squirrel gun in hand, to volunteer to ride with Quantrill's Raiders. Upon talking to the boy, Amos soon learned that Jim held no motives beyond answering the call to defend his homeland after the war had claimed the life of his father at Vicksburg, and he had traveled all the way from his home in Tennessee to find Quantrill. The notorious Rebel guerrilla leader was killed in May 1865, and it had been Jim's lot to end up riding with a remnant band that had split off from the original. Although young and inexperienced, Jim was welcomed by Henry Butcher to join his ragtag gang of ruffians. The more Jim thought about it, the more convinced he became that he should have listened to Amos Barfield. He was right about Henry Butcher, Jim decided; he was little more than a common bushwhacker and a bully who intimidated his followers with fear. There was a difference between ambushing Union patrols and riding roughshod over small civilian settlements, and Jim had decided that the latter was not to his liking.

Back on the banks of the Solomon River, Butcher's men took advantage of the time to rest while Jim was scouting the countryside ahead. Joe Coons, a short stocky man of thirty-four years of age, took it upon himself to build a small fire to boil some coffee. Joe was unofficially second in command and had always been the first to back any plan Butcher came up with. "We'll have us a little coffee in a minute or two," he announced as Butcher settled himself on the ground beside the fire.

After the horses were watered, the rest of the men gathered around to partake in the pot of boiling coffee. Joe gazed around the circle at the gaunt faces, evidence of their desperate endeavor to stay one step ahead of their Union antagonists. Maybe it was time, he thought. Maybe Amos and the others had been right. It was a treasonous thought and he hesitated to mention it to Butcher, but he was noticing signs from the other men of a definite lack of dedication to the original cause. It had been over three weeks since they had held up that train depot and they were all short of supplies and ammunition. "You know, Henry," he started reluctantly, "the pickin's around here is got pretty damn lean. Maybe we oughta forget about the Confederacy and go on down to Texas. I mean, hell, the war's officially over."

Joe's remark brought a squint to Butcher's eyes and an instant lowering of his heavy eyebrows as he sent a piercing gaze in Joe's direction. Before Butcher answered, Quincy spoke out. "I been thinkin' 'bout that myself. Hell, this damn war was over when Lee surrendered. It'd be a lot safer down Texas or Mexico way, I reckon, but Montana's where the gold is." His comment captured the attention of the others gathered around, causing some nodding and grunts of agreement, as well as a darkening scowl from their leader.

"Maybe you boys are thinkin' somebody else oughta be callin' the shots," Butcher replied, his voice low and carrying a warning. His words were aimed mostly in Quincy's direction, for he had pegged him to be the most dangerous challenge to his authority.

"Ah, hell no," Joe Coons quickly responded, however. "No such a thing, Henry. You're the boss." He glanced around him for support. The others were equally as quick to respond with signs of reassurance. No one of them was anxious to challenge Butcher's authority. "I was just sayin' that, since we're really raiding just for profit right now, we might as well go somewhere where the damn army ain't lookin' for us."

"That's all we're sayin'," Quincy added, somewhat indifferently. "You're the boss. Just thought it's about time to think about movin' on to someplace where they don't know us."

Butcher continued glowering at them for a minute or two while he considered what Billy and Quincy had suggested. It had in fact never crossed his mind to give up the pretense of carrying on the war, but what they said made sense. He relaxed his scowl and said, "Well, as a matter of fact, I was plannin' to do just that very thing, but we need one more good raid for supplies first. Maybe there's a town up the road where we can take care of that." His announcement was met with approval by all, and an instant lightening of the somber mood.

"Yonder comes the kid," one of the men called out.

"Good," Butcher answered, "we'll see what we've got now."

Jim hopped down from the saddle and turned the sorrel loose to drink. "Come on over and get you some coffee, boy," Joe said.

Butcher gave him only a few seconds before demanding, "Well, what did you see? Is there a town up there?"

"Nossir," Jim replied as he held his cup out while Tom Banks poured. "There ain't nothin' but a right good-sized farm—nice house and a big barn, but there ain't nothin' we'd want to bother with. Just peaceful folks tryin' to make a livin'."

"The hell you say," Butcher responded. "Sounds like easy pickin's to me—just what we're lookin' for. We'll ride in there and take what we need."

Jim was not comfortable with the response. The scene he had discovered was a typical family farm—a man and his two sons working to clean out some hedgerows between two fields, his wife and daughter picking late beans from the fall garden. He felt compelled to express his opinion. "They're peaceful folks. They don't have nothin' to do with the war."

"Well, by God, they do now," Butcher replied with a wicked smile upon his face.

Seconding his boss as usual, Joe said, "They most likely fed a lot of Yankee soldiers with all the wheat raised in them fields we passed. It's time they paid for it."

Jim was suddenly sickened by the gleeful reaction of the men, all anticipating an easy romp over this Kansas family. He remembered then something that Amos Barfield had said. "You watch. Pretty soon they'll be stealin', rapin', and murderin' with no conscience at all."

"This ain't right," Jim stated. "I don't want no part in it."

His comment received an immediate response from Butcher. "I'm the one says what's right and what ain't," he roared, glaring at Jim. "Why, you ain't much more than a snot-nosed kid. This is war! What the hell do you know about what's right?"

"I know this ain't right," Jim calmly replied, and turned at once to go to his horse.

"Grab him!" Butcher shouted. A couple of the men reached for him, but they were not quick enough to stop him from reaching his horse and galloping away with just one foot in the stirrup. "Shoot him!" Butcher commanded when Jim headed back toward the farm. In the confusion, several of the men scrambled to get off a shot, hoping for a lucky hit, but Jim was already beyond the accurate range of their revolvers.

"Dammit!" Quincy exclaimed in anger when he missed with his revolver. "That damn boy is gonna warn 'em!"

"Get after him!" Butcher ordered. "He might warn 'em, but we'll be right behind him, so they ain't gonna have much time to do anything about it." All twelve were soon on his heels.

"Come on, boy," Jim implored as the tired sorrel's hooves pounded the dirt with a steady tattoo, giving

the best it had to offer. He looked over his shoulder
at the gang of riders gradually shortening the distance
between them, their horses fresher than his. He was
determined to warn the innocent folks of the hell that
was about to descend upon them. At the same time he
was reprimanding himself for not choosing to see the
obvious evidence before that Butcher's gang had trans-
formed from Confederate guerrilla fighters to common
outlaws. "Don't let me down, boy," he encouraged the
rapidly failing horse.

The house and barn were in sight now, but Butcher
and his men were charging no more than one hundred
yards behind him. Galloping into the barnyard, he
heard shots from his pursuers and realized that the men
he had ridden with for a year and a half were trying to
kill him. "Take cover!" he shouted. "They're comin'!"
But he saw no one in the field or garden where they
had been before. "Grab your guns!" he yelled. "Raiders! Raiders!" He could hear Butcher right behind him
as they poured into the yard.

He wasn't sure what happened next until some
time later. At that moment, he vaguely remembered
a glimpse of the barn doors opening and a wave of
Union soldiers flowing out and the popping of rifles
as the sorrel went down head first, throwing him from
the saddle. Unable to move for a few seconds until his
brain stopped spinning around in his head, he finally
attempted to get to his feet in an effort to gain cover
behind the carcass of his horse. He had taken no more
than two steps when he was slammed in the shoulder
by a rifle slug, spinning him around before landing
him on the ground again. Trapped in the cross fire be-

tween his former companions and the Union soldiers, he was forced to lie where he was, next to his dead horse, while a swarm of hot lead flew overhead.

Riding at the head of his gang, Henry Butcher was the first to slide from his saddle, fatally wounded. "It's a trap!" Joe Coons yelled as he backed his horse while emptying his six-gun at the charging cavalry. In the chaos that followed, two of the outlaws fell from their saddles as the raiders tried to retreat. Taken completely by surprise, the outlaws could do little but scatter, every man for himself, but in the confusion of horses bumping into each other amid the cursing and shouting of their riders, they were easy targets for the soldiers' rifles. Only four of the twelve-man gang managed to escape to scatter across the Kansas countryside, and only one was able to effectively return fire. Quincy managed to get off one shot, killing one of the soldiers before he fled with the others.

Lieutenant Jared Carrington stood over the body of the fallen soldier as his men checked the bodies of the outlaws. He was far more irritated than sad to have lost a man in the ambush. He looked at the unfortunate occurrence as a mark against his ability to take care of his men. "This'un's alive, Lieutenant," a soldier called out, and raised his Spencer carbine to finish the job. He hesitated before pulling the trigger. "He don't look much more'n a boy," he said after a closer look at the thin mustache and scraggly beard on the otherwise smooth face.

The lieutenant walked over to look down at Jim, whose revolver was still in his holster. He quickly reached down and pulled the weapon and tossed it to a short stump of a man dressed in a fringed buckskin shirt and trousers. "Boy or not," the lieutenant said, "if he's old enough to shoot at us, he's old enough to hang."

Johnny Hawk turned the Colt Army model revolver over in his hands, examining it before he spoke. "This here weapon ain't been fired no time lately. It's stone cold." He continued to gaze down at the wounded boy, who was now staring back defiantly. "From where I was over yonder by the porch," he continued, pointing at the farmhouse, "it looked more like he was being chased—and he was hollerin' somethin' like 'grab your guns'—almost like he was tryin' to warn these folks."

Lieutenant Carrington gave the elflike scout's words a few moments' thought before deciding. "It sure looked to me like he was leading the attack." He shrugged indifferently. "At any rate, he was riding with them, so we'll take him on back to Fort Riley for trial." He ordered two troopers to take Jim over by the barn to guard him while the rest of the patrol chased after the four escapees. He then went back to the house to reassure the Thompson family that they were safe.

An interested bystander to this point, Johnny Hawk studied the wounded boy carefully. He didn't strike the scout as typical of the trash who rode with the outlaw bands. He followed the soldiers over to the barn. "I'll take a look at the boy's wound," he said. "See how bad it is."

"Suit yourself," one of the soldiers said. "I wouldn't waste my time."

Jim sat down with his back against the wall of the barn, his shoulder now starting to throb. Still, he had not spoken a word, resigning himself to the turn of events that had placed him in this situation. His two guards made themselves comfortable on one side of him, content to be spared further time in the saddle. Jim glanced up when the scout stood over him for a few moments. "Let me take a look at that there wound," Johnny said. When Jim made no reply, he asked, "You ain't gonna bite, are you?" Jim paused for a second, considering the gray-bearded little man before slowly shaking his head. "You was pretty wild lookin' when you come chargin' in here," Johnny continued. "Looked like you was bein' chased yourself."

"I was," Jim said, speaking for the first time.

"Now, why would I wanna believe a tale like that?" Johnny asked, just to test the boy's reaction.

"It doesn't make much difference whether you believe it or not, does it?" Jim replied stoically.

Johnny studied the clear dark eyes that met his gaze defiantly, never blinking or avoiding contact. He had a feeling about the boy, yet he was not one to be easily misled. "Why was that bunch chasin' you?" he asked. "They were all your friends, weren't they? How come they was shootin' at you?"

Jim merely shrugged, convinced that nothing he said would be believed, so Johnny pressed further. "It wasn't like you was tryin' to warn these folks here." Jim did not reply, but his eyes confirmed what Johnny suspected. He finished tying Jim's bandanna across the boy's shoulder and under his arm, then stood up to fix him with his gaze. "I figure you was tryin' to warn these folks before that bunch hit 'em. Is that about the size of it?"

Jim's expression shifted from one of morose resignation to that of mild surprise, causing him to wonder why the scout was even interested enough to question him. "That's about the size of it," he replied, and studied the curious man intently. He was an odd little man, standing a hair under five feet tall, Jim estimated. His face was covered from his ears on down with a gray set of whiskers. And his lower jaw protruded beyond his upper lip, causing a prominent display of the lone front tooth on the bottom. Jim was reminded of a picture of a leprechaun in a book his grandfather had once been reading.

"What's your name, son?" Johnny asked.

Jim hesitated, wondering if he should tell him or not, before finally stating, "Jim Moran, Quantrill's Raiders."

Johnny nodded thoughtfully. "Quantrill, huh? How long have you been ridin' with this bunch that chased you in here?" Little by little he was able to increase the boy's responses until finally he was successful in piecing together Jim's history as a member of Quantrill's Raiders. The conversation was ignored by Jim's guards, who were unconcerned with the guilt or innocence of the prisoner. Johnny continued, "So you found yourself ridin' with a gang of outlaws after the war was over?"

"That's about it," Jim said, as Lieutenant Carrington came from the house, accompanied by William Thompson, effectively ending Johnny Hawk's interrogation.

His two guards jumped to their feet as the officer approached and Johnny stepped aside.

"So that's one of the scum that was plannin' to murder my family!" Thompson blurted as he marched up to stand over Jim. "Why, he ain't much older than my boy, Edgar." He turned to Carrington. "What are you gonna do with him?"

"We'll take him back to Fort Riley for trial," the lieutenant answered.

Thompson looked around at the bodies lying in his farmyard before asking, "Why don't you just shoot him now . . . or hang him? I've got plenty of good rope in the barn and a stout beam to string it over."

"That would be a lot less trouble for me, but I'm afraid I can't do that," Carrington replied. "I have to take him back to be tried." He glanced down at Jim. "I've no doubt they'll hang him afterward for killing one of my men. I can understand how you feel, but that's the way it'll have to be unless he tries to escape. Then I guess we'll have reason to shoot him." The last comment was for Jim's benefit, in case he might be entertaining thoughts of escape.

Thompson, staring down again at Jim, goaded him. "Why don't you try to escape, boy? Just take off runnin'. Maybe they'll miss." He punctuated his taunting with a kick to Jim's leg.

Silent until that moment, Johnny Hawk decided to speak. "I can understand why you got your backbone up, mister, but you're maybe owing to this young feller more'n you think. He was tryin' to head them outlaws off and warn you and your family."

Thompson immediately looked to Carrington for

confirmation, but the lieutenant simply shrugged, unconvinced himself. "How do you know that?" Thompson asked Johnny then. "Is that what he told you? Hell, he'd say anything to save gettin' his neck stretched."

"Mostly that's what I saw for myself, since he was so far ahead of the others, and the shootin' had already started before the soldiers came chargin' outta the barn." He reached up and stroked his chin whiskers as if giving the matter serious thought. "Add to that the fact that I just bandaged his wound, and the bullet went in the back of his shoulder . . . tells me he wasn't hardly hit by a shot from the barn."

The scout's comments were enough to give the lieutenant pause, but he was still reluctant to accept Johnny's version of the events just witnessed in the barnyard. After a few moments' consideration, he said, "That's not my responsibility to decide. We'll let a judge decide. All I know for sure is that he came charging in here at the head of that outlaw gang and one of my men was killed. Somebody will have to pay for that." He grinned at Johnny Hawk then. "I believe you're getting softhearted in your old age, Johnny. Maybe that's the reason you said this was your last patrol for the army."

"Maybe so," Johnny replied with a chuckle. He had no intention of scouting for the army six years ago when he passed through Fort Riley on his way back to the high country in Montana. Recognized by the commanding officer, who had employed him as a scout some years before in Wyoming Territory, he had been persuaded to accompany a regimental campaign against a hostile band of Sioux. He had been threatening to quit and head west ever since. This time he had made it final. Now he was asking himself why he gave a damn one way or the other what the army did with this wounded young man. It just struck him that somehow it didn't seem fair to hang him when he was convinced that Jim had been trying to do what he thought was right. He decided to make one more attempt to influence Carrington's decision. "You know, Lieutenant, that boy ought'n be treated no different from any other prisoner of war, and most of them has already been let go to go back home. Hell, there was a whole lot of boys—boys younger'n him—that fought with the Rebs durin' the war."

"This is different," Carrington replied, obviously weary of discussing the matter. "This was no military unit he was riding with. He's no more than a common outlaw, and young or not, he has to answer to a court. Then it's their decision as to what punishment is justified."

Johnny nodded, thinking that Carrington's stance was typical of most military points of view. Like so many officers, the lieutenant seemed incapable of thinking outside *the book*, when he could just as easily have let the boy go and no harm done. *Well*, he thought, *it ain't no concern of mine. Maybe Carrington's right. Maybe if he let him go, the boy might sneak back and take a few potshots at the soldiers.* He returned his thoughts to his decision to quit his job as an army scout. "I reckon this little business is finished," he said to the lieutenant. "You don't need me no more. You'll be headin' back to Riley when your men get back, and I expect I'll be headin' the other way. By the way, your prisoner's name is Jim Moran, in case you wanna know."

"Jim Moran, huh?" Carrington responded, making a mental note of it. "You sure you won't change your mind?" he asked. "You're the best damn scout in the regiment, and you're not ready to retire yet. What are you gonna do?"

"I've got a heavy cravin' for the high mountains," Johnny replied. "This flatland gets to a man after a while, and I wanna see some things I ain't seen yet while my eyes are still sharp enough to see 'em." He didn't mention the strong desire to see a wife who waited for him in a Crow village near Fort Laramie. It had been over a year since he had seen her and he wasn't too old to have cravings in that direction as well.

"I guess there's no use trying to convince you to stay," Carrington said, and extended his hand. "Good luck. I hope you find what you're looking for." He was sincere in his wishes. He had never ridden with a scout as capable as Johnny Hawk.

"Thank you, Lieutenant," Johnny said. "Same to you." He cast one more brief glance in Jim's direction before turning to leave. The boy nodded in response as if to express his appreciation for the scout's efforts, and Johnny returned the nod in acknowledgment. Then he walked briskly away to collect his horses, a spotted gray and a sorrel packhorse.

Carrington turned his attention back to his prisoner, who was still sitting quietly with his back against the barn wall. He studied him for a moment, Johnny Hawk's words still in his mind. Maybe the scout was right about the boy. He quickly discarded the thought, once again deciding there was no alternate course of action for him. "Maybe you'd better tie his hands behind his back," he told the two privates. Then he changed his mind. "Might be too painful for him with that shoulder wound, though." He hesitated, thinking the prisoner should be bound in some way. "Tie his hands, just leave them in front."

"'Preciate it," Jim said, surprising the lieutenant. His shoulder was already throbbing. It would have been uncomfortable indeed to have his arms tied behind his back.

"Don't get the idea I'm going to be easy on you because of your age," Carrington quickly responded. "You're just a common thief and murderer as far as I'm concerned, and the court will deal with you appropriately."

It was late in the afternoon by the time the rest of the patrol returned to the Thompson farm, horses hot and weary from the chase. Much to Carrington's disappointment, none of the four escapees were captured. After the bodies of the outlaws were tied across the saddles of their horses, it was too late to start back to the fort that day, so the lieutenant gave orders to make camp at the edge of the barnyard, leaving the outlaws' horses to carry their loads overnight. Fires were built and the troopers prepared their supper. Extra coffee and fresh-baked biscuits were provided by Esther Thompson, much to the delight of the soldiers. With Thompson's permission, the prisoner was locked in the smokehouse behind the barn with one soldier stationed at the door as guard.

Inside the house, William Thompson sat down by the stove to finish his coffee, conversing with his wife about the excitement of the day. "I reckon we can thank the Lord that the soldiers knew that gang was headin' our way," he said. "Four of 'em got away, but I doubt they'll stop till they get to Texas. I hope they're plannin' on leavin' out of here early in the mornin', though. All them dead bodies might start to stink before long."

A compassionate woman, Esther Thompson expressed a curious thought about the prisoner. "You said that wounded man wasn't much more than a boy."

"That's a fact," her husband responded, "maybe a year or two older than Edgar."

At that moment, Edgar and his younger brother came in from the yard where they had been talking to the soldiers as the troopers ate their evening meal. Still thinking about the prisoner, their mother asked, "Did anybody feed that boy in the smokehouse?"

"I don't know," Edgar replied. "I don't think so—least I didn't see nobody takin' no food to the smokehouse. Did you, Peter?" His brother shook his head.

Noticing the look of concern on his wife's face, William said, "I'm sure the soldiers know what to do about their prisoner. Anyway, it ain't none of our business. I still think they oughta just shot him and been done with it."

"Edgar heard them talking about what that funny-looking little man dressed like an Indian said," Esther went on. "He thinks the boy was trying to warn us. What if he was? And him sittin' out there in that dark ol' smokehouse."

"Esther," her husband insisted, "it ain't for us to worry about."

"I don't care if he is a Rebel," she firmly announced. "There's no reason to starve the boy."

"Esther . . ." William protested, but she ignored him. Taking a couple of biscuits from a plate on the kitchen table, she then went to the pump, filled a fruit jar with water, and proceeded out the door.

Over by the fire at the edge of the yard, Lieutenant Carrington paused when he saw the woman heading toward the smokehouse behind the barn. Placing his cup on the ground next to his saddle, he quickly cut through the barn to head her off. "Mrs. Thompson," he called, "we're holding the prisoner in the smokehouse. Is there something in there you need?"

"I know you've got that boy in there," she answered. "Did you give him anything to eat?"

"Well, ah, no," Carrington stammered. It hadn't occurred to him, and the prisoner had not complained.

"Well, there's no need to starve the boy. Here's some water and a couple of cold biscuits." She handed them to the guard by the smokehouse door. "Give him these," she said, then turned to leave.

"Yes, ma'am," the private said, and slid the bar back to open the door.

"Thank you, ma'am." The words came softly from the darkened building, causing Esther to pause a moment before continuing back to the house. She shook her head slowly, thinking of her own son, and how the mother of this boy must be worrying herself sick wondering if her son was safe that night.

Inside the windowless little outbuilding, the object of her concern eagerly accepted the food from the guard. There was no mother worrying about him. She had left him with his grandfather and gone to Nashville when his father went off to war. He had heard nothing from her since, and there was no mention of her in his grandfather's house. The old man had never had much respect for his daughter-in-law, and felt justified in his opinion of her when she abandoned her son.

Trying to take his mind off his aching shoulder, he thought about how quickly his fortunes had changed— from bad to worse, he had to admit. The words of warning from Amos Barfield returned to his thoughts. He had cautioned him about the designs of Butcher and Joe Coons, but he had told him to be especially careful about Quincy. "That man's got a black heart," he said. "He'll likely move to take over the leadership of the gang, and he'll probably have to kill Butcher, and maybe Joe, to do it." Jim remembered then, looking back over his shoulder and seeing the first gun aimed at him in Quincy's hand. Less than twenty-four hours before this moment, he had harbored no ideas of betraying the band of guerrillas he had ridden with for a year and a half. Even with the turn of events that now placed him in custody of a Union cavalry patrol, however, he knew that what he had done was the right thing. He never considered himself anything less than a warrior, and although he had been slow in realizing it, the war was over. And yet he had no intention of being incarcerated in a federal prison, so escape was foremost in his mind. He resigned himself to wait for the opportunity, for there was none for him under the present circumstances.

*   *   *

The hours passed slowly as he sat in the dark hut, listening to the sounds outside that told him the noisy camp was gradually winding down to sleep. Finally all was silent until he heard the changing of the guard outside the door, and he guessed that it was probably midnight. He could hear nothing but the shuffling around of the new guard for a few minutes; then the quiet returned, broken only a short time later by the sound of snoring. It would have been his opportunity to escape, had not the smokehouse door been bolted on the outside. He settled down once more, trying to sleep.

His attempts to sleep proved hopeless, however, so he sat and waited for morning, hoping there would be some time when he could make a run for it. It couldn't have been much more than an hour when he heard the bolt slide back on the door. A moment later, the door swung slowly open with a soft complaint from the rusty hinges. Framed in the opening, silhouetted by the moonlight behind him, stood the short, square form of Johnny Hawk. "Come on," he whispered, "let's get outta here before the guard wakes up." He then drew a knife from his belt and stepped into the hut. After making quick work of the rope binding Jim's wrists, he whispered, "Can you stand up all right?"

Astonished by the sudden appearance of the little man, Jim replied without hesitation, "I sure can," and got to his feet.

"Be quick and don't make a sound," Johnny cautioned, "'cause if that guard wakes up, it's gonna be hell to pay for both of us."

Outside in the moonlit barnyard, Jim paused to look at the guard sleeping peacefully by the door while Johnny carefully closed the door and slid the bolt back to lock it. Then motioning to Jim to follow, he led him around behind the smokehouse and across a field. Once on the other side of the field, they headed toward the river where Jim could see the dark forms of horses in the trees. It was not until they had reached the riverbank that Johnny spoke again to the mystified boy following him. "Well, I reckon it's up to you, but you can stick with me if you're of a mind to," he said. "I got you some things you'll be needin'—a horse and a rifle, some cartridges."

"Mister, I don't know how to thank you, and I reckon I don't know why you did it," Jim said. "I thought you rode scout for the army."

"I did," Johnny replied, "but there ain't no doubt in my mind that you was tryin' to warn them folks about that bunch of outlaws. Was I right?"

"You were."

"Well, then, it don't make no sense to haul you off to jail. And once them military courts got to hemmin' and hawin', they mighta decided to string you up. Hell, the war is over—don't matter which side you fought for. It's over and done."

"Well, sir, I 'preciate it. I surely do, and I'll take you up on that offer to go with you, as long as it's away from here."

"Not a'tall," Johnny replied. "Come on, we'd best get ourselves goin' then. Right now I expect we'd best ride till we get to a place where I can take a look at that wound again." He started toward the trees and the horses. "I took the liberty of borrowin' a horse from the army for you. I figure it didn't belong to the army, anyway, so it ain't like we stole it. We need to unload him first, though."

In the darkness among the trees, Jim had not noticed that the horse behind Johnny's saddle horse and his pack animal had a body draped across the saddle. Johnny explained that there hadn't been time to dump the body, saying that he was lucky just to be able to lead the horse away from the others without being caught. Leading the buckskin out into the moonlight, Jim could not help being startled when he recognized the corpse of Henry Butcher. After Johnny cut the rope tied under the buckskin's belly, Jim took hold of Butcher's feet and shoved him off on the ground, causing the horse to sidestep away from the falling body. To Jim's way of thinking, it was a sign that the animal was expressing its contempt for the bully. Johnny waited for Jim to climb into the saddle, then turned his horse toward the river, heading for the other side.

Chapter 2

It struck Jim as ironic that he was now riding Henry Butcher's horse, for he had always admired the buckskin for its strength and stamina, often putting his faithful old sorrel to shame when it came to long marches or difficult terrain. Butcher had often bragged about the buckskin, saying it had better bones and harder feet than other breeds. Accustomed to a cruel master, the horse seemed a bit nervous at first, as if unsure of what his new master required. Jim felt pleased for the horse, knowing that he would now be treated a great deal better than he had been in the past. It didn't take long for the horse to realize it, and the two of them developed a partnership by the time Johnny picked a place to camp just before sunup.

"Lemme get a fire built and some coffee made, and I'll take a look at that hole in your shoulder," Johnny said.

Jim tried to help out as best he could with one hand, but about the most he could do was gather wood for the fire and water the horses. After that, he was reduced to sitting down and watching his rescuer go about cooking some breakfast for the two of them. He could not help being fascinated by the mysterious little man, dressed in animal skins as he fried up bacon and beans. When they had finished eating, and Johnny drained the last of the coffee, he was ready to examine the wound.

"It's swelled up a-plenty," Johnny decided as he peered at the hole in Jim's shoulder. "I expect it's sore as hell." Jim confirmed that and added that it was stiff as a board as well. "I reckon I'd best dig that bullet outta there, or it ain't never gonna get well."

"Mister, I sure 'preciate everything you're doin' for me," Jim finally stated. "What I ain't been able to figure out is why."

Johnny laughed. "First off, quit callin' me mister. My name's Johnny Hawk, and to answer your question, I done told you why back there in the smokehouse. You just looked like you could use a hand. And it 'peared like I was the only one back there that believed you wasn't leadin' that gang of outlaws. Now let's see if we can't get that bullet outta your shoulder, 'cause I think you'll feel a whole helluva lot better without it." He started to sterilize his knife in the fire, but paused to ask, "What was your name, again?" He had already forgotten.

"Jim Moran."

"Well, Jim Moran, this is gonna hurt like hell."

The operation didn't take long because Johnny went after the bullet with a vengeance, figuring that it was better to get the pain over with as soon as possible. Luckily, it was not as deep as he had anticipated, but it would soon have begun to infect the tissue had he waited much longer. "I've knowed men to walk around all their lives with a chunk of lead in 'em," he said, "and no bother at all. This'un looks like it wants to fester the muscle around it. It's a good thing we're diggin' it outta there." Throughout the procedure, the boy never made a sound, except for an involuntary grunt when the bullet was removed and Johnny cauterized the wound. The pain he experienced, however, was evident by the expression on his face. Johnny was impressed. "You're a helluva man, Jim Moran, 'cause I know that hurt like a son of a bitch. But you oughta start feelin' better pretty soon."

Now that the initial pain from Johnny Hawk's none-too-gentle surgery was over, Jim was left with an aching in his shoulder, accompanied by the stinging of the cauterization. His discomfort must have been evident in his eyes, because Johnny suggested that they could both use a couple of hours' sleep before climbing back in the saddle. Jim was grateful for the suggestion.

While Jim was undergoing Johnny Hawk's crude medical procedure, some fifteen miles behind them Lieutenant Carrington was scratching his head over the mystery of the missing prisoner. A few minutes earlier, he had sent Corporal Ellis to get the prisoner. Now he and the corporal were questioning the guard about the whereabouts of the wounded young man. "The door was still locked when I went to get him," Ellis said, "but he wasn't in there. I looked around the sides, but there ain't no sign of him diggin' out under the wall, and he didn't go out the top."

Carrington just shook his head in disbelief. "When

did you come on?" When the guard replied that it had been at four o'clock, Carrington asked, "Did you hear anything inside? Any noise that would let you know he was still in there?" The guard stated that all had been quiet, causing the lieutenant to curse and say, "So there's no telling when he got out of there."

"You went to sleep, didn't you?" Ellis accused.

"No, I didn't," the guard protested. "Honest to God, Corporal, I was awake the whole time."

Carrington sent for the other men who had pulled guard duty during the night. None could report hearing any sounds from inside the smokehouse, and all swore they had not fallen asleep on their tour. The lieutenant knew at least one of them was lying, but there was no way to prove it. And since the door was still locked that morning, someone had to have walked past a sleeping guard and released the prisoner. It was impossible to know how much head start the boy had without knowing what time he had escaped. As for the boy's accomplice, the first name that came to mind was Johnny Hawk, since he had tried to speak on the boy's behalf. Another possibility was Esther Thompson, or one of her sons, since they had shown compassion for the prisoner. Giving the issue some hard thought, he had to conclude that Hawk had already left before evening, and he doubted the grizzled old scout cared enough to risk freeing the prisoner. That left the woman, and he knew there was little he could do if she denied it. To add further irritation to a morning that had already caused him undue frustration, a trooper came to report that one of the captive horses was missing along with the body that had been on it, so that told him that the fugitive was not on foot and probably miles away by now. A short time later, the missing body of Henry Butcher was discovered in the trees by the river.

The decision to be made at this point was whether or not to try to go after the prisoner. *I wish to hell Johnny Hawk had not left yesterday,* he thought. *I need him to track that boy.* He thought it over for a long moment. His patrol was low on supplies, not prepared to extend the mission. And his objective had certainly been accomplished. He had effectively stopped the raiding by this band of bushwhackers and had the bodies to prove it; unfortunately one of the bodies was that of a soldier. Coming now to influence his decision, the weather was showing indications that the past few weeks of fair skies might be coming to an end. Clouds had been rolling in since early morning and he suspected they might soon see some snow. There was little value in questioning Esther Thompson, he decided. "To hell with it," he said, and turned to Corporal Ellis. "Get the men mounted. We're going back to Riley." He couldn't help wondering, however, when he saw Esther's smiling face as she and her sons waved good-bye as the patrol passed out of the yard. In spite of his efforts to dismiss the incident in his mind, it would continue to plague his conscience.

Although he had not slept at all during the preceding night, Jim was still unable to get more than a few minutes of fitful sleep owing to the discomfort of his wound. As a consequence, he was feeling tired and sore when Johnny stirred from his blankets, ready to ride. Lieutenant Carrington had permitted Jim to take his own blanket and a few personal items from the carcass of his sorrel, which he was thankful for, since the weather was turning colder.

"We'll run into some snow before noon," Johnny predicted as he cast his blanket aside and replaced his .44 in its holster. When Jim seemed surprised to see he had slept with the revolver in his hand, he shrugged and commented, "Hell, I didn't know how far I could trust you. You mighta had some ideas about goin' on alone."

"That'd be a helluva way to thank you," Jim said. Johnny never slept with his pistol under the blanket after that. The tone of the boy's response was enough to assure him that he could trust him.

As Johnny had predicted, a light snow began to fall as they left the river and angled more toward the northwest. By nightfall, there was a small accumulation of snow on the short grass plains when they reached a small stream bordered by a line of willow trees. "Don't look like we're gonna find anythin' better before hard dark," Johnny said. "Leastways we can pull some of these willows over to make us a shed." After the horses were taken care of, he went to work bending several of the willows over and tying them together to make the framework. Next he unrolled a buffalo hide he carried on his packhorse and laid it over the willows to make a roof for his shed. In the meantime, Jim gathered enough sticks and branches to make a fire. Soon they were settled comfortably inside the makeshift hut enjoying a meal of boiled jerky, again courtesy of Johnny Hawk.

"I reckon you're wonderin' how long I'm gonna tag along with you, eatin' up all your supplies," Jim suddenly commented.

"The thought had struck me," Johnny replied.

"Some of the stiffness has already left my shoulder. I reckon I might be able to use it a little in a couple of days. I guess I could go on my own tomorrow and let you go about your business."

Johnny didn't say anything for a moment while he studied the young man's face. "Maybe you could," he finally said, "but maybe we'd better wait till mornin' and see how you saddle your horse with that lame shoulder." Jim's expression told him that he wasn't confident in his ability to use the shoulder. "Say you do take off in the mornin', where are you gonna go?"

In fact, Jim had not given it any thought. He didn't know what he was going to do or where he was heading. He just didn't want to burden Johnny any further. "I don't know," he said. "There's lots of places I ain't seen yet."

Johnny continued to study his young companion. There was something about the boy that led Johnny to believe he was made of the right kind of iron, and he always fancied himself a good judge of character. After a moment, he spoke again. "Have you seen the Yellowstone? Or Big Timber? Three Forks? Or the Musselshell?"

"Nossir, I reckon I ain't."

"Well, that's where I'm headin'—back to God's country where there's still game and fur for them that know how to find it. It's a right tough country if you don't know what you're doin'—and I expect I could use a partner. Whaddaya say?"

The invitation caught him by surprise, but there was no hesitation before he responded. "That suits me just fine—if you think you can put up with me," Jim replied. It trumped any idea he might have had of his own, and he already liked the comical little man.

Johnny extended his hand and they shook on it. "All right, Jim Moran . . ." He paused then. "I don't know if they'll still be lookin' for you or not, but I'm sorry to say they know your name and they wanna hang you for the death of that soldier. So maybe you oughta use another name just to be safe, especially when we get to Fort Laramie. You think of any name you'd want?"

The necessity of a name change had not occurred to Jim. He thought it over for a few moments while Johnny patiently waited. There was his mother's maiden name, but he wasn't inclined to recall that unpleasant period of his life. His father's middle name was Percy, so that was out. Finally he replied that he couldn't think of any alias at the moment.

"Well, I'm gonna call you *Rider*, 'cause that's where we hooked up, where Rider Creek empties into the Solomon River. All right with you?"

"I don't care," Jim replied.

It took a full week, maintaining a steady northwest course over grasslands blanketed with a six-inch snowfall, before the gaunt buildings of North Platte appeared in the distance. Located at the confluence of the North Platte and the South Platte rivers, the town had only a few permanent structures but appeared to show a bustling population since the last time Johnny Hawk had ridden through. They soon found out the reason.

The Union Railroad had just recently completed their tracks to that point and the men that Jim and Johnny saw milling about were camped in tents along the tracks, preparing to push the line on to Ogallala in the spring.

The change was not a welcome sight to Johnny, for he had planned to spend some time there to hunt buffalo and restock their food supply. With the railroad there, he could naturally expect a passel of buffalo hunters to feed the workers, and that meant the game was more than likely hard to find. "Damn," he swore as he reined his horse up short to avoid running over a drunk who came staggering off the boardwalk in front of a saloon that hadn't been there six months before. He peered down the short street, looking for the trading post where he had previously done business. It was still there, but now it had added a shed on the back. "Well, I reckon we can get some coffee beans and some salt. I swear, I'd like to have a little drink or two while we've got the chance." Not waiting for Jim's response, he stepped down from the saddle and led his horses up to the hitching rail.

Inside the canvas walls of the tiny saloon, they found about a dozen patrons at various stages of drunkenness from near sober to near unconsciousness, the most part of them obviously railroad workers. Near the end of the bar, a trio of men were sharing a bottle of rye whiskey, and based on their loud talk and laughter, they had probably consumed all the alcohol missing from the bottle. They seemed not to notice the short, stocky man and the tall gangly boy when they stepped up to the bar. "I'm partial to corn whiskey," Johnny said, standing only a head above the level of the bar.

"I ain't got no corn whiskey," a bored bartender replied.

"Then we'll take what you've got," Johnny responded cheerfully. "How 'bout it, Rider?" he said, turning to Jim.

"I reckon," Jim responded, and the bartender filled two shot glasses.

Jim tossed the fiery liquid back and set the empty glass on the bar. When Johnny did likewise, then motioned for a refill, Jim waved the bartender off. "One's all I want," he said. He had been drunk only once in his life, and he didn't like the effect it had on his mind and body. As one who didn't like not having complete control over his faculties and reflexes, he swore never to get drunk again.

"Pour me another," Johnny told the bartender. "It's been a while since I found a saloon, so I need to do some catchin' up."

Aware of the rough-hewn appearance of the crowd of men, Jim felt some concern for his and Johnny's possessions outside on their horses. He had just gained the horse and an 1863 model Sharps carbine that had been converted to accept metal cartridges, and he wasn't comfortable leaving them unguarded on the busy thoroughfare outside. "I think I'll wait outside where I can keep an eye on the horses," he told Johnny.

"All right, partner, I'll be along directly. I just want a couple more."

Sufficiently liquored up and looking for further entertainment, one of the three railroad men took notice of the stumpy little man at the bar. The sight was especially amusing to him, and he called his friends' attention to what he figured would be a source of entertainment. They immediately responded with a howl of laughter. One of them, a large, heavy-built man with a drooping handlebar mustache, decided to take it further. "Hey, there, Shorty. Does your mama know you're in here?" His remark brought the round of laughter he hoped for.

Oblivious of the three men until that moment, Johnny turned his head unhurriedly to face the heckler. Having been the object of like remarks all of his life because of his short stature, he chose to ignore it, wanting simply to enjoy his whiskey. His reaction served to only encourage Mustache to further entertain his companions. He moved over closer to Johnny. "All dressed up in your little Injun suit. You wanna box to stand on so you can see over the bar?"

Johnny tossed his drink down before replying to the grinning bully, "No, I'm just fine right where I am, but I expect you're gonna have to get on your knees to kiss my ass. Why don't you get to it?"

The foolish grin disappeared immediately from Mustache's face. "Why, you sawed-off little bastard," he roared, and grabbed Johnny by the back of his collar. The saloon suddenly became dead silent, alerted to the possibility of a fight, most of them unconcerned about the discrepancy in size. Caught with no weapons but his fists, Johnny took a swing at his antagonist, but because of the length of his arms, was woefully short. This served to spark the laughter from the onlookers again. "Now I'm gonna teach you a lesson, Stumpy," the bully said, and drew back his fist.

"I wouldn't." The words were accompanied by the unmistakable click of a rifle being cocked. All eyes turned to discover the lanky young man standing in the doorway, a bandanna supporting one arm, and a Sharps carbine pointed at Mustache.

None could mistake the cold resolve in the boy's eyes, but Mustache attempted to bluff anyway. With his hand still clutching Johnny's collar, he blustered, "You crazy? Put that damn gun down or I'll make you eat it."

He jumped, startled, when Jim pulled the trigger and the rifle slug breezed by his face, ripping a hole in the canvas wall of the saloon. "Let him go," Jim demanded as he quickly cranked another cartridge into the chamber and brought the rifle around to point more directly at the man's chest.

"Whoa!" the bully yelled. "Wait a minute!" He quickly released Johnny's collar and backed away, convinced that it was no time to bluff. One of his two companions let his hand drop slowly toward the revolver in his belt. A slight shift of Jim's eyes brought his baleful gaze to focus on the man, enough to convince him it was not worth the gamble.

"I expect we can go now, Johnny," Jim said, his eyes still promising lightning at the first hint of movement from any of the patrons.

"Right," Johnny replied, then stepped quickly up before his antagonist, staring him in the face for a moment before bringing his foot up sharply between the man's legs. With Mustache bent over in pain, the two new partners backed cautiously out the door. They wasted no time jumping in the saddle and galloping away toward the trading post. "That went well," Johnny said when he caught up to Jim's buckskin. "With all the fuss, the bartender forgot to charge me for the whiskey."

This would be the day Johnny would remember as the first indication that he had a partner who would always watch his back. After buying some supplies, they wasted no more time in North Platte, striking out for Fort Laramie, which Johnny figured was a good six days' ride with the weather that had set in. Following the North Platte River along the trail countless immigrants had traveled on their way to Oregon, they were in the saddle three days when the weather cleared and the sun reappeared. Pushing on, they came upon a great swath trampled across their trail. "Buffalo," Johnny pronounced, "and they crossed here not long ago." Knowing they would not likely have a better opportunity for meat and hides, they immediately went in pursuit of the animals.

Jim was fascinated. He had never seen buffalo, and he was anxious to join the hunt. They followed the wide black swath in the snow for almost half a day before coming upon the rear animals in the herd. They had gathered in a low basin near the South Platte, and were milling about, snorting and pawing the snow for grass. Jim had been told before about the magnitude of the buffalo herds, but all he had heard was not sufficient to prepare him for the sight he was now seeing with his own eyes. All the way to the banks of the river, there was a wide sea of dark massive bodies, bobbing and pawing, like a black flood flowing toward the river.

Following Johnny's lead, he guided the buckskin along a ridge that formed one side of the basin until they reached a point parallel with the middle of the herd. There they left the horses and prepared to descend the ridge on foot to get a little closer to their quarry. "Here," Johnny instructed, and handed Jim a deerskin from his packhorse. "Put this over your shoulders. You're gonna have to get a helluva lot closer to do any good with that carbine."

"Won't that spook 'em?" Jim asked.

"Nah," Johnny drawled. "With that hide on your shoulders, they won't think nothin' about it. They're used to havin' wolves sniffin' around the herd, lookin' for a calf or a lame cow. With that weapon you're usin', you're gonna need to shoot 'em right behind their front legs. Try to get a lung shot—might take two or three shots to bring one of 'em down." Satisfied that Jim was all set, he then untied another deer hide from his packhorse and unrolled it to reveal his special buffalo rifle, a Remington Rolling Block .50/70, leaving his Henry in the saddle sling. "This boy'll knock 'em down," he said with a grin. "I've shot more'n a few with this here rifle."

As Johnny had advised, Jim threw the deerskin over his shoulders, and hunched over as much as possible, he moved in closer to the edge of the herd. The beasts began moving away from him, so he wasted no time in selecting his targets. Picking two young cows closest to him, he quickly pumped two shots into each of them, behind the front leg as Johnny had instructed. Matching him, Johnny dropped two also, spending only one shot on each animal. "That'll do," Johnny crowed. "That's as much meat and hides as we'll be able to handle without no more packhorses. In fact, I ain't sure but what we'll have to waste some of it."

Jim got to his feet and watched the buffalo closest to him break into a trot until moving a few dozen yards from the carcasses. Then they slowed to a walk again. "They don't even know they're bein' hunted, do they?" he commented.

"It takes more'n three or four dropping before the rest of 'em break into a run," Johnny said. He turned and started back up the ridge to get the horses. "Let's get to work skinnin' and butcherin'. Ain't no tellin' who mighta heard them shots and we're pretty much out in the open."

Jim immediately caught the urgency in his voice and hurried up the slope after him. About halfway up, Johnny turned to say, "That wasn't bad shootin' back there."

"This carbine shoots a mite high," Jim responded. "I didn't have a chance to shoot it before, so I ain't got used to it yet." Johnny didn't comment further, but he was thinking that if the two shots in each cow were any closer together, there would be but one hole.

Jim got a valuable lesson on the quickest and most efficient method of skinning a buffalo. The butchering was somewhat different than portioning a deer or an antelope, which Jim had done on many occasions, because of the size of the animal. But left alone, he would have butchered the animal the same way Johnny favored. After the hides were harvested and the best cuts of meat and the liver were packed, they left the rest to a pack of wolves that had already discovered their kill. "Everybody gets to eat," Johnny proclaimed, satisfied that there would be no waste. "Now let's get away from here. We're gonna have to find us a good place to camp for a couple days so we can cut up this meat and smoke-cure it, and then we'll have food for a good while."

They headed back toward their original trail on the North Platte, where they selected a campsite by a creek where it flowed into the river forming a small island. There was ample coverage in the willows that ringed the island to conceal them from the view of any passersby. The successful hunt was celebrated by a feast of roasted meat while they cut most of their kill into strips to be cured over the fire as the sun dried the hides staked out on the ground. It was a good time for Jim. They ended up staying at the camp for almost a week.

"We need to get you a packhorse," Johnny announced one afternoon when Jim returned from a short trip upriver to try his hand at fishing.

"How we gonna do that?" Jim wondered. "I don't have any money to buy a horse."

"The same way an Injun gets one. We'll steal it." This captured Jim's attention, and Johnny continued. "There's a couple of different bands of Injuns between here and Fort Laramie, mostly Crow, but Arapaho, too, last time I rode through. I'd prefer we steal it from Arapahos. I'm kinda partial to the Crows, since I married one a few years back."

"You married one?" Jim responded, surprised. He

tried to picture the little gnomelike man with an Indian woman. It was a picture that was hard to conjure. "What happened to her?" Jim asked.

"Oh, she's still with her people, I reckon. I ain't seen her in more'n a year—lives in Two Bulls' village. I figured on visitin' her after we get to Fort Laramie. Two Bulls usually camps between the North Platte and the Laramie River in the winter—at least he has for the last three years." He paused and grinned. "Morning Flower, you'll get to meet her if Two Bulls is campin' where he usually does." Jim made no comment, but he found the prospect of meeting *Mrs. Hawk* extremely interesting.

Quincy walked across a low rise about a quarter of a mile from the Smoky Hill River. As he walked, leading his grateful mount, he frequently looked back over his shoulder to make sure no one was following him. "That damn kid," he muttered to himself, thinking of Jim Moran, never conceding the fact that the gang of raiders would have ridden into an ambush by the soldiers regardless. The soldiers had guessed where they might strike next. Quincy blamed Butcher for that. They had damn near ridden in a straight line from Salina, hitting every farm and ranch they came to. *Hell, any damn fool could have seen that*, he thought.

As far as he could tell, only three of the others had gotten away from the ambush, and it was every man for himself. *At least I got one of the bastards*, he thought, thinking of the soldier he had shot before running. He saw Joe Coons and Ben Roberts, hightailing it off to the west, and one other, maybe Maynard, heading toward the river—he couldn't be sure, as he was pretty busy saving his ass at the time. After he lost the soldiers chasing him, he had cut back toward the west in hopes he might find Coons and Roberts at the camp they had left on the Smoky Hill. Now as he walked toward the creek, he suddenly stopped when his eye caught some movement in the cottonwoods that lined the river. Not sure if he had been spotted, he hesitated, standing behind his horse in case he was greeted with a rifle shot while he strained to see who or what might be in the trees. Maybe someone else had stumbled upon their old camp. After watching for a few moments more, he spotted a gray horse through an opening in the trees that looked like the one Joe Coons rode. He decided to risk it. There weren't many horses as downright ugly as Joe's horse.

As soon as he hailed the camp, he was met with two rifles aimed at him from the edge of the trees. Still using his horse for cover, he called out, "Joe, is that you? It's Quincy."

"Damn, it's Quincy," Coons said to Ben Roberts, relieved. "Come on in, Quincy," he called, then, and walked out in the open to meet him.

"That was a fine mess Butcher got us into back there," Quincy commented as he led his horse into the trees.

Still visibly shaken, Ben Roberts said, "I don't think but four of us got away. I saw Maynard headin' off the other way. I decided to follow after Joe—we figured Maynard might make his way back to this camp, too, but we ain't seen no sign of him."

"I'm pretty sure we're in the clear now," Joe said.

"We ain't seen no sign of any soldiers for at least a week." He shook his head and said, "I thought we was all done for back there at that farm, though."

"You boys got anythin' to eat?" Quincy asked. "I'm down to a few coffee beans and a strip of salt pork." When Ben volunteered that the two of them had a little more than that, but would need to find a new source pretty damn soon, Quincy took the lead in planning the next move. "We'd do well to move on up into Montana, where they're diggin' all that gold outta the ground. We'll find us some grub somewhere—maybe do some huntin', now that we're sure the army ain't just over the next hill." He hesitated then, thinking their reaction was not especially receptive to his proposal.

"We've been talkin' over what we're gonna do," Joe said. He paused to look at Roberts for support before continuing. "Me and Ben pretty much decided we was gonna go on back down to Texas."

"Texas?" Quincy responded, surprised. "Hell, the gold's in Montana. There ain't nothin' in Texas but cows."

"Well," Joe countered, "that's what me and Ben are good at, rustlin' cattle." A discussion on the subject followed and was soon upgraded to an argument. Quincy needed the two of them, but he could not convince them to join him, and it was already obvious to Joe that Quincy was planning on being the boss. The result was a standoff. "Well, I reckon this is where we part company, then," Joe concluded.

Plainly irritated, Quincy nevertheless said, "I reckon that's the way it's gonna be, then—no hard feelin's."

"Ah, hell no," Joe said, relieved that Quincy accepted the split-up, so much so that he failed to notice the casual drop of Quincy's hand to rest on the handle of his six-gun. Caught completely by surprise, both he and Ben were frozen for the fraction of a second that it took Quincy to draw the weapon and pump two rounds into Joe's chest, then turn and slam Ben with two in the back when he scrambled for his rifle.

Quincy moved casually over Ben as the mortally wounded man tried to crawl the last few feet to his rifle. One more shot in the back of the head finished the job. Then he went back to stand before Joe Coons while the dying man agonized through his last few seconds on earth. "Like I said," Quincy told him, "no hard feelin's, Joe. It's just business. I need your guns and your horses. I reckon I'll just have to find me a couple men up Montana way." He watched Joe for a few moments more to see how long it was going to take him to die. He could have helped him along, but he'd already spent an extra cartridge on Ben. Then he decided to end it with his knife. He was not concerned for his former partner's suffering as much as the remote possibility that he might live. He was saved the trouble, for as he drew his knife from its sheath, Joe accommodated him by expiring. "It'da been a whole lot easier if they'da just come on with me," he commented.

Chapter 3

With their horses tied in the brush below the riverbank, Jim and Johnny edged up to the top of the bluffs, where they could see the village and the horse herd beyond. After a few minutes, Johnny said, "Arapaho. Good. We can wait till dark before we go around the village and pick up a horse on the other side." Jim nodded his agreement. "Course, the best ponies are the ones tied up by the tipis," Johnny continued. "A warrior usually keeps his best war pony by his tipi." He shrugged then. "We're only lookin' for a packhorse, so we'll just take the best one we can find in their herd." He got no argument from Jim because he doubted he could find one he liked as well as the buckskin he was riding.

They returned to their horses just as a light dusting of snow began to powder the riverbank. Using the buffalo hides for shelter, they sat up close against the bank and waited for darkness, unconcerned about being spotted since the village was obviously starting to settle in for the night. It was a while, however, before hard darkness set in, so they chewed on strips of smoked buffalo and did without the hot coffee that Johnny was so fond of. It was unlikely it would have been noticed, but they were a little too close to the Arapaho village to build a fire. Watching his young companion testing his healing shoulder repeatedly as he sat shivering slightly in the cold winter evening, Johnny said, "When we get to Laramie, we'll find Two Bulls' camp, and Morning Flower can make you a warm coat outta one of them buffalo hides. It'll sure beat the hell outta that wool coat you got on." Jim looked at him and nodded, causing Johnny to comment. "You don't talk much, do you?"

"Ain't been no need to," Jim replied.

Johnny chuckled. "I reckon you're right. I can take care of the talkin' all by myself." He sat back and gave his partner a long, hard look. "Rider," he pronounced. "Maybe we oughta name you somethin' else—like gloomy or somethin'. You don't smile very much—got a kinda dark look in your eyes like you're 'bout to give a person some bad news. Ain't nothin' good ever happened in your life?"

The little man's assessment took Jim by surprise. He wasn't aware that he exhibited a brooding countenance. He had never really thought about it—he was what he was and figured that was good enough for him. Considering Johnny's question, he took a few seconds to think back over his young life, and in truth could not actually recall any part of it that he could call happy times. He was about to confess as much when Johnny abruptly changed the subject with a sharp release of flatulence, no doubt a consequence of the beans he had eaten that morning. "Jaybird," he announced, a contented look upon his face. Jim made no comment. Johnny always seemed to announce these occurrences with the one word, *Jaybird*, as if the sound itself was not sufficient. Jim never asked about the relevance of the term. It was just one of many characteristics of the odd little man. At any rate, he was happy to avoid the subject of the lack of happiness in his life.

The confiscation of a single horse from the Arapaho herd was not a difficult task for the two thieves, even though some of the young boys from the village had come out to move the ponies in closer to the village for the night. Johnny led their horses along the riverbank on the opposite side until past the tipis while Jim made his way on foot into the herd. His walking among the ponies caused a mild disturbance as he tried to approach a likely looking prospect, an occurrence that was repeated several times until he was finally able to slip his rope on a gray mare much like the gelding Johnny rode. With still no sounds of alarm from the peaceful village, he led his stolen horse away from the herd and back to the bank where Johnny was waiting. "Looks pretty good," Johnny commented when joined by his partner. "Looks a helluva lot like mine. When we get far enough away from here, I'll show you how to make an Injun packsaddle and we can shift some of this load. I know my sorrel will be damn glad to share it with her."

They found Fort Laramie to be a busy army post when they arrived in early January. Most of the activity, however, seemed to be toward recovery and regrouping from the campaigns of the year just past. Some had been successful thrusts against Sioux and Cheyenne hostiles. Some, notably the Powder River Expedition under General Conner, had proven to be costly to the army and proof enough that Red Cloud and the other principle chiefs were gathering forces to repel the white invaders.

"It don't surprise me none a'tall," Johnny commented upon learning that Conner's men had staged no aggressive action against the Sioux. They had destroyed a harmless village of Arapaho. Beyond that, their combat had been strictly defensive as they were harried all the way back to Camp Conner with most of the cavalry on foot as a result of horses frozen to death in the harsh winter storms. "Red Cloud ain't about to let folks keep followin' the Bozeman Trail up to Montana," Johnny said. "Ever'body calls it the Bozeman since John Bozeman and John Jacobs cut a trail up there a few years ago that's a little easier for wagons to travel on. But the truth of the matter is Injuns been travelin' that trail runnin' north and south through the Powder River country for longer than the white man ever thought about it. Hell, it's their prime huntin' ground."

He was proven quite the prophet when they learned that the army was already talking about closing the trail to all civilian traffic because of the threat of Indian attacks. The government hoped to settle the problem peacefully. Just a week prior to their arrival at the fort, runners had been sent out to all the hostile camps inviting them to come in to Fort Laramie for a great peace council in June.

Cold and tired, Jim and Johnny rode across the parade ground and tied the horses at the sutler's store.

"Well, I'll be damned," William Bullock sang out when the two weary travelers walked in. "Johnny Hawk. I ain't seen you in a year or more. I thought sure you'd gone under out there in the mountains somewhere."

"Not hardly," Johnny replied with a wide grin. He had known Bullock for over ten years, since he was first hired by the sutler, Seth Ward, to manage the store. He swaggered up to the counter, as much as his stubby legs would allow, to grab Bullock's hand. "I got snagged by the colonel down at Fort Riley in Nebraska to scout for 'em. Took me a damn year to get shed of 'em." He nodded in Jim's direction. "Say hello to my partner, here."

"Howdy, young feller, I'm William Bullock," he said with a smile. "You musta been in a desperate situation to have to partner up with the likes of this ol' badger. What's your name?"

"Rider," Johnny quickly answered for him, afraid Jim might slip. "His name's Rider."

Bullock laughed. "Does he talk?"

"Very seldom," Johnny came back. "That's the reason I took him on as a partner."

"Well, I'm pleased to meet you, Rider, in spite of the company you keep." He hesitated then, curious. "Is that your first name or last name?"

Jim shook the hand extended to him. "It's just Rider," he said.

"All right," Bullock said as he studied the somber young man. It was not unusual to meet a man in these parts who went by only one name for whatever reason. Bullock gave it no more thought.

"Maybe you can tell me where ol' Two Bulls is camping," Johnny said.

"Last I heard," Bullock replied, "his bunch was camped on the Laramie, about ten or twelve miles from the fork. I haven't seen any of his people in the last week or so. They mighta moved back up closer under the mountains since the weather's turned so cold." He chuckled then. "I expect you're anxious to see that little wife of yours." They both laughed at that, leaving Jim to wonder about the joke.

Johnny brought in a few hides he had been accumulating over the last six months and traded them for some staples the two of them were running short of. After that, they lingered long enough for Bullock to bring Johnny up to date on the news concerning the Indians and the action the army had taken to secure the Bozeman Trail to the Montana gold mines. It was a topic that was of interest to Jim, because he was of a mind to see that country for himself—maybe in the spring. They said farewell to Bullock and turned their horses toward the Laramie River.

Jim glanced at his partner from time to time as they followed the Laramie River south. The stumpy little man looked about him constantly with an air of eager anticipation. Jim guessed that Johnny was reacquainting himself with an area that he knew well, checking to see if anything had changed since he was last here. When they came to a sharp bend in the river, Johnny stood up in the stirrups to get a better look ahead. He explained to Jim that the crook in the river was a favorite camping spot for Two Bulls. There was water and game, and plenty of grass for the ponies, but there was no one there on this day. "Don't surprise me none," Johnny said while looking the wide area over, reading the signs that told of the recent presence of a village. "Bullock guessed about right. I expect Two Bulls moved 'em back to the North Laramie, up closer to the mountains when the cold weather set in."

It didn't take long to confirm his speculation, for the movement of a large village left indelible tracks, even with a light covering of snow. "Yep," Johnny said, looking toward the shoulders of the Laramie Mountains about ten miles distant. "That's where they headed, and I know the spot he picked to camp." He went on to tell Jim about a grassy meadow where a strong stream made its way down from the mountain above to empty into the North Laramie. "It's a right pretty spot," he said. "I expect it would be a good place to camp year-round if the stream didn't dry up some in the summer."

They were spotted by a couple of Indian hunters when they were about two miles from the base of a mountain near the lower end of the range. The hunters halted their ponies and sat watching them until they approached close enough to be recognized. Then one of the Indians let out a whoop and charged straight toward them with the second hard on his heels. Jim could not help dropping his hand to rest on the butt of his carbine, but Johnny simply grinned from ear to ear and continued on at the same steady pace. When within about fifty yards, the Indian in the lead held up his hand and shouted excitedly in the Crow tongue. "What did he say?" Jim asked, catching the excitement when he saw that whatever the hunter said, it seemed to be friendly.

Johnny answered the greeting, also in the Crow tongue. Then he answered Jim's question. "He called the name the Crows gave me—Little Thunder. That's Deer Foot and White Fox."

"Little Thunder?" Jim questioned.

"Yep. That's because of my Remington buffalo rifle," he explained as the two riders pulled up to circle around beside them.

Jim sat patiently on his horse while Johnny greeted his friends. Excited as children, the two Crow hunters could hardly have been more jubilant to see the little man had he been the great white father in Washington. Jim was convinced that Johnny must certainly be well liked by the tribe. Scarcely noticing him for a few minutes in a confusion of Crow words, the two suddenly stopped their chattering and cast their gaze upon him, and Johnny switched the conversation to English. "Friend," he said, pointing to Jim. "Rider." Then he repeated the name in Crow so they understood the meaning. Deer Foot repeated Rider several times. Satisfied then, he said, "Welcome, Little Thunder friend."

"Much obliged," Jim responded, in lieu of anything more appropriate to say.

The reunion over, they continued on to the village. Deer Foot and White Fox galloped on ahead of them to announce their arrival to the people. Jim glanced at his partner. The little man was grinning happily, his lone front bottom tooth prominently displayed as he was obviously enjoying his apparent status in the Crow village. When they reached the lodges at the foot of the mountain, it appeared that everyone in the village had come out to greet Johnny—like the homecoming of a figure of royalty, Jim imagined. Because he was a friend of Johnny's, Jim was received graciously as well, with people crowding around the two of them when they dismounted, smiling and touching them.

A moment before he stepped down from the saddle, Jim had noticed a group of women standing to one side of the gathering, and he could not help noticing one who stood head and shoulders above the others. Not only tall, she was big also, a heavyset woman with a stern face until it had suddenly lit up with a wide smile when some of the other women appeared to be saying something to her. He thought no more about it until the mob parted to give Chief Two Bulls room to greet his friend. Once again the crowd converged around them, only to part once again when the large woman came toward them. The people suddenly became quiet, although the smiles remained in place, as they backed away to let her through. Mystified, Jim moved away from Johnny's side, since the huge woman appeared to be heading for the little man.

Turning to see her, Johnny stopped talking, but a happy smile still shone upon his whiskered countenance. She walked directly up to stand looking down at the stumpy man whose upturned face sought her eyes from a level just even with her generous breasts. She spoke softly to him in her language, then bent down and lifted him up in her arms, holding him as she would a child. There was an immediate outburst of approval from those watching the reunion, with only one person silently amazed. It was a scene Rider would remember many years hence, and it would never fail to bring a smile to his face. It was not an insignificant feat. Johnny was short, but he was husky and by no means a lightweight. Jim remembered a comment made by William Bullock in the sutler's store earlier, realizing now why Bullock and Johnny enjoyed a hardy chuckle when Bullock speculated that Johnny was probably anxious to see his little wife.

It was the custom in the Crow tribe for the husband to move into the wife's mother's tipi, so Jim followed the unusual couple to Jim's mother-in-law's lodge when Johnny signaled for him to come along with them. With Johnny in Morning Flower's arms, that left Jim to lead their four horses. Uncertain at the moment whether he wanted to remain in the village, or to make a camp away from it, he decided that he would see that Johnny's horses were taken care of before he settled on it. When they got to a large tipi on the inner circle, Morning Flower kissed her grizzled lover and put him down, much to the delight of an old gray-haired woman Jim assumed was the mother-in-law. Then the three of them, and the others that followed the procession, all enjoyed a great laugh—and Jim realized then that it had all been in fun. Still, he had to marvel at the size and apparent strength of Johnny's big wife. She was certainly not the average Crow woman, but it appeared she felt a genuine affection for the little man more than twice her age.

When the crowd began to disperse, Johnny told Morning Flower that he would tend to his horses now. "I fix you and Rider food," she said, still beaming.

"That'ud be good," Johnny said. "There's meat a-plenty on the packhorses. We can have us a feast." He turned to Jim then, who was still standing there holding the horses' reins. "Come on, Rider, let's unload these horses. Then we'll let 'em out to graze. Ol' Two Bulls said he's callin' for a dance to celebrate my homecomin', but it'll be a while yet, so we'll eat somethin' first." He reached over and pinched his wife's bottom as she started toward the horses. "Morning Flower's a right fine little cook."

Morning Flower squealed girlishly and playfully slapped Johnny's hand. Then grinning at Jim, she stepped up close to him to look him in the eye. "Rider tall, like Morning Flower," she said. Then she squeezed his forearm. "Need meat. I fix." She laughed then and proceeded to the packs.

"Don't you worry 'bout Rider," Johnny said. "He ain't much more'n a boy. He'll fill out, I expect."

The weeks that followed the triumphant homecoming of the miniature scout saw his friend Rider settle into the daily life of the Crow village. Morning Flower's mother, Owl Woman, had a large tipi and Jim made his bed on one side, near that of the old woman's, while Morning Flower and Little Thunder slept on the other side. It was not an especially comfortable arrangement for Jim for the first few nights, owing to the couple's version of lovemaking. Judging by the sounds that came from the blankets, which Jim tried unsuccessfully to muffle by pulling his blanket over his head, it was more closely akin to a wrestling match, or possibly the copulation of buffalos. It was an assortment of grunts and groans, occasionally accompanied by an identifi-

able blast that was usually followed by the announcement "Jaybird." Jim was struck by the suspicion that
possibly Johnny had earned the name Little Thunder
by means other than his Remington Rolling Block buffalo rifle. Initially, he felt embarrassed for Morning
Flower's mother until he found out that Owl Woman
was almost stone deaf, and could not have cared less
even if she could have heard her rambunctious daughter's antics.

After a week or so, Jim became oblivious of the activity on the other side of the tipi, and in short order
the frequency of their mating fell off dramatically as
the younger Morning Flower drained the energy of her
older lover. Soon Johnny began to complain to Jim that
he feared Morning Flower was going to wear him out
completely, and to avoid the possibility, they planned
a hunting expedition for antelope. Some of the men of
the village had recently returned from the grasslands
to the north where they had found a sizable herd of
the animals. It was unusual to find a large herd in this
part of the country this time of year, so Johnny suggested that they should ride up toward the Lightning
River to see if the pronghorns were still in the area.
Deer Foot and White Fox asked to go along. The big
hunts with the entire village involved had been made
earlier, but they could always use more meat. Before
they left, Morning Flower took some measurements
for a shirt and coat for Rider, planning to use hides she
had already cured and dried. Johnny was quick to in-
struct his wife that Rider wanted a shirt like his, with
no tribal trimmings—a fringed sleeve was all right, but
nothing more. "There ain't no tellin' where you and

me'll end up, and you don't wanna be tryin' to convince a Blackfoot warrior that you ain't a Crow."

Luck was with them. After riding for two days, they caught up with the antelope. The herd was not as big as the other hunters had reported, but numbered thirty or forty animals, plenty for this small hunting party's needs. The problem facing them was in the form of terrain, an open grassy plain that stretched to a line of hills several miles beyond. To give chase would be a waste of their horses' stamina, for the swift pronghorns would soon outrun them. With no possibility to even get within effective rifle range, they paused to decide on the best plan. After watching the herd for a while, they decided that the antelope seemed to be moving in the general direction of the hills to the northwest.

"We'll let 'em be," Johnny said, "go around 'em and wait for 'em in the hills yonder."

"How do you know where they'll strike the hills?" Jim asked. "They might not even keep headin' toward those hills."

"I reckon we won't know for sure till we get in the hills and see," Johnny replied. "But I got a feelin' there's water somewhere up there, and that's most likely where they're headin'." None of the other three had any better suggestion, so they swung wide of the herd and headed for the hills to set up an ambush.

The hunters had plenty of time to set up their trap once they reached the hills, because the antelope were moving slowly as they pawed the snow in search of grass. Consequently, they reached the foothills while their game was still distant on the prairie. Reaching the first hill, they tied the horses and climbed to the top where they could watch the progress of the herd. From this vantage point, it was still just a guess as to where the antelope were going. Finally Johnny said, "They're heading for that draw yonder." He pointed toward what appeared to be a passage between the two highest hills. They wasted no time in getting back to the horses.

"This is it, all right," Jim confirmed when they reached a narrow passage that led through to a wide creek on the other side. It looked to be an oft-used trail by antelope, deer, and maybe buffalo at one time or another.

"Let's get down there and get to work buildin' a fence," Johnny said, and started to climb back in the saddle.

"Wait!" White Fox said, and pointed toward a stand of cottonwoods near the creek. There among the trees, Jim saw the reason for the Crow warrior's caution. There were about a dozen ponies tied there. Someone had the same idea for acquiring meat, and that someone was a step ahead of them.

Uncertain now as to whether or not they had been spotted, they quickly backed away from the brow of the hill to discuss their possibilities. The first thing to do was to try to find out who was down there, for judging by the number of ponies, they could fairly well figure they were outnumbered. But if they were friends, they might still share in the meat. "We're gonna have to get a lot closer," Johnny said. Then he glanced at Jim. "Those two boys ain't got nothin' but bows," he pointed out, nodding toward their two companions.

"So if these folks aren't friends, and there's more'n you and me can handle, we might have to run for it."

Not ready to give up without seeing what the odds were, Jim replied, "Let's get a closer look. I told Morning Flower I'd bring her some hides to pay for my new clothes."

Johnny grinned. "Fair enough. Let's go."

Crossing over to the next ridge, they left the horses halfway up the slope and continued on foot. The situation was what they had assumed. Below, where the narrow valley closed in between the hills to form a passage only about thirty yards wide at the tightest point, half a dozen Indians were hurriedly building a fence with branches and brush. The four hunters on the ridge watched in silence for a few minutes before Deer Foot muttered, "Cheyenne!"

"Damn the luck," Johnny whispered to Jim. "Cheyenne don't like Crows and vice versa."

"I don't see but six," Jim said.

Johnny shook his head. "There's bound to be some more of 'em hidin' back at the mouth of that draw, waitin' to box them antelope in."

Jim was still reluctant to turn tail and run, and go back with no meat. He watched the Cheyenne hunters for a few minutes longer while they finished their fence. When it was done, and the hunters found places to hide on either side, he said, "That little ol' fence ain't gonna stop 'em. My horse can jump that fence."

"They could jump it all right," Johnny patiently explained, "but they won't. Antelopes is peculiar that way. They won't jump over anythin'. They'll turn away, try to go around, or go back the way they came. All them Cheyenne have to do is set there and shoot 'em, and they'll have some more of their friends comin' up behind to keep 'em in a box." He shook his head again and said, "That's what we was gonna do."

Jim looked over at Deer Foot and White Fox. Their anger was clearly evident in their faces as they watched their enemies preparing to slaughter the unsuspecting antelope. As Johnny had told him, this was considered Crow country and he was surprised to find a Cheyenne hunting party this close to Fort Laramie. Watching the two Crow warriors talking quietly together, he wondered if they were contemplating an attack on the Cheyenne hunters. That might prove to be a mistake without knowing how well the Cheyenne were armed and how many more were waiting at the mouth of the canyon.

Maybe there's a better way to look at this thing, he thought, after studying the situation for a few moments more. He moved over next to Johnny. "I'm thinkin' we've got a good chance to get the meat we came after and maybe get some horses, too." His comment captured Johnny's attention right away. Hearing his remark, White Fox and Deer Foot moved over closer to hear his proposal. Jim continued. "If the three of you can work your way down closer to the bottom and stay hid, I'll circle around the base of that hill where their horses are tied. When they start killin' the antelope, I'll take off with their horses. Unless I miss my guess, they'll sure as hell go after me or they'll be on foot. Might give the three of you time to throw some of those carcasses on your horses and skedaddle before their friends know what's happenin'."

"That's the craziest plan I ever heard of," Johnny responded. "It just might work." It was unnecessary to ask the two Crows what they thought. The satisfaction it would bring from humiliating their enemy was written on both faces. "Maybe one of us oughta go after the horses with you," Johnny said.

"You're gonna need all three of you to get that meat loaded in a hurry before the other Cheyennes find out what's goin' on," Jim said. "Besides, I've been studying how they've got those ponies tied—same way the cavalry does it. They tied a hitchin' rope between two trees and tied the reins to it. All I've gotta do is untie that rope and lead the whole bunch outta there." While Johnny thought it over, Jim added, "Course, if they've got somebody watchin' the horses, I might have to run like hell, and you fellers would have to watch out for your own asses. If we pull it off, I'll meet you back where we crossed the river."

Johnny could think of no reason to object to the plan, and the Crows were eager to implement it, so Jim made his way back down the ridge to his horse, then proceeded to the bottom of the hill. He got in the saddle then and rode away from the draw until he had gone far enough to circle back to the other side. He felt secure in the speculation that the Cheyenne party would not have posted a lookout at the top of the ridge to watch the plain behind their antelope trap.

Completing his circle, he walked the buckskin slowly up through the cottonwoods by the creek until reaching a point some fifty yards upstream from the Indian ponies. There he waited for the show to begin. He didn't have to wait long. From his hiding place, he could not see the pen the Indians had erected, so when he heard the animals stampeding into the canyon, he moved closer just as the shooting began. He had harbored some doubts when Johnny said the antelope would not jump the barrier, but the half-pint was right. The forward animals refused to jump the brush fence, and the Cheyenne hunters were shooting them as fast as they could pull their triggers or notch another arrow. In a way, it was a somewhat sickening sight for a skilled hunter like Jim Moran, but he understood the object was to acquire as much meat as possible.

With the noise of the slaughter ringing through the trees, Jim led the buckskin slowly toward the picket line of horses. So far, he could see no sign of a guard. He could assume that all six were participating in the slaughter. When he reached the line of ponies, he could clearly see the Indians busy in their killing, oblivious of his actions behind them. Speaking low in an effort to calm the horses already nervous from the shooting, he untied one end of the rope, then the other. With an eye constantly on the slaughter, he tied the ends of the rope together and led the whole bunch back to his horse. They followed obediently, satisfied to put the noise of the shooting behind them. In truth, he had not been sure that the ponies could be led on one rope, but they continued to follow along behind the buckskin, bumping and jostling together as he guided them across the creek.

He had figured the sound of the horses splashing through the water would alert the Cheyenne at the fence, but the sound was drowned out by the noise of the slaughter. To be heard was essential to his plan, so he drew his revolver and fired a couple of shots in the air. It was enough to catch the attention of one of the Indians, and when he saw what was happening, he cried out in anger. In a matter of seconds, all six were screaming their fury and running after their horses. Although he could hear the distinctive snap of rifle slugs as they zipped through the air, he held the horses to a lope, hoping to lure the Indians farther out on the prairie and give Johnny and the Crows more time to steal the meat. When he had worn the last Cheyenne runner out, he turned his little herd of horses back toward the southeast and the North Platte River. His part of the raid was successful. Now he wondered how Johnny had fared.

It was early evening by the time the party joined up at the river. The stolen ponies were drinking at the water's edge when Johnny and the two jubilant Crows showed up with an antelope carcass draped before each rider and two each riding on the two packhorses they had brought. Their arrival was accompanied by shouts of triumph and glee when they saw that Jim had managed to get away with all twelve horses.

"Hot damn!" Johnny exclaimed as he shoved the carcass off his horse and dismounted. "That was slick as owl shit, partner!" White Fox and Deer Foot gathered around to pat Jim on the shoulder, their faces beaming with their accomplishment. The confiscation of the meat and horses was a great feat in itself, but the added satisfaction of the humiliation afforded their enemy was almost equal in importance. "We got down there in a hurry when they chased after their horses," Johnny continued. "And we didn't waste no time."

"What about the other Cheyenne," Jim asked, "the ones chasing the antelope into the trap?"

"They were late to the party," Johnny replied, chuckling. "There warn't but two of 'em, and we were loaded and gone by the time they got there." He enjoyed another chuckle before commenting, "You know, that little trick you pulled is gonna make you big medicine back at Two Bulls' village." Much to the delight of his companions, Jim divided the horses equally, so each man returned to the village the owner of three Cheyenne ponies.

Chapter 4

Johnny Hawk was right, the raid on the antelope hunt was the beginning of the legend of Rider Twelve Horses. A dance was held to celebrate the triumphant return of the hunting party, and Rider was looked upon with smiles of admiration as Deer Foot repeated many times the story of how Rider stole the Cheyenne ponies right out from under the hunters' noses. Morning Flower and Owl Woman swelled with pride because he was living in their tipi, and several mothers made it a point to parade their daughters before the astonished young man. Unnoticed by the joyous crowd, a young Crow maiden looked upon the white warrior with eyes reflecting thoughts beyond simple admiration.

The major difference to Jim was a feeling that he was accepted by the people, not only as a friend of Little Thunder, but as a member of the village. All through the winter of 1866, he enjoyed the closest thing to a family that he could remember, hunting with Deer Foot and White Fox, as well as other men of the village. It was not enough, however, to dim his desire to see the high mountains, and as winter faded into spring, the urge to see beyond the horizon began to pull at him.

Feelings and emotions were not the only changes in the tall white man, for this winter proved to be a year of physical maturity as well. In a few short months' time, he shot up in height another two inches, so that Morning Flower had to look up to him. He wasn't sure her cooking had anything to do with it, but he also began to fill out his towering frame. By the end of spring, the lanky boy had completed his metamorphosis into manhood. As a final touch, he shaved his mustache and beard, and let his hair grow longer to be more like the young Crow men. Morning Flower complained that she had to alter all the clothes she had sewn for him, but she also took credit for the change in his development.

"Wish to hell you'd loan me some of that height," Johnny said, joking.

"No, Little Thunder," she said, laughing, "you perfect now."

None noticed the change in Rider Twelve Horses more than the young Crow girl Yellow Bird, Deer Foot's young sister, though she told no one of her approval. Realizing that she was little more than a child in Rider's eyes, she continued to admire him from afar.

Jim's natural ability as a marksman soon earned him a reputation among the Crow hunters, but he was always envious of Johnny Hawk's Henry rifle. Nothing Jim owned could tempt Johnny to trade with him for Jim's Sharps carbine. The price tag on a new Henry was a steep forty-two dollars, and Jim had not one dollar to his name. If he was ever to obtain one of the lever-action rifles with the shiny brass receiver, it would have to be in a trade. His opportunity came that winter when an ex-soldier, down on his luck, sold his 1860 model Henry rifle to Seth Ward for a grubstake on his way to Virginia City. Seth, with no use for another rifle, decided to sell it. Resolved to own the rifle, Jim was determined to trade for it, for the final cost of the rifle and a ten-dollar box of cartridges was three horses and his Sharps carbine and ammunition. Johnny maintained that he could have gotten the weapon cheaper, but Jim didn't care. He had the rifle he had craved, and that was enough for him.

Because of the cost of the rifle and the expense to keep it supplied with cartridges, he knew that he was going to have to conserve his use of the Henry whenever possible. The solution to this problem was provided by Deer Foot. Jim had admired the Crow hunter's skill with a bow, and expressed a desire to try his hand with one. Eager to assist him, Deer Foot went with him to find a suitable piece of cedar, which was Deer Foot's preference. He then showed Jim how to shape it into a three-foot length, telling him that anything longer would be too difficult to handle on horseback. To strengthen it, he applied strips of buffalo sinew backing and made the bowstring also from sinew. After learning the proper method for making his arrows, Jim had a practical weapon to supplement his rifle. It did not take him long to become proficient with it when hunting, much to Deer Foot's delight, for he took credit for teaching Rider Twelve Horses how to shoot.

*   *   *

Like Jim, Johnny had not forgotten his plans to return to the mountains of Montana with which he had enticed Jim when they had first formed their partnership. Whereas his love for the mountains was real, an underlying attraction to the area were the gold mines of Virginia City. In conversation with William Bullock at the sutler's store in Fort Laramie, Johnny Hawk learned that the principal chiefs of the Sioux and Cheyenne had agreed to come into the fort on the first of June to discuss peaceful passage of white men on the Bozeman Trail. Bullock's boss, Seth Ward, was not confident that the peace talks would be successful since he had learned that Colonel Maynadier was expecting a large expedition force commanded by Colonel Henry Carrington to arrive sometime in early June, their mission being to build forts along the Bozeman. Johnny persuaded Jim to wait until after the peace talks, figuring it might make the trip on the Bozeman Trail less hazardous.

June first came, and with it the Sioux and Cheyenne, with an estimated three thousand in all. Two Bulls was not at all comfortable with the huge number of enemies camped around Fort Laramie, and had great concern that the soldiers might not be able to defend against them if the talks turned ugly. It was time to move from the winter camp, anyway, so Two Bulls decided to leave the North Laramie for another camp down the Laramie. Since they had already talked about going to Montana, Rider Twelve Horses and Little Thunder said farewell to their adopted family.

"You go along now, honey," Johnny bade a tearful

Morning Flower. "You take care of your mama, and I'll
be back." Still, she was reluctant to leave him. "Don't I
always come back?" He tried to reassure her. "Maybe
I'll find some gold to buy you some fine things."

Finally she released him and turned to Jim. "Take
care of Little Thunder," she pleaded.

"I will," Jim promised. There was a certain sad-
ness in his heart to see them go, but he realized that
he was ready to move on. He hardly noticed Deer
Foot's younger sister standing alone to watch him and
Johnny as they rode out of camp.

The peace talks started well enough, but before they
could be concluded, a case of bad timing wrecked the
entire procedure. Colonel Carrington arrived at the fort
with two thousand heavily armed troops and equipment to build forts on the Bozeman Trail. Red Cloud,
leader of the Sioux, was infuriated when he saw the army's intention to establish forts through land that the
Sioux considered sacred whether he agreed to a treaty
or not. It was the end of the negotiations, for the other
Indians followed him when he promptly withdrew. "I
will fight any soldiers who try to invade Sioux lands,"
he informed the commission.

With stocking up on supplies in mind, Jim and Johnny
rode into Fort Laramie to trade some of the winter
hides they had collected. With the departure of the
Sioux and Cheyenne, they figured they might as well
start west and rely on their skills and instincts to keep
out of harm's way. Just as they started to enter the
sutler's store, they heard a voice behind them. "I'll be
damned if it ain't Johnny Hawk."

They both turned to see a lean, muscular man strid-ing up to them with a wide smile on his face. Johnny grinned back and replied, "Hello, Jim, how the hell are you?" He turned to Rider then and said, "Rider, this here's Jim Bridger. He's the chief scout here." Turning back to Bridger, he said, "Or should I call you Major Bridger?"

Bridger laughed. "Jim'll do. Howdy, young feller. I didn't catch the name."

"Rider," Johnny quickly answered.

"Rider," Bridger repeated, then turned his attention back to Johnny. "Last I heard you were ridin' scout down at Fort Riley."

"I was, but me and Rider, here, decided to head out to Montana country—got a cravin' to see the high mountains again—but from what I just heard, it might be a risky trip if we take the Bozeman Trail."

Bridger shook his head and chuckled. "It was a mighty short treaty, all right. Red Cloud told Colo-nel Maynadier and those boys from Washington to go to hell when Colonel Carrington showed up with the Eighteenth Infantry and a couple companies of cavalry."

"That's what I heard," Johnny said.

"Colonel Carrington asked for me to scout for him—show him the way up the Bozeman, so he can look over spots to build his forts," Bridger said. "If you and Rider are still wantin' to go, I can have you hired on as scouts. How's that sound?"

"Sounds good to me," Johnny replied. "All right with you, Rider?" Jim nodded.

Bridger took a closer look at the tall young man, not-

ing that he had to look up at him—and Bridger stood
a shade over six feet. "Well," he said, "looks like he's
big enough to take care of himself, and he sure ain't too
noisy, is he? He does talk, don't he?"

"I do," Jim said.

"All right, then. I'll put you on the payroll. Maynadier knows you well enough, Johnny. I reckon you
can vouch for your partner." He paused to scratch his
chin as he thought about it. "God knows Colonel Carrington brought some sorry-lookin' scouts with him. I
could use some men I can count on. The colonel ain't
gonna be ready to start out before a week or two, so
you got plenty of time to do whatever you need to do."

Bridger shook hands with both of them before continuing on his way toward the post headquarters building. "I wonder if that Colonel Carrington is any kin to
the lieutenant that arrested me on the Solomon," Jim
said after Bridger had gone. "Wasn't that his name?"

"As a matter of fact, it was," Johnny replied, then
thought about it for a moment. "I don't know much
about the lieutenant. He was just sent to Fort Riley
about the middle of last summer. That patrol on the
Solomon was the first time I ever rode with him. He
seemed all right, except he was too much by the book
to suit me." He paused to chuckle then. "He was sure
gonna take you back to Riley to hang, though, wasn't
he?"

"How in hell am I gonna be a scout worth a damn
when I ain't ever been in the Powder River country?"
Jim asked.

"I know the country up that way," Johnny said, "almost as good as Bridger, I expect. You just stick close to

me. Besides, Bridger will be leadin' the column. We'll most likely be sent out to scout ahead and make sure there ain't no Injuns about to hit 'em."

Jim was satisfied with that—as long as he wasn't asked to tell anyone the best way to get to Fort Reno or some other specific spot. Left on his own, he was confident that he could find just about any place, just not the quickest route to it. He had always felt at home in the forest and on the plains, and the past winter and spring he had spent with Two Bulls' village had taught him even more. Johnny Hawk was always eager to teach him on any given facet of living off the land, but he knew that he learned more about the spirit of the earth and the animals from Deer Foot. He was more at home with Rider Twelve Horses than he had ever been with the boy Jim Moran. He could feel his strength, and he feared nothing that might lie in his path. He would miss Deer Foot and White Fox, as well as Morning Flower and Owl Woman, but he might see them again one day. Who could say? For now, his thoughts were for the trail west and the mountains beyond.

They started out from Bridger's Ferry on the Platte early one morning late in June with Colonel Carrington's headquarters marching in advance, followed by the infantry command and the battalion trains, supply wagons, and mounted troops bringing up the rear. Rider and Johnny Hawk were sent out ahead with the other scouts to act as the eyes of the column. None of the scouts reported seeing any sign of Indians during the first two days of the march, nor were any expected so close to Fort Laramie. The trip to Fort Reno took over a week since the column could only move at the pace set by the wagons. After crossing the Lightning River, there were almost daily reports of Indian sightings, usually small parties that were obviously watching the progress of the column from afar. It was close to midnight when the command finally reached Fort Reno, located on a high plateau on the banks of the Powder River, near the mouth of Dry Fork. The garrison at the fort consisted of two companies of the Fifth Regiment of Volunteers, which Carrington relieved from duty to return to their regiment and replaced them with an officer and men from his command. Upon reaching Reno, he discovered several wagon trains waiting for the protection promised them to continue their journey over the Bozeman Trail.

Lieutenant Jared Carrington, nephew of Colonel Henry Carrington, walked his horse slowly around the encampment on a routine inspection of the guard posts. It was the first time he had drawn officer of the day since his transfer to his uncle's command. He stopped to accept a cup of coffee at the campfire of F Company, near that of the scouts' encampment. Sipping the hot black liquid from the equally hot metal cup, he stood contemplating his luck at having been able to transfer out of Fort Riley to participate in this grand expedition into the Powder River country. As he cast an eye toward the scouts' camp several dozen yards away, his attention was caught by a tall man dressed in animal skins, standing next to the fire. There was something about the man that seemed familiar, but at that distance, he could not place where he might have seen him before. "Sergeant," he asked the soldier who had offered the coffee, "do you know who that man is?" He pointed toward the camp. "The tall one close to the fire, you know him?"

The sergeant turned to follow Carrington's finger. "Him? No. I don't think anybody knows much about him. He don't say very much—name's Rider. He's a friend of that little runt Johnny Hawk—everybody knows him."

"Johnny Hawk?" Carrington replied, surprised. Assigned to one of the cavalry companies, and always riding in the rear of the column, he had very little contact with any of the civilian scouts. Consequently, he was not even aware that Johnny Hawk was with the column. His first thought upon hearing the news was one of amusement, thinking of Johnny's declaration that he was through with riding scout for the army. *I just might go over and say hello,* he thought, *and ask him what happened to his plans to go to Montana.* The smile on his face turned quickly to a concerned frown when he glanced at the dark figure now turning away from the fire. It struck him then that it was a strange coincidence that Johnny Hawk had reappeared with a friend that Carrington felt sure he had seen somewhere before. *Moran,* he recalled after a moment's recall, *Jim Moran. Could it be?* he wondered. The man he had just been looking at was maybe a bit taller than the boy, and much more filled out, but there was something about the way he carried himself that certainly resembled Moran. *I've got to satisfy my curiosity,* he decided.

There was no mistaking the officer approaching their campsite as far as Jim was concerned. He was stopped abruptly when he recognized the lieutenant leading his horse toward him. Lieutenant Carrington was the last person he had expected to see on this campaign. In an effort to appear casual, he slowly turned away and walked over to the temporary rope corral to check on his horse. Seated on the ground a few yards from the fire, using his saddle as a backrest, Johnny Hawk glanced up to see where Jim was going. When he did, he also noticed Carrington striding toward their campfire. He immediately scrambled to his feet to intercept the lieutenant. "Well, lookee here," he said, "if it ain't Lieutenant Carrington."

"Hello, Johnny," Carrington called out. "I thought you'd surely be in Montana by now. What are you doing here?"

"Well, you know how it is. One thing leads to another, and before you know it, you wind up doin' somethin' you hadn't really planned on—the same way I wound up in Fort Riley. How did you get hooked up with this little party?"

"The colonel's my uncle," Carrington replied, "and he requested my transfer to his unit."

"Well, like they say, it's a small world, ain't it?" In an effort to avert any suspicions the officer might have, Johnny asked, "Whatever happened to that young boy you caught on the Solomon? Did the army hang him?"

The question served to cast some doubt in Carrington's mind. "No. As a matter of fact, he got away somehow during the night." He went on then to relate the story to Johnny, and the little man displayed the proper reaction of surprise and amazement.

"And he even stole a horse with a dead body on it?" Johnny asked incredulously. "That do beat all."

"As I recall," Carrington said, recovering a bit of his suspicion, "you argued pretty hard for that boy's innocence."

"Ah, well," Johnny scoffed, "I was just feelin' sorry for him. You know, being young as he was and all. But you was probably right in arrestin' him." Attempting then to change the subject, he blurted, "So, the colonel is your uncle—I wondered if there was any kin there."

Ignoring the attempted switch in conversation, Carrington pointed to the tall figure standing at the rope, stroking the buckskin's face and neck. "Who is that man there? I'm told he's a friend of yours."

"Who, him?" Johnny replied, trying to maintain an indifferent air. "He's just one of the scouts—name's Rider. He was livin' with Two Bulls' village. That's where I met him. My wife lives in that village. I think he was some big medicine with the Crows. They call him Rider Twelve Horses. That's all I know about him."

Carrington considered Johnny's comments for a few moments. He was still not satisfied. If he could believe the grizzled little scout, he was just imagining a strong resemblance between the boy he had captured and the man at whom he now continued to stare. But something else told him that Johnny Hawk could lie with the best of liars. "I think I'd like to talk to him," he decided. Johnny shrugged as if it was immaterial to him, but he watched with great concern as the lieutenant walked over to the corral.

"Evening," Carrington said as he walked up to

Jim. Jim turned to face him and nodded, looking him straight in the eye. "That's a fine-looking buckskin," the lieutenant continued. "Yours?" Again Jim nodded. Carrington searched the face and the cold expressionless eyes as he tried to recall the horse that Henry Butcher's body had been loaded upon, but he could not be sure if it happened to be a buckskin or not. Looking at the powerful shoulders that filled the antelope-skin shirt, he wondered if it was even possible for the lanky boy he remembered to grow into a man in that short time. "Johnny Hawk said your name is Rider." There was no response, not even a nod. Carrington began to get flustered; it was like talking to an Indian who had no knowledge of the English language. "You don't talk a helluva lot, do you?" Again, there was no response, so he attempted a question that could not be answered with a simple nod. "How long have you known Johnny Hawk?"

"Not long," Jim answered.

"So you do talk, after all," Carrington said. He studied the blank stare for a few moments more before giving up, undecided. "Rider sounds like an Indian name. What's your real name?"

"Rider," Jim answered stoically.

"I think you've been living with the Indians too long," he said, and turned to leave, impatient with himself for asking such a stupid question. If he was Jim Moran, he would hardly admit it.

Jim waited until the lieutenant climbed back in the saddle and rode away before returning to the campfire. Johnny was waiting expectantly. "Hadn't counted on that," he said. "What did he say to you?"

"Nothin' much," Jim replied, "and I didn't say much to him."

"You didn't have to tell me that," Johnny quipped. "I think he smells somethin' funny, but I don't believe he's sure a'tall. You have changed a helluva lot since that day." He stroked his chin thoughtfully while he speculated upon it. "I expect he'll just go on about his business and forget about it."

"I hope you're right," Jim said. He picked up his rifle and blew a grain of sand from the brass receiver plate. "I ain't goin' to jail," he declared as he cradled the nine-and-a-half-pound weapon across his arms.

"Don't go gettin' edgy now, partner. If Carrington looks like he's gonna cause you any trouble, we'll just take off and get on up to Montana. This damn column is gonna take the whole summer, anyway, and we'll find ourselves up there trying to camp in the snow."

Johnny had been wrong when he predicted that Carrington would forget the whole matter. While he had not suffered even a reprimand for the mysterious escape of his prisoner and the loss of one of his patrol after the action at Thompson's farm on the Solomon, it had been the source of some embarrassment for him among his fellow officers. A man killed in a skirmish was to be expected, but to permit a wounded prisoner to escape showed negligence on the officer's part. The thought of the possibility of further embarrassment if it turned out that the boy who had escaped him had actually ridden to the Yellowstone with him was enough to cause him to pursue his suspicions. The problem facing him was the fact that there was no way he could prove that the man Rider was the boy Jim Moran—other than a confession from Rider, himself, or confirmation from Johnny Hawk. It was a frustrating situation to a young officer who liked all i's dotted and all t's crossed. He promised himself that he would not permit the possibility of a hoax at his professional expense. He decided to take his suspicions to his uncle.

It was not a good time to bother the colonel with suspicions that he could not prove and accusations based on nothing more than a slight resemblance to a fugitive. Added to all the preparations to be made upon arriving at the post, Colonel Carrington was concerned with a report that Indians had run off the stock of the sutler, a man named Leighton, that very morning. On another day, the colonel would most likely have been receptive to his nephew's problem, but on this occasion he suggested that the young officer should talk to Jim Bridger, since Rider was one of his scouts. Feeling that he was being rather rudely handed off to the chief scout, Carrington decided to let the matter drop for the time being and return to his duties. There would be time later, he decided, after the column had settled in at the post.

"Let's go, partner," Johnny Hawk called out as he returned to the campfire where Rider was waiting. "Some Injuns run off the sutler's mules, and they're sendin' out a detachment to go after 'em. Bridger wants you and me to go with 'em."

It was welcome news to Jim. He was not comfortable sitting around the fort in the presence of so many Yankee soldiers. He had accepted the fact that the war was over, but there was still a lingering loyalty to the South. He had been more at ease at Fort Laramie when he and Johnny had actually lived with the Crows. There was little time wasted in saddling the buckskin and checking his new Henry rifle.

The detachment of ninety mounted infantry was commanded by Captain Howard Marks with three lieutenants as adjutants and four civilian scouts. Since the troops did not leave the fort until early afternoon, Johnny didn't see much hope for success. "Hell," he said, "they've had time to eat a couple of them mules and ride to hell and gone with the rest of 'em." There was no problem following the trail left by the raiders until reaching Crazy Woman Creek just before dark. While the detachment went into camp, Johnny Hawk and Rider crossed over to the other side of the creek to see if they could pick up the trail where the Sioux came out. The other two scouts seemed to show no interest in anything beyond the cook fires. Even in the growing twilight, it was easy enough to find. "I was wonderin' when this was gonna happen," Johnny said as they stood on the creek bank, for the raiders had scattered in at least three different directions. From what they could determine in the fading light, it appeared that each of the three parties had driven some of Leighton's stock with them. "We might as well go tell Captain Marks he's got a decision to make," Johnny said.

As they expected, Marks was not happy to hear Johnny's report. He had already ridden close to thirty miles chasing the Indians. Now he must decide whether or not to split his command and continue the hunt in the morning. Marks was not new to Indian warfare and was consequently reluctant to divide his troops into three patrols, aware as he was of the Sioux penchant for setting up ambushes. "I'll have a look in the morning," he said. "Then I'll decide whether it's feasible to continue."

Johnny and Jim took their horses to water, then fed them oats supplied by the army. "You're gonna get spoiled," Jim told the buckskin. "I don't want you to get too used to eatin' these oats." Like the Crow ponies in Two Bulls' camp, the horse had learned to live off grass, and Jim hoped to keep him that way.

"You ever name that horse?" Johnny asked.

"Nope," Jim replied. "Reckon I oughta, though. I just never gave it much thought."

"I expect you oughta, 'cause you spoiled him so much he thinks he's one of the family."

"I'll think about it," Jim said, since he had no inspiration at the moment.

When the horses had been taken care of, they led them back to the bivouac and hobbled them. Then they went about finding wood for a fire and having a little supper. Johnny put a pot of coffee on to boil; then they dined mainly on some deer jerky they had brought with them. This they supplemented with some hard bread the army issued, although it was of poor quality with considerable mold. It was enough to satisfy, however, and they relaxed by the fire to finish the coffee. Their leisure was to be disturbed, however, in the form of visitors.

The other two civilian scouts were two prime examples of the "sorry-looking" scouts that Jim Bridger had spoken of. It didn't take long to see the two were hardly earning their pay and would never voluntarily venture far from the column of soldiers. Jim and Johnny had no patience for the two and that was the reason they made their camp apart from them. They had very little else in common and preferred to leave them to their own. It was plain to the other two scouts that they were being avoided by the stumpy little man and his tall friend, and it was a cause of resentment on their part. "Looks like we got visitors," Johnny muttered when he saw them approaching.

Jim glanced up to see the two men as they swaggered over to the fire. In the lead, a big surly brute of a man called Bodine grinned maliciously as he came to stand over Johnny Hawk. "Well, we thought we'd make a social call on you two birds," he said. He looked over at his partner, Billy Hyde, a thin, weasel-faced half-breed. "Lookee here, Billy, two birds, a hawk and a raven. Maybe you'd better make that a half a hawk," he added with a contemptuous chuckle.

"What the hell do you want, Bodine?" Johnny asked.

"We just wanted to set down with you boys and maybe have a cup of coffee or somethin'. You know, be sociable, since we're all doin' the same job on this little shindig."

"Sorry. You fellers are out of luck," Johnny said. "Me and Rider just finished the pot—maybe some other time—like next time it snows."

"Now, that ain't no way to talk to a friend," the bully replied. "Me and Billy was just tryin' to be neighborly. Warn't we, Billy?"

"That's a fact," Billy replied. He had been trying to think of some clever insult to add to Bodine's remark about birds, and when Rider casually got to his feet, it occurred to him. "Maybe they ain't two birds— more like a tree and a stump," he said, grinning at his partner.

"Bodine," Johnny stated flatly, ignoring Billy's attempt at sarcasm, "in the first place, you ain't no friend of mine, so why don't you take your weasel friend and get on back to your own business?"

Bodine was clearly irritated then; his contemptuous grin turned into an undisguised sneer as he continued to study the obstinate little man, still lolling against his saddle. He glanced briefly at Rider, standing quietly close to the fire, and made the mistake of reading his failure to speak as a sign that he chose not to be involved. Encouraged, he turned his attention back to the man on the ground. "You know somethin', you little runt. It's time somebody taught you some manners, so you can start out by sayin' 'I'm sorry, Mr. Bodine.'"

"Maybe you're right," Johnny replied. "We oughta kiss and make up. You can start it off by kissin' my ass."

"Have it your way, you sawed-off little son of a bitch. I gave you a chance. Now you're gonna get a lesson the hard way." He bent down, reaching for Johnny's ankle, fully unprepared for what happened in the next instant. The flaming limb that struck him beside his head caught him off balance, causing him to stagger several feet, trying to keep from crashing to the ground. Still stunned, he tried to regain his stability, but was knocked to his knees by a second blow, this one a solid strike to the back of his head. Still without having uttered a word, Rider stood waiting to see if the bully was going to retaliate, but Bodine was too dazed to offer combat. Rider glanced at Billy Hyde, whose hand was lingering over his revolver.

"Pull it and you're dead, Billy," Johnny Hawk warned, his .44 aimed at Bodine's hesitant sidekick. Billy immediately put his hands out to the side, away from his weapon. "Now, you get that piece of horseshit on back to your own camp and mind your own business."

Billy did as he was told, helping Bodine to his feet. Still dazed, the lumbering brute made no effort to resist when his partner led him away from the resolute man holding the smoking limb in his hand. The altercation did not go unnoticed as several nearby soldiers witnessed the brief explosion of fury by the silent scout. The word reached Captain Marks and resulted in a personal investigation of the incident that very night. Calling an assembly of the four, he laid down the law that he would not tolerate fighting among his scouts. Bodine, his head and one side of his face bleeding and covered with smut, had regained his bluster and threatened to avenge his blindsided attack. Marks threatened to put him in chains if he did not stay away from Rider and Johnny Hawk. Bodine grudgingly agreed to let the matter drop, but his eyes conveyed an unmistakable message that told this would not be forgotten.

After the respective antagonists had withdrawn to their separate campfires, Johnny expressed his thanks to Jim. "Damn, partner, I 'preciate you steppin' in back there, but I didn't aim to get you into that little spat."

Jim grunted, astonished. "You didn't?" he replied.

"He was fixin' to drag you across that fire. I thought I'd better stop him if I didn't want a roasted runt on my hands."

Johnny laughed. "Hell, he wouldn'ta drug me very far. I'da shot him. I pulled my pistol out as soon as I saw them two buzzards comin' our way and stuck it under my leg. But I 'preciate it, partner. That's the second time you've watched my back."

"You'da shot him?"

"I expect I woulda," Johnny replied emphatically, and farted for emphasis. "Jaybird," he announced.

The night passed without further incident and the morning found Captain Marks with no desire to split his command into three different units to chase after the thieves. So after a quick breakfast, the patrol started back to Fort Reno.

Chapter 5

Upon returning to Fort Reno, they discovered some new arrivals in the form of twenty-nine wagons with forty men, headed for Virginia City. It was led by a tall, lean man named Jack Grainger. With solid white hair crowning the ruddy face of a man who likes his liquor, Jack had left Fort Leavenworth in the spring with wagons loaded with tools and equipment for the "diggings" in Virginia City. He planned to "lay over" at Fort Reno for a day or so, long enough to burn charcoal and weld the tires on some of the wagon wheels that needed repair. His company more than met the requirements set by Colonel Carrington for trains to be allowed to continue on past the post. The colonel had posted a long list of rules for permitting emigrant wagons to travel through Indian country, and foremost of these was the requirement for at least thirty armed men. The arrival of the heavily armed train was met with much optimism by the emigrants who had been hoping for more wagons to enable them to leave for Montana.

Grainger was not especially enthusiastic about the idea of taking on the pilgrims. There were no women or children in his company, men only, and most of them veterans of the war recently ended between the North and the South. Well armed, he was confident in crossing Indian lands, and planned to move at a demanding pace. Emigrant families would slow him down, he feared, and he was anxious to reach Virginia City. Already there had been reports that the placer mining was drying up in Alder Gulch and folks were beginning to leave for Helena. Jack wanted to deliver his goods before the merchants who had ordered them might try to refuse shipment. After strong persuasion from Colonel Carrington, however, he relented and agreed to take a small party of six wagons that had been there for several weeks—and they were permitted to go because they were driving mules. A more recently arrived party with oxen was denied. "You'll have to keep up with my wagons if you go," Grainger told the families with mules, "and be ready to pull out of here tomorrow or the next day. We leave at four in the morning and stop for breakfast at ten. We rest the stock then and get under way by noon and stop for the day at four. I need to get ten hours a day driving, weather permitting." He got no argument, even though the routine might have been more difficult than some of the families desired. Colonel Carrington informed the families that he planned to remain at Fort Reno for two weeks before moving on to the Big Horn. He would escort the other wagons to that location if they did not continue waiting at Reno, but there would be no facilities for them on the Big Horn.

*   *   *

Tessie McGowan climbed up to put the supper pans away, carefully nesting them to fit in their place in the tightly packed wagon. She turned then to take the plates and silverware handed to her by her sister, Lucy Taylor. "Sounds like we're gonna be travelin' like soldiers when you hear that Grainger fellow tell it," she said as Lucy stepped back to give her room to get down.

"I guess he hoped he could discourage us," Lucy replied with a laugh. "He doesn't know much about farm folks, does he?"

"I guess not," Tessie said. Their daily routine was not a great deal different from the one Grainger described. It wouldn't have mattered if he had said they were going to ride all night. Lucy, Tessie, and Lucy's brother-in-law were eager to get to Montana to join Harvey's uncle, who operated a dry goods store in Virginia City.

Word that had come back east from there recently, of people leaving the town, was enough to cause concern on Harvey's part, but they had come too far to have a change of heart. Tessie, like her sister, was of a stout constitution and fierce determination, and she had told her husband that if things didn't work out for them in Virginia City, they'd simply follow the crowd to Helena, or wherever the tide carried them. She and Lucy both had a notion to try their hands at panning for some of those nuggets other folks were finding in Montana's streams. None of their brave optimism was enough to ease Harvey's mind. He was a born worrier, as most farmers were, accustomed to the fate that befell him at the hands of the weather and pestilence, believing he had no power to influence what the seasons held in store for him. He knew nothing about panning for gold, and for that matter, he knew just as little about managing a dry goods store. But Harvey's uncle Ralph had assured him in his letters that he would teach him all he needed to know, and thus allow his uncle to open a second location. It seemed a better opportunity than remaining on their small farm in Illinois. They had begun to worry that their journey had ended in the middle of Indian country, as they had been stalled at Fort Reno for the last three weeks. Grainger's arrival had been the answer to a prayer.

"Looks like we'll be leavin' tomorrow mornin'," Harvey McGowan announced as he returned to the wagon. "Mr. Grainger said they got their wagons fixed, and he didn't see no sense in hangin' around here any longer. Barfield is goin' with us. He changed his mind about waitin' for some more family wagons." That was good news to the women, since Mary Barfield had become their closest friend on the trip after leaving Omaha.

"We're ready to go right now," Tessie replied, and flashed an eager smile in her sister's direction. "Breakfast won't be until ten o'clock tomorrow morning, but we've got some biscuits left to keep our stomachs happy till then."

The McGowan wagon was not the only place where someone contemplated the coming morning. "I've been thinkin' 'bout this thing," Johnny Hawk said as he and Jim finished the last of their evening coffee. "Whaddaya think 'bout hookin' on with this feller Grainger's outfit and leavin' outta here in the mornin'?"

"It would suit me just fine," Jim replied, "but what about our jobs as scouts?"

"Hell, Bridger won't care," Johnny snorted. "He knows we're just ridin' along on our way to Montana. He won't feel like we're backin' out on him. You heard him say he had a full complement of scouts before we joined up. We've been talkin' 'bout takin' off on our own, but these fellers will be movin' pretty fast." He drained the last drop from his cup and smacked his lips. "I'll talk to Bridger." He peered into the empty cup as if hoping to find more in it. "Wish that was whiskey," he said, then continued. "These soldiers ain't goin' on to the Big Horn for a couple of weeks yet, and when they get there, who knows how long they'll be there before headin' up the Yellowstone? Bridger said Carrington's supposed to locate another fort up near Piney Fork somewhere and then go on to the Yellowstone. We'll be in Virginia City by then if we tag along with Grainger." A grin spread across his face then. "Of course you won't be able to ride scout with your friends, Bodine and Hyde." His face screwed up into a frown and he grunted, "Bodine—jaybird."

"Whatever you want is all right with me," Jim said, and shifted his position away from the fire.

"Good, let's go talk to Grainger."

They found Jack Grainger talking to Jim Bridger. "This'll save some extra talk," Johnny said when he saw the two together, as Bridger turned to see who was approaching.

"Well, here comes some trouble," Jim Bridger called out with a laugh, and turned to Grainger. "You know these fellers, Jack?"

"I don't believe I've had the pleasure," Grainger responded as he looked the odd pair over.

"The stumpy one's a bigger liar than I am," Bridger joked.

"Now, hold on there, Jim," Johnny came back. "Ain't nobody west of the Mississippi can tell as many tall tales as you." He walked up to shake Jack Grainger's hand. "My name's Johnny Hawk," he said. "My partner's name is Rider." Grainger nodded to Rider as Johnny continued. "I'm glad we caught you and Bridger together, 'cause what I'm fixin' to say is liable to break Jim's heart."

With a pretty good notion of what Johnny had in mind, Bridger interrupted. "I know what you're fixin' to say, and I hate to have to tell you, but you're fired— you and your friend, there, too."

"The hell we are," Johnny exclaimed. "We quit ten minutes ago. You can't fire us."

Bridger threw his head back and laughed. "I figured as much." He then explained the situation to Grainger, who, up to that point, was not sure if it was all a joke or not. "These boys just rode along with the colonel on their way to Montana," he said. "I expect they came over to see if they could hook up with your outfit in the mornin'."

"That's a fact," Johnny said.

Bridger continued to speak for them. "I've known Johnny Hawk for more years than I can remember. He's a first-rate scout and won't let you down. I don't know much about his tight-lipped partner there, but Johnny vouches for him, so that makes him all right in my book."

Grainger didn't hesitate. "I always welcome a couple more good rifles," he said, "but I ain't lookin' to add no more to my payroll."

"We ain't lookin' for pay," Johnny replied. "We'd just like to tag along. We'll take care of our own food, and we'll help out if you run into any of Red Cloud's boys. That's all we're lookin' for—same as these families you're pickin' up here."

"Fair enough, then," Grainger said.

As they turned to leave, Bridger said, "Take Bodine and Billy Hyde with you. I fired both of 'em this mornin'."

"We'd sure love to do that," Johnny replied, joking. "If we see 'em, we'll invite 'em to come along. I never figured you'd fire two fine scouts like them. You sure you ain't makin' a mistake?"

Bridger got serious for a moment. "I fired 'em, all right. That little tussle you boys had with 'em wasn't the first trouble they've caused, and as far as I've been able to see, we ain't likely to lose nothing with them gone."

The company wheeled out of Fort Reno in the predawn darkness, on a northwest trail to strike Crazy Woman Creek, and from there forward to the Clear Fork of the Powder, a distance of approximately sixty-five miles, they figured. Grainger hoped to make the trip in two days without undue strain on the mules. They reached the Crazy Woman in less than a day's time, in spite of the weather, which reached one hundred and twelve degrees in the shade. Grainger decided to go into camp there for fear the mules would suffer if pushed any farther. The wagons were circled, with the front wheel of each wagon locked inside the rear wheel of the wagon in front of it. The wagon tongues were all turned to the outside of the circle. An opening was left on one end so that the stock could be driven in for the night.

After a hot day in the saddle, Jim decided to cool off in the creek while Johnny went about making camp. Since the teamsters and their mules were busy churning up the water close by, he decided to ride upstream to find clearer water. So he rode past the emigrants' wagons near the end of the circle, and kept riding until he spotted a place where the cottonwoods were thickest. Guiding the buckskin through the cool shade of the trees, he dismounted and led the horse to the water's edge to drink before he saw to his own comfort. Although the buckskin continued to drink until satisfied, Jim noticed that the horse's ears, which were seldom still, always flickering, were now pricked up and still as if alert to something. It didn't snort or even blow, as it would have if it thought there was a threat of some kind. Still, there were signals enough for Jim to become alert. There was always the possibility of a Sioux scout working his way in close to the camp to evaluate the strength of the wagon train, so he let his hand casually drop to the butt of his rifle while he strained to listen.

There was no sound other than the buckskin's drinking and an occasional bird calling as Jim stood frozen on the bank of the creek. Just then, he heard a rustle of leaves, faint at first, but then a definite disturbance as if someone or something was moving in the berry bushes near the water. Jim jerked the Henry rifle from the saddle sling and turned to face the bushes as he dropped on one knee, his rifle aimed at the trembling branches.

"Wait! Don't shoot!" a woman's voice cried out, and a moment later a pale, bare arm appeared through a gap in the bushes. Astonished, Jim lowered his rifle as the hand waved back and forth for a moment before withdrawing into the shrubs again.

"What are you doin' in there?" Jim asked, not sure if he should be worried or not. "You better come on out where I can see you."

"I can't come out," Lucy Taylor called back. "I'm not dressed properly."

Still baffled by a woman in the bushes and quite a ways from camp at that, he questioned her. "Well, what are you doin' in the bushes?" As soon as he said it, it occurred to him that she might be in there doing her business.

Lucy was rapidly losing her patience with the seemingly clueless man dressed like an Indian, staring at her leafy screen. He was obviously one of the scouts who had joined the train at Fort Reno, although she had not seen him before. In answer to his question, she responded, "Up until a minute ago, I was trying to take a bath in the creek." She thought that sufficient to suggest to him that he should simply leave her to her privacy, but still he remained.

"Miss, it might be a whole lot safer for you if you took your bath a little closer to the camp," he cautioned. "There's Sioux and Cheyenne raidin' parties scoutin' this country, and it's not unlikely for a Sioux warrior to slip in close to see what kind of firepower they might run into if they attack the train. It'd be best if you put your clothes on and I'll see you safely back to your wagon."

His comment was sobering, but she was still perturbed by the intrusion upon her one opportunity for privacy. Straining to hold her temper, she replied, "I can't put my clothes on. They're over by the creek on that log. If you would just get on your horse and leave, I could get out of this damn bush and get my things."

Jim looked up and down the bank then, and sure enough, there was a skirt and blouse a couple of dozen yards upstream that he had failed to notice before. *Damn*, he thought, *how could I have missed seeing them?* "I see 'em," he said. "I'll get 'em for you."

"Just leave and I'll get them myself," she insisted.

"All the same to you, miss, I'd feel better about it if I saw you back to camp."

In exasperation, she rolled her eyes heavenward. "All right," she relented, "bring them over here and put them on the bush. And no peeking, understand?"

"Yes, ma'am," he replied, and promptly went to fetch her clothes.

"That's far enough," she warned as he approached. "Just lay them right there on that branch, then turn your back." When he did as she bade, she hurriedly put on her blouse and slipped into her skirt, desperate to escape from the bush in which she had chosen to hide. "All right," she said when finished. She paused a moment to brush some sand from her skirt before going to the log to recover her shoes and stockings, keeping a wary eye on the tall, rough-hewn scout as she did.

Jim, no less uncomfortable than she with the awkward situation, stared openly at the source of the voice in the bush. She was a young woman of slight build with light brown hair, and would have been an easy catch for any Sioux warrior who happened upon her. Although, he conceded, she had a sufficiently sharp tongue. If the Indian who stole her was as green around women as he was, it might be weapon enough. The flash of a milky white calf caught his eye as she raised her skirt to pull her stocking on. With an eye still on him, she said nothing, but motioned with her forefinger for him to turn around. When he did, she continued to study the tall figure with shoulders that seemed as wide as an oxbow while she finished putting on her shoes. "Are you an Indian," she suddenly asked, "or what they call a half-breed?" Her question was prompted by the animal skins he wore, even down to the beaded moccasins.

Turning to face her again, he replied, "No, ma'am, I just lived with the Crow people for a while." Thinking she might have been fooled by his lack of facial hair, he added, "None of the Crow men had whiskers, so I reckon I got in the habit of scrapin' mine off." His comment seemed to puzzle her, so he quickly changed the subject. "You ready to go back to camp now?"

"I expect I'd better," she said, and picked up her sunbonnet from behind the log.

"You can hop up behind me and I'll give you a ride back," he offered.

She cast a wary glance his way and replied, "No,

thanks. I can walk. You've done your masculine duty now, so you can be on your way. No wild Indians carried me off."

He ignored her hint of sarcasm. "It's still a good little piece back to the camp. I'll go along with you."

"It's not that far," she insisted. "I can see the wagons from here. I'll be fine now."

He looked toward the wagons, then turned to look behind them along the banks of the creek. She was right, but for his own peace of mind, he thought he might as well see her safely to her wagon. "I'll just ride along behind you," he said, equally insistent, "see you back to your husband and family."

Her impatience unraveling and rapidly being replaced with open irritation, she stated emphatically, "I don't have a husband, and I don't need one, so why don't you just go on about your business and I'll tend to mine?"

Her message could not have been clearer, so he apologized. "Sorry to have bothered you, miss." He reined the buckskin to a halt as she continued walking, her stride purposeful and strong.

After walking for a few minutes, she allowed herself a quick glance behind her and discovered that he was keeping pace with her from a distance of perhaps fifty yards. "Oh, good grief," she muttered to herself, and increased her pace. By the time she reached her brother-in-law's wagon, she felt that she needed another bath, due to the briskness of her walk. Glancing behind her then, she saw him wheel the buckskin around and head back upstream at a lope.

Without consciously thinking about it, he made a

mental note of the wagon she went to. It certainly appeared that he had managed to thoroughly irritate the woman, although it had been his intention to see that she was not in any danger. As he rode back upstream to finish what he had started to do before encountering the lady in the bush, he didn't know what to think about the woman—but he did think about her, and for some time after this evening's encounter.

The wagon train set out the following morning, hoping to camp that night where the Bozeman Trail crossed Clear Creek. The wheels started rolling precisely at four o'clock, as Jack Grainger had mandated, with no slackers tolerated. The emigrant wagons had been warned from the first day that to fall behind would result in that wagon being left on its own. Grainger was smart enough to take advantage of Johnny Hawk's knowledge of the Powder River country. Jim Bridger had assured him that no man knew it any better, so he put Johnny and Rider out front during the early hours of darkness. After the sun came up, he was able to lead the train, himself, relying on his memory of the one time he had made the trip before, and guided by the occasional signals of Johnny as he and Jim scouted the country up ahead of the wagons.

At ten o'clock, the train stopped by a stream to eat breakfast and rest the stock. Jim and his partner rode in to take their breakfast as well, building their fire close to the wagons. Jack Grainger walked over to their fire to discuss the afternoon's plan of travel.

"Who is that man over there?" Lucy Taylor asked her brother-in-law when he walked up to the fire after tending the mules. When he turned to see where she pointed, she continued. "That one, the tall one talking to Mr. Grainger."

"I don't know," Harvey replied. "Scout, I guess. Him and the little short one joined the train back at Fort Reno, same as us. I think Sam Barfield said his name is Rider."

"Rider?" Lucy responded. "What kind of name is that?" Harvey shrugged. Lucy continued to question. "Rider *what*? Or *what* Rider? Is it his first name or last name?"

"I don't know," Harvey said, more interested in the coffeepot just then reaching a boil. "You'll have to ask him."

Tessie paused to give her sister a puzzled glance before turning the bacon over in the pan. After turning the sizzling strips of fried pork, she stood erect and stared toward the scouts' campfire, taking a good look at the man in question. "Why are you so interested in the man, Lucy?" She favored her sister with a knowing smile.

Lucy blushed. "I'm not interested in him," she said. "I was just wondering, that's all." When Tessie continued to fix on her with that wide smile, she tried to explain. "He just chased me in the bushes yesterday when I was taking a bath."

"What?" Harvey and Tessie replied, almost in unison. "Why didn't you say something about it yesterday?" Harvey asked, obviously concerned that the man had accosted Lucy.

"Whoa," Lucy exclaimed. "It's nothing like you're thinking. What I should have said is that I hid in the bushes when he happened to come down to the creek right where I was taking my bath. He didn't do anything. He didn't even know I was there." She went on to relate the encounter by the creek.

"So now you want to know his name?" Tessie said, seeing an opportunity to tease her sister. "He is tall, isn't he? I can't tell much about him from this distance. He looks like an Indian."

"He's not an Indian," Lucy said, "and I'm not the slightest bit interested in him, so let's drop it."

Harvey had already put the matter aside, relieved that he was not going to be called upon to defend his sister-in-law's honor. He could tell from that distance that he *was* tall, and broad-shouldered as well, and he would not have enjoyed taking him to task. Tessie had to turn her attention back to the breakfast she was cooking, so Lucy was spared further taunting about the tall scout. Always the imp, however, Tessie would be sure to broach the subject again, if only to see her younger sister blush. She delighted in teasing Lucy about her proclaimed attitude toward men in general and the competitive nature she tried to exhibit to others. Lucy insisted that she could get along just fine without some lazy husband to contend with—an attitude that would have offended Harvey had he not so readily fit the profile. In fact, he enjoyed the benefit of Lucy's help with the team of mules.

The breakfast break over, the wagon train set out again, following the Crazy Woman for five or six miles before leaving it to take a more northwesterly direction. With the route established, Jim and Johnny Hawk rode out away from the train to scout the country ahead.

The prairie gradually transcended into rolling grassland as they approached the foothills, dotted with stands of pines. And off to the west of their route, Jim could now see the taller, stark, and foreboding peaks of the Big Horn Mountains. The sight of them seemed to fill his veins with their call to his primitive soul, regenerating a feeling that he had always felt that he was somehow born to the mountains. He had a strong urge to turn the buckskin's head directly west and ride into the midst of the majestic peaks. Such notions of fantasy were restrained, however, by his responsibility to scout the foothills while Johnny ranged east of the wagon train.

Loping along comfortably, he let his gaze sweep the hills before him, from one ridge to another, some with wide meadows while others were ringed with thick bands of pines. Suddenly his eye caught a movement of some kind near the base of a hill. It was just for a moment, but he was certain his eyes had not played tricks on him. It could have been a deer or some other animal passing through the pines, or it could have been something more dangerous, like a Sioux war party. He knew he had to find out what, if anything, was on the other side of that stand of pines. Of concern to him then was, had that something or someone spotted him as he rode along nonchalantly daydreaming and admiring the scenery?

Without thinking about it, his initial reaction was to pull his rifle and crank a cartridge into the chamber. Then he replaced it in the sling and guided his horse down across a grassy draw and up the ridge on the other side, hurrying to gain the cover of a ravine leading up the slope toward the stand of pines. Before reaching the top of the ravine, he pulled the Henry again and dismounted. Dropping the buckskin's reins to the ground, he crawled up close to the edge of the ravine. What he saw convinced him that he would have ridden into a real hornet's nest had he not caught sight of that slight movement in the trees. On the uphill side of the trees, a Sioux war party rode, using the pines to hide them as they paralleled the train of wagons in the valley below. The movement Jim had spotted was no doubt one of their scouts who had been following the progress of the wagons. From his position on the topside of the ravine, Jim could see the prairie ahead of the wagons, speculating on the spot the war party might be thinking about attacking. It was a sizable party, he estimated maybe sixty or seventy strong, but he could not tell how well they were armed. Whatever their strength, Jim had to believe that the well-armed men of Grainger's freight train would be more than a match for the Indians—but only if the wagons were not surprised before they could go into a defensive position. His job was obvious. He had to warn Grainger before they reached a point parallel with the edge of the pine belt.

Even then as he was withdrawing from the top of the ravine, the Sioux warriors were crowding up to the edge of the trees, awaiting the signal to attack. In the saddle on the fly, he urged the buckskin impatiently down the ravine and crossed over the ridge between him and the valley at a gallop. With hooves pounding the short grass prairie, he emerged in the open and raced after the wagons.

*   *   *

There seemed to be no relief from the heat of the previous two days as the wagons trudged forward at their monotonous pace. Lucy could have enjoyed the view of the mountains as she drove the mules, in relief of Harvey, had it not been for a long barren stretch where the grass had evidently been burned in a prairie fire. Whether set by lightning or Indian, it had left a large section of the prairie scorched. Aided by a stout summer breeze, the wagon train stirred up a dingy gray cloud of smut-filled dust that billowed out behind them, an unfortunate occurrence for those bringing up the rear. Consequently, the emigrant wagons got the worst of it.

Never one to follow the rules when they inconvenienced her, Lucy soon rebelled against the cloud of soot in her eyes, and pulled the wagon out of line, driving them a good fifty yards out to the side before the constant wave of dust. "We're gonna get in trouble with Mr. Grainger," Tessie warned when Lucy drove the team out of line.

"I don't see him back here choking to death on this dust," Lucy replied. "Besides, what's he gonna do, tell us to get back in place?"

Tessie shrugged, equally glad to escape the soot and grime. There was no argument from Harvey, who had taken the opportunity to get a nap in the back of the wagon.

Since the trail was wide and gentle enough, she continued on away from the train even after the scorched patch of prairie was passed. Suddenly Tessie turned in the wagon seat when she saw a lone rider clear the top of a low ridge, racing toward them. "Somebody is sure in a hurry to . . ." She paused then. "Isn't that your Indian scout?" Before Lucy could turn and see for herself, the rider fired his revolver in the air three times, the signal to circle the wagons.

"Oh, Lord," Lucy muttered, and hauled away on the traces. "Gee, mules, gee!" she yelled, and applied the whip.

The wagon lurched to the right, bringing a confused Harvey clawing his way up to the seat behind her. "What is it?" he yelled, confused when he saw how far they were out of position.

"Circle up!" Lucy answered, still urging the mules on, still fifty yards from the other wagons already forming up. A few seconds later, the pine forest on her left seemed to explode into a screaming horde of savages that poured out upon the prairie, heading for the wagons.

"Holy Mother of God," Harvey uttered when he saw the hostiles. "We're not gonna make it," he said, and reached for the shotgun behind the seat.

With the buckskin stretching its stride to cover ground as quickly as it could, Jim bent low in the saddle. "What the hell are they doin' way out there?" he exclaimed when he topped the ridge and saw the lone wagon apart from the rest. Looking back at the host of warriors descending the slope, he saw that it was going to be a close race even if he headed straight for the circle already forming. The wagon was going to be swarmed over before it could reach the circle. With no choice, he holstered his pistol and drew his rifle. Then he made for the lone wagon, still at a full gallop. The errant wagon did not go unnoticed by the Sioux warriors, and a dozen or more split off from the others to go after it, unleashing a barrage of gunfire and arrows. Jim looped his reins loosely around his saddle horn so he could use both hands to fire his rifle. Stretching flat out in the gallop, the buckskin provided a steady platform for his Henry and he fired it as fast as he could pull the trigger and cock it again. The twelve warriors chasing the wagon were bunched closely, so he simply aimed in the middle of them. One by one they slid from the saddle as his deadly fire found them while their bullets zipped harmlessly on either side of him.

When four of their number had gone down, the rest wisely scattered to escape the deadly killing machine bearing down on them, shooting wildly at him as they fled to join their brothers. In the meantime, Grainger, at Johnny Hawk's suggestion, left a fifty-foot opening at one end of the circle of wagons and waited to see if the hostiles would charge through it, thinking to slaughter what they might believe to be a train of white families. Back on the prairie, Jim pulled up even with Lucy's wagon and pointed toward the opening in the circle. She nodded that she understood and urged the mules on. Seeing the lurching wagon as it raced toward the circle, the Sioux immediately tried to cut it off. But Lucy beat them to the opening and raced through it, Jim right beside her, with bullets and arrows flying after them. Unaware of the trap set for them, or the firepower of the teamsters, the raiders rode inside the circle after Lucy. Caught in a cross fire from both sides, and finding repeating rifles in the hands of men who knew how to use them, the war party soon fled back out of the trap as fast as they could get their ponies turned around, leaving their dead behind in their panic to escape.

"By God, I don't think they'll be back," Johnny Hawk crowed as he walked out from behind a wagon, reloading his rifle.

Over by the McGowan wagon, Jim stepped down from his weary horse and looked up at Lucy. "Are you all right, miss?"

Thoroughly shaken, now that it was over, yet game enough to hold herself together, she smiled and replied. "Yes, thanks to you mostly, I guess."

Harvey McGowan climbed down, then helped Tessie and Lucy down, his shotgun propped behind the seat again, having never been fired. "I was bouncing around so much, I couldn't get steady enough to take a shot," he explained. He extended his hand then. "Mister, I wanna shake your hand. You sure came along at the right time."

Jim didn't have time to respond before Johnny walked up. "I swear, partner, I didn't think you was gonna leave any Injuns for the rest of us to shoot."

Motioning toward the bodies lying within the circle of wagons, Jim replied, "Oh, I don't know. It looks to me like you fellers did all right. Besides, mine were ridin' pretty much in a bunch. A man would have to be a pretty poor shot not to hit somethin'." Feeling someone's eyes upon him, he turned to face Lucy just as she averted her gaze in order to miss his.

There wasn't much time for further talk. Already Grainger was summoning his men to get their teams ready to roll and leave this place behind, not knowing if there were more war parties in the vicinity. The next one might be bigger, but he was still confident in his superior firepower to see them through attacks by raiding parties of any size. He came over to talk to Harvey. Of interest at the moment was the condition of Harvey's mules. They had been pushed to a long, hard run in Lucy's sprint for the rest of the train, and Grainger was concerned that they were in no shape to keep up. Harvey and Lucy, in particular, were subjected to a lecture by the captain of the wagon train for their departure from the line. "If those mules are too tired to keep the pace," he complained, "they're gonna slow up the whole train, and it's best that we leave this place as soon as possible."

Jim listened to the lecture without comment. The expansive area of burned-out prairie would indicate that the valley had been the site of an earlier attack upon an emigrant train. It might be a favorite spot for Sioux warriors to sit in ambush, since the valley narrowed slightly, making it further suitable for ambush. It was not a good spot for McGowan's wagon to lag behind. When Grainger had finished his admonishing, Jim spoke up. "If they can't keep up, I'll hang back and ride with 'em."

Although not yet recovered from the terrifying dash for life, Tessie glanced quickly at her sister to see her reaction to the scout's offer. But Lucy was still smarting somewhat from Grainger's remarks, too much so at that moment to read anything personal into Jim's words. Though she was prone to recover quickly from stressful situations, her disposition at the moment was one of defiance. One spectator, who found the incident amusing, was Johnny Hawk as he read the faces of Jim and Lucy, and wondered if his somber young partner had more than a casual interest in the rambunctious young lady. Harvey was quick to apologize for impeding the progress of the train—not so with Lucy, however. "We'll keep up," she declared emphatically. "Don't worry about us." Her statement raised Grainger's eyebrows, brought a faint smile to Johnny's face, and an expression of alarm to Harvey's.

"All right, then," Grainger said. "Let's get ready to roll." He returned to his own wagon, leaving them to stand looking at each other in silence.

It was Tessie who spoke first. "Let's get away from here and all these dead Indians," she said.

"These mules need water," Jim said, stating the obvious. "That looks like some kinda stream up ahead there." He said pointing toward a line of trees and bushes that usually defined water. "My horse needs it, too."

Harvey nodded and prepared to follow the column of wagons already pulling out. Shaken by his first experience with hostile Indians, he was grateful for the presence of the broad-shouldered scout.

"I expect it would be a good idea if we rode out a ways and took a look around, partner," Johnny said.

"I expect so," Jim returned. "I need to water my horse first." He stepped up in the saddle and turned the buckskin around. "I'll be keepin' an eye on you folks," he said, looking directly at Lucy.

The train continued on with no further contact with Indians. Harvey's mules proved to be up to the task, never falling seriously behind the others, so Jim was never required to hang back with them. But he was seen from time to time to appear for a few moments on a distant ridge, or at the edge of a stand of pines, before disappearing again. It was enough to tell Lucy and Tessie that he was watching over them.

They camped that night between the forks of the Little Piney Creek, and Tessie called for a celebration in honor of the successful defense of their wagons. In view of that, she announced that she was going to use some of her precious flour and make pan bread to go with their beans and bacon. "I think it would be nice if you took some bread over to Rider's fire," she said to Lucy, "to sort of thank him for protecting us today."

"Why me?" Lucy replied, her guard up immediately. "Why don't you take it over—or Harvey?"

Tessie favored her sister with an impatient gaze, much like a mother with a difficult child. "Because you're the one who drove the wagon way outside the column," she retorted. "You're the one who's been eyeing him when you think nobody's looking. And you're the one he's been eyeing. Besides," she giggled, "I've already got a husband."

"Tessie Taylor McGowan!" Lucy charged. "Bite your tongue. I haven't been *eyeing* anybody. Even if I was, it wouldn't be a wild man who looks like an Indian." She pulled herself erect in an exaggerated huff. "I've a good mind to pour some of this coffee on you," she said as she moved the boiling pot away from the coals. "Harvey," she called, "whip your wife."

Harvey looked at her bewildered, with no notion if she was serious or not.

Jim and his partner got some pan bread that night,

but it was Tessie who brought it to their campfire, telling them how pleased she was that they had joined the train back at Fort Reno. Jim was slightly disappointed that Lucy did not deliver the bread, but he and Johnny enjoyed the treat. "I swear," Johnny commented, "this is better'n that bread Mornin' Flower bakes, but don't ever tell her I said that. She'd kick my ass."

It took a little extra time for Lucy to fall asleep that night, for there were many thoughts that captured her mind, most of them concentrated around the rugged dark-haired scout called Rider. The strong, sharply chiseled face and the dark moody eyes were things that a woman would notice. She had to question the many times he was on her mind when she should be thinking about other things. Long before this day, she had vowed to herself that she would never marry for love, unless it was accompanied by wealth. Still, it was interesting to fantasize about a union with a man like Rider. *It would be like mating with a panther,* she thought, and allowed a devilish smile to creep across her face.

The wagon train started out early the next morning as usual. There was no further threat from Sioux or Cheyenne war parties the entire trip as they crossed the Tongue and traveled on to the confluence of the Big Horn and the Yellowstone. After crossing over to the north side of the Yellowstone, which required the major part of the day, the train went into camp a few hundred yards from the ferry. With the wagons circled up and the stock driven in for the night, there was nothing more to do but finish the last of their supper and drink up the remaining coffee.

"When we get to Bozeman City," Johnny said,

"we're gonna need to trade for some more coffee beans, and that's a fact."

Jim didn't answer, caught more deeply in thought than usual, even for him. Johnny had a suspicion about what the problem might be. The closer they came to the end of this trip with Grainger's train, the more his young partner seemed to withdraw into himself. Jim was never much for talking, but over the last few nights, he almost never said a word. Johnny was sure the problem had to do with Lucy Taylor, and to Johnny it was very much like lancing a boil. If Jim didn't release some of that worry inside him, he was in for some powerful suffering. So he decided it was time to lance the boil. "I swear, you've been a bit off your feed lately, and I know you've been thinkin' 'bout that gal." There was no response from Jim at all, but Johnny was not discouraged. "I've seen enough buck fever to know when it's hit somebody, so you might as well come on out with it."

Jim gazed unblinking into Johnny's eyes, a look Johnny had become accustomed to from his serious young friend. Then for a second, his sober expression softened, the burden he had been carrying on his mind weighing too heavily to hold any longer. He spoke hesitantly in the beginning, but as his feelings flowed, he emptied his heart to the only man he would trust with his inner yearnings. "I don't know what to do," he confessed. "I've never had any doin's with a girl before. I never cared whether I did or not. But dammit, from the first day I found her in the bushes at the Crazy Woman, I ain't been able to get her out of my head."

"That's what I thought," Johnny said, satisfied that

his diagnosis was accurate, and ready to subscribe the medication. "I ain't been blind to the way she's been lookin' at you, so I'm willin' to bet you ain't the only one thinkin' 'bout the other'n."

"But what should I do about it? She acts like she don't like me most of the time I'm around her."

"Now, see," Johnny was quick to explain. "That's what they do. They don't want you to think they're gonna be easy, like pickin' a gooseberry off a bush." He paused then. "What kinda hurtin' have you got for this gal? Roll in the hay hurtin'? Or marryin' hurtin'?"

"I expect it's marryin' hurtin'," Jim confessed. "I wanna take care of her, go somewhere where we can live together."

"Hmm," Johnny murmured. "You've got it worse than I suspected."

"I don't know what to do," Jim repeated.

"There ain't nothin' to do but tell her how you feel. That's the only way you'll find out how she feels about it. Then you have to take it from there. Two young folks like yourselves, you can make it right fine, do enough huntin' and trappin' to get what you need."

"You think I'm crazy?" Jim asked humbly.

"Hell no. Look at me and Mornin' Flower. We get along just fine, and I ain't even there half the time. Go tell that gal what you got on your mind. She's getting way past marryin' age, anyway. I expect she's been wonderin' if she was gonna have to pop the question to you."

"You think so?"

"Sure I do."

"I reckon I might as well do it," Jim decided.

"Go get 'em, boy," Johnny encouraged happily.

Lucy walked down by the busy stream as the evening softened. It was the last camp before reaching Virginia City. It had seemed like a trip of a million miles and it was hard to believe they had actually made it with everyone safe and sound. The thought of seeing Virginia City the next day was cause for excitement after so many days traveling in a wagon through land so foreign to civilization, but she felt stronger because of that trip, and confident that she could tackle any task. There were some things that had made the trip interesting, and her thoughts went directly to Rider. *What an odd name,* she thought, remembering her reaction to it the first time she had heard it. *Surely he must have a second name.* Her thoughts were interrupted then by the sudden appearance of the tall, silent scout. She glanced up to see him leading his buckskin horse toward her along the stream bank, and knew that he had come to find her. "You found me by the water again," she said in greeting him.

"Yep," he replied. "Only this time you ain't hidin' in a bush."

"Where are you going?" she asked, guessing that she knew the answer.

"Lookin' for you," he replied, then paused before trying to go on with what he had determined to say to her, his nerve wavering now that he was face-to-face with her. "I got somethin' I need to tell you," he found the courage to say.

"Well, I'm right in front of you," she replied, wondering now if she could possibly be right in thinking what she suspected he was gathering his nerve to confess.

It was difficult to speak of his feelings for her, harder than Johnny had said it would be, but he had opened the door and he was determined to go through it. "Well"—he stumbled over the words—"I ain't—I mean—I reckon I oughta tell you that my real name ain't Rider. Johnny gave me that name, after a creek we camped on. My real name is Jim Moran. Johnny gave me the name Rider because the Yankees were lookin' for me because I rode with Bill Quantrill's boys durin' the war."

"Is that what you came down here to tell me?" Lucy asked, somewhat surprised.

"Well, that and another thing. I just thought I oughta be honest with you before I asked you, and I didn't want you to think I was an outlaw usin' another name."

"Asked me what?" she promptly responded before he could finish.

"I've been watchin' you ever since that day on the Crazy Woman," he said. "I never thought about ever hitchin' up with a woman, but I ain't been thinkin' about much else ever since that day. I know I ain't got a lot to offer you right now, but I'm strong and able. I know I can make a good life for you—or die tryin'. I guess I just need to know how you feel about it."

"You do?" she asked after listening to his stumbling attempt to confess his feelings. He nodded. "You're asking me to marry you?" she asked.

"I reckon I am," he replied.

Before answering, she gazed intently at the bashful young man standing nervously before her. Fearless in the face of charging Sioux warriors, he fidgeted bashfully in her presence. She thought carefully about her response. "Rider—or Jim, whichever—I wouldn't marry you if you were the last man on earth. It's nice of you to ask, but I don't intend to spend the rest of my life like a squaw in some log cabin, raising a houseful of young'uns for a husband who's off somewhere hunting or trapping." It was cruel, she admitted that to herself, but she wanted to be sure he didn't harbor any hope that she might change her mind.

Chapter 6

Virginia City was a proper town in 1866, with schools and churches and stores for respectable citizens, a newspaper, and more than a thousand buildings—all mushroomed up from Alder Gulch and Daylight Gulch from the first strike of gold in 1863. Gone were the lawless times of the vigilantes. There was law and order now in Virginia City and the town had recently been designated the Territorial Capital of Montana Territory. Just this year, the town boasted the first telegraph in Montana. Much to Johnny Hawk's relief, the other face of Virginia City was still evident—the bawdy houses and saloons. It was an amazing sight to Jim Moran's eyes. Virginia City was a proper town, all right, but it was a dying town. Placer mining had all but played out, and the gold strike in Last Chance Gulch near Helena was pulling even the die-hard miners away from their claims. It was only a matter of time before the whole place would dry up.

That Virginia City was in her death throes was plainly seen by Harvey McGowan, an observance that

was immediately verified by his uncle's boarded-up
store on Wallace Street. Easily discouraged, Harvey felt
his hopes draining into his boots as he stood staring at
the empty windows of the store, for he had counted
totally on his uncle's help in establishing a successful
living in what had been a boomtown. Never prone to
despair as a rule, Tessie stood beside him wringing her
hands, the air of bravado she had shown before leaving Fort Reno having faded. Of the three, Lucy Taylor
remained the determined tower of strength she had
willed herself to be.

"We'll go to Helena with the rest of the people," she
said. She stepped up on the boardwalk and peered
through a crack in the shuttered window. "There's a
lot of stuff in there. I don't think your uncle has left
town yet, or if he has, he's left an awful lot of inventory
here." She turned back to her sister and her husband,
who were still in deep despair. "We'll find your uncle's
house. He sent for you, Harvey, so he'll damn sure welcome you to help him build a new business. Snap out
of it." She then told her sister, "I didn't come all the
way out here to be poor." She stepped away from the
window to stop a passerby. "Excuse me, sir. Do you
know the man who owns this store?"

"Why, sure, miss," the man replied. "That's Ralph
McGowan's store. You looking for Ralph?" When Lucy
replied that she was indeed, he turned and pointed.
"He lives in that white frame house on the hill."

"Thank you, sir," Lucy said, then turned to Harvey
and Tessie. "See, he's still here. Now, let's get in the
wagon and drive up there to let him know his new
partners are in town."

* * *

Ralph McGowan was a self-made man. He had built his store in the summer of 1864 when Virginia City was still at her peak. Losing no time, he accumulated his fortune while the town was desperate for dry goods and prices were high, mining his gold from the men who labored to extract it from the mines and streams. For that reason, he was disappointed, but not surprised, when the gold petered out, and certainly not discouraged. A single man, Ralph had no ties to keep him in any spot he didn't deem promising to his financial possibilities, so he promptly turned his closed sign to face out, and locked his door, and looked forward to new prospects in Helena.

The one thing he had not been sure of was the arrival of his nephew. When things were booming, he wrote that he would put Harvey to work for him if he came out to Montana, but to be honest about it, he wasn't certain Harvey had the gumption to uproot and make the journey. And since that was sometime back and he had received no word from Harvey, he had all but forgotten his offer. So he was somewhat taken aback when his nephew pulled a wagon up to his house, accompanied by his wife and her sister. "Harvey?" he questioned in disbelief.

"Howdy, Ralph," Harvey responded. He never called him *Uncle Ralph* even though Ralph was almost twelve years older than he. "Well, we made it," he announced, then climbed down from the wagon. "This is my wife, Tessie, and her sister, Lucy," he said as he helped each one down.

Ralph was temporarily suspended in a moment

of indecision, but only for a moment, before he responded appropriately. "Why, good Lord," he managed, "I see you did. I was beginning to wonder." He hurried down the porch steps to greet them, pumping Harvey's hand enthusiastically, then a hug for each of the ladies. All the while his mind was working over his reaction to the unexpected appearance of his nephew at a time when he was set to move on to another prospective spot. Always one to see the silver lining around every dark cloud, and a firm belief that the silver was there for him to mine, he quickly concluded that Harvey's arrival was a good thing. He was positive that he would be as successful in Helena as he had been in Virginia City, and he would need a good man to help with the expansion of his business. He remembered his nephew as an honest, hardworking individual, although short of ambition. Just the kind of man Ralph figured he needed, someone who could run his business, but unlikely to press for a partnership. There was also the added attraction of Tessie's younger sister, a fine-looking woman who graced him with an engaging smile.

"Excuse my manners, ladies," Ralph went on. "Come on in the house. You must be hungry. I'll have Pearl fix you something to eat. It's a little past suppertime, but I'm sure she can rustle up some coffee and a little something to go with it." When Harvey raised an eyebrow, Ralph explained, "Pearl's a Shoshoni woman who cooks for me. I can't pronounce her real name so I just call her Pearl."

"I gotta take care of my mules," Harvey said, looking around at somewhat of a loss as to what he could do with them. There was no barn or corral that he could see.

"You must have seen the stables at the foot of the hill," Ralph said. "You came right by them. You can unhitch 'em and leave your wagon right where it is, and take your mules down to the stables." When Harvey seemed to be taking a moment to think that over, Ralph guessed his indecision. "Tell Percy at the stable that I'll pay for their feed and board."

"That's mighty generous of you, Ralph," Harvey replied gratefully.

"Not at all," Ralph said. "We're gonna need those mules when we pack up and head for Helena." His remark caused raised eyebrows in all three guests. In answer to their unspoken question, he explained, "We'll load everything up in the next couple of days, and take our business to Helena. That's where the gold is flowing now, so you folks got here at just the right time." He stood aside then and waved the women up the steps while Harvey unhitched the team. "You take those mules on down to Percy and I'll take this opportunity to get acquainted with these lovely ladies you brought with you."

The reaction to the news that they were going to Helena was varied among the three new arrivals. Harvey was relieved that his uncle showed every indication of including him in his plans. He had been concerned about his future ever since learning of Virginia City's decline. Tessie was dismayed that another long trip was in the immediate offing after just having survived the long trek from the east. Helena was about one hundred miles away. Lucy, on the other hand, was eager for the new adventure to begin, and felt fortunate to have an alliance with someone who had material and financial backing. Her ambitious eyes saw only opportunity.

His young friend was in pain. It was not necessary to ask what had happened upon his profession of affection for Lucy Taylor. The results were written in Jim's face, and as was his habit, he withdrew to a place inside himself, but this time it was a deeper room inside his mind in which he permitted no entry. Johnny tried to get him to talk about it several times, but Jim would only shake his head and respond that it was a bad idea from the beginning. For three days, they camped at an abandoned claim by a stream near the town while Johnny satisfied his cravings for strong spirits and loose women. Jim remained in camp, declining the little man's invitations to accompany him and wash away his hurt with whiskey and a go with one of the many available whores. Finding it difficult to believe that this remedy did not tempt his young friend, he finally stopped trying and left Jim to wrestle his demons alone.

After the third day Johnny had to admit that his capacity for rotgut whiskey and mattress grappling was exhausted, along with his money, and much like his partner, he was in need of the solitude of the wilderness. "I know what you need," he said one evening as he looked across the campfire at his morose companion. "We need to get outta this place and head for Helena where the boom is going on now. I don't know how much longer I can stand to look at that droopy

face of yours without gettin' the melancholies myself."
When Jim started to speak, Johnny interrupted him.
"I know what you're fixin' to say, but you ain't heard
what I'm talkin' about yet. I ain't talkin' about goin'
where the people are. I'm thinkin' you need to get up
in the mountains with the hawks and the deer and the
badgers, where the country is still like the good Lord
made it. We can do some huntin' and trappin' in a place
I know that ain't many souls seen. It's a place where I
made a camp a long time before there was a place such
as Helena in what some folks call the Big Belt Mountains. We won't even go into Helena. Whaddaya say?"

The suggestion struck a chord in Jim's bruised
mind, reminding him of his early quest to embrace the
high mountains. Johnny was right. This was what he
needed—to let the solitude of the high country heal
his heart. They left for Three Forks the next morning,
following the Madison River north. There were plenty
of signs that the trail had been well traveled of late,
both horses and wagons, attesting to the exodus out
of Virginia City. "Looks like we're always a day late
and a dollar short," Johnny opined over the profusion
of tracks. "I'd like to get in on a new strike once, but it
don't look like it'll ever happen."

After a while, Johnny grew tired of talking and
they pushed on in silence, a state that Jim favored.
The stubby-legged little man had thought to take his
friend's mind off his disappointment by jawing away,
but nothing he said was able to penetrate the stony silence of the man following along behind him. But Jim's
mind was not resting, for he had learned that he could
be hurt by having feelings for someone, and he made a

silent promise to himself that he would never let himself be put in that position again. In fact, he decided that the less contact he had with people, the better off he was, so he rode on, anxious to reach the place Johnny had talked about and vowing to put Lucy Taylor out of his memory.

When they camped that night at Three Forks where the river they had followed combined with two others to form the mighty Missouri River, Johnny was in a high state of concern, worrying that his partner had withdrawn into a state of melancholy from which he might never recover. *I ain't never seen a man take rejection so hard*, he thought. "You know, I hope there ain't no hard feelin's agin' me for tellin' you to go talk to that gal," he finally said.

Much to his relief, Jim smiled, although sadly as he told himself that he had moped around long enough. It left a scar, just as the bullet wound had left in his shoulder, and like the bullet wound, his heart would heal. "No, partner," Jim replied softly. "It ain't your fault I don't have sense enough to tell when a woman ain't got no use for me. I expect I've learned a lesson."

The next morning, they stocked up on the basic supplies they needed to start out for Helena—using the last of their money, a small sum that Johnny had given Jim to hold on to to ensure that it did not contribute to some prostitute's or bartender's gain. Starting out once more, they were in the saddle for a long day before reaching the wide valley between two mountain ranges and making their camp by a slow-moving stream. "It ain't very big, but it tastes all right," Johnny said after sampling the water. "I reckon it won't kill the horses," he joked. "I still got so much of that damn whiskey in me that it'll kill anythin' that crick's got in it."

After the fire was made and they had eaten, Johnny sat back and gazed at the mountains in the distance. "Yonder's where we'll head in the mornin'," he said, pointing toward the northeast, "Big Belt Mountains." Then he made a sweeping motion with his arm. "When I was last in this valley, all that ahead was home to a couple of villages of Blackfeet. I've been to that place they named Last Chance Gulch—wish I'd had enough sense to pan some of that gold—but, hell, I thought pelts was my gold and there were too damn many Injuns near that gulch to be healthy for a lone trapper. Blackfeet never have been partial to white men. It's best to avoid 'em whenever it's possible, and that's a fact—jaybird."

Jim shook his head slowly, amused by the little man's ramblings. Looking away toward the mountains Johnny called the Big Belts, he could feel an excitement inside himself over the prospect of riding deep into the bosom of their solemn peaks. It was what he needed at this time of his life, and already thoughts of Lucy were gradually fading to gray, although they would never be gone completely. He fell asleep that night thinking of the mountains, feeling that he had no place in what man called civilization. He thought about White Fox and Deer Foot, and Morning Flower—and wondered if he would ever see them again. Perhaps, he reasoned, when Johnny developed another yearning to visit his "wife."

As Johnny had said, his old camp was not easy to find, even for him after all the years since he was last there. In fact, they climbed deep into the mountains, following steep ravines and narrow passes through slopes covered with thick pine forests, searching for some familiar sign that would put Johnny on the right path. Jim felt an immediate peace as he guided the buckskin over rocky areas with rocks so small they reminded him of gunpowder, to huge magnificent boulders protruding from grassy meadows near the tops of the mountains. The ground seemed dry, but there were springs everywhere, even this late in the summer, with grass growing in the bottom and moss covering the rocks on the sides. Looking off to the east, he could see some peaks softened by grass. Other mountains had no trees at all except near the bottom, where he saw antelope sign. Higher up there were scarred trees that looked like elk had rubbed antlers there. It was a good place, he decided.

They were not successful in finding Johnny's one time camp, however, much to his chagrin. "Well, I told you it was a hard one to find," he said. "With nobody but Blackfeet warriors ever'where, I had to have a good place to hide."

"We've got plenty of time," Jim told him. "Maybe we'll find it tomorrow."

"If I can just find that little notch near the top of the mountain," he said. "There's a tall pine bent like an S right at the edge of a stand of trees in front of a cliff of solid rock. Leastways it looks like solid rock, but behind that screen of trees there's a notch just big enough to let a horse through. 'Bout thirty or forty feet in, it opens up to a space big enough to keep a small herd of horses, with a strong stream that runs all year.

In the spring, it's so full of snow runoff it makes a little waterfall." He shook his head, perplexed. "I swear, I wish I could find it, but nothin' looks the same as it did then."

"Maybe we'll find it tomorrow," Jim repeated. It sounded like the perfect place he was looking for.

"I wouldn'ta found it the first time if I hadn't shot a mountain lion and didn't kill it." He hastened to explain. "I didn't have time to draw a bead on him, and he jumped at the same time I pulled the trigger—got him in the hind leg. I followed that cat halfway around this mountain, and he woulda got away if I hadn't seen him crawl between those trees in front of that cliff. Let me tell you, I was mighty careful when I pushed through those trees, expectin' to find him between them and the rock face of that cliff. But he had dragged hisself through that notch. I was tickled to find that place."

"There was a cliff like that on the mountain we were on this mornin'," Jim said.

"Yeah, there was," Johnny replied, "but there was no crooked-shaped pine at the edge of it, like at my camp." He leaned back and tried to recall the morning he had shot the mountain lion. After thinking about it for a while, he started from the beginning when he crossed over the foothills and went up into the thickest of the pines. The more the image of that day came into focus, the more he suddenly remembered until it came to him what was different. "Son of a bitch!" he blurted. "We're on the wrong damn mountain. That place we saw this mornin' was the right spot. It's just growed up more since then. But there weren't no crooked tree.

Maybe it got struck by lightnin' or somethin', although I didn't see no sign of a fire. Did you?"

"Nope," Jim replied. "It's too late now, but we can go take another look in the mornin'."

They got an early start the following morning, retracing their steps of the previous day. When they reached the rock cliff about three-quarters of the way to the top of the mountain, they stopped while Johnny took another hard look, trying to spot something that would tell him this was the right place. Jim, meanwhile, led his horse over to the edge of the belt of pines and dropped the buckskin's reins while he went into the trees, where he found what he searched for. "Here's your crooked tree," he called to Johnny, and waited beside a fairly large stump about waist high until Johnny made his way into the trees to join him.

"Damn," the little man muttered when he saw the rotted, twisted log lying on the ground between the trees. "Wonder what knocked it down?" He looked around the ground in search of signs of a fire, but there was none.

Inspecting the stump, and then the log, Jim said, "Looks to me like the tree was sick and some kinda borers got to it." He pointed to another tree not far from where they stood. "Looks like they're workin' on that one now."

With no interest in tree borers, Johnny started weaving his way through the thick belt of pines toward the rock wall. "Come on," he called to Jim. A minute later, he exclaimed, "Here it is! By God, we found it!"

The secret camp of Johnny Hawk was much the way he had described it. Formed by rock walls on all four sides, nature had formed an enclosed meadow with a stream coming up from the ground and running through the center of it to disappear underground again at the lower end. Looking up, Jim could see that the camp was protected overhead by trees and boulders. He could not imagine a more ideal camp for a man alone in hostile country.

The grass on the floor of the enclosure had grown so thick that it concealed any signs that anyone had been there recently, but Johnny scratched around in it until he was able to uncover remains of his campfire. He looked up at Jim and grinned. "Ain't nobody found this place since I left it," he said. Then his grin grew wider, his one sentinel tooth protruding prominently from his lower gum, and he declared gleefully, "Ain't this somethin'? Two Crows smack dab in the middle of Blackfoot country—Little Thunder and Rider Twelve Horses!"

Jim had to smile. "I reckon," he said.

Although they had not sighted any Blackfoot hunters, or seen sign that any had been in the area recently, there was still cause for caution. The Indians had left the broad valley west of the Big Belt Mountains to the thousands of gold seekers that rushed into the gulch. But they had not gone far away, settling in the valleys to the north and east of the Big Belts, and were certain to hunt in these mountains. Of concern then, to the two white intruders, was to find a way to disguise the entrance to their hidden camp. The sharp eye of a Blackfoot hunter would no doubt discover an oft-used trail to and from the thick stand of pines, but Johnny showed Jim a clean apron of stone and shale on the far end of the trees where careful entry would leave no sign. Once they were in the pines, the floor was so thick with needles that even horses, when led slowly, would leave no trail.

Their camp secure, they now had a good deal of work to do in order to supply it with firewood and build a lean-to for their horses before winter came, as well as construct a hut of some kind to protect them in foul weather. There were plenty of pines close at hand, but pine was not good firewood. It burned too quickly and it produced too much smoke for people who did not want to be discovered. To further complicate the issue, they chose not to cut trees for firewood too close to their camp, also to prevent anyone from knowing they were there. So it was necessary to scout the lower foothills for hardwood to supply their fuel. The lean-to and hut were problems also due to the fact that they could not snake large logs through their screen of trees without leaving a clear trail for anyone to follow. To solve this problem, smaller pines were hewn at some distance from their camp, and through Jim's skill with hatchet and vine, a small but sturdy shelter was constructed. Johnny counted himself a keen judge of men for having picked young Jim Moran for a partner, for he was not afraid of hard work. What Johnny failed to understand was Jim's motivation was sparked by the notion that he was building his home and not just a camp to soon be abandoned.

After several weeks in their mountain camp, life had become more enjoyable for Jim Moran. There was abundant game close at hand and there was no lack of anything the two of them needed except coffee, flour, and salt. Jim could do without any of the three, but he missed coffee, so he welcomed Johnny's proposal to go into Helena to see if he could trade some of the hides they had dried. They were not prime since they were summer pelts, but he figured they should be at least worth some coffee beans and maybe a little flour. Since Jim was still reluctant to have anything to do with civilization, Johnny volunteered to make the trip into town alone. Jim quickly accepted the offer. "I 'preciate it, Johnny," he said. "I'm thinkin' about scouting up through the northern end of the mountains to see what kinda game I can find."

"Sounds like a good idea," Johnny replied, "but you better keep a sharp eye. You'll be gettin' awful close to that Blackfoot village."

"I will," Jim said. "I'm more worried about you. You know they don't sell coffee and flour in a saloon, don't you?"

"Why, Rider, now you've gone and hurt my feelin's," Johnny replied, feigning insult.

After Johnny disappeared down through the wooded ravine leading away from the camp, Jim strapped his bow on his back, picked up his rifle, and made his way on foot down the slope toward the adjacent mountain. He was not looking for large game, planning to use his bow for anything worth shooting, but the rifle was always with him for emergencies. Walking along a high ridge that connected two mountains, he found sign of elk, but no sighting. Beyond that ridge and up the next mountain, there was sign of deer, but he was not looking for deer on this day. Still, he was glad to see plenty of sign, for they would need a lot of meat put back for the winter.

Descending the ridge, he slowed his pace to keep his balance on the steep slope. Just before reaching the bottom where a strong stream cut a ribbon in the narrow pass, he suddenly came to a halt. He was sure he had heard something and he stood still to listen. There it was again, and this time he identified it as the warning growl of a grizzly. He could see nothing in the direction the growl had come from, and not certain if it was him who was being warned or something else, he inched forward cautiously to see if he could spot the source. Now the growl came again, this time louder and more of a roar. He decided he wasn't the cause of it, so he made his way down to a large boulder close to the stream, and there he saw the problem. Below him, a young Indian boy stood on the near side of the stream, frozen by the ferocious spectacle of an angry grizzly with its ears pinned back and its head and neck thrust forward. He had evidently crossed between the bear and her cubs. Seeing the boy, the cubs had scattered in three different directions, leaving the sow confused and agitated because she was unable to make an orderly retreat with all of her cubs in tow. Growing more agitated by the second when the boy remained frozen with fear, she began to shift her weight back and forth from one forepaw to the other.

Jim knew she was about to attack. He roared as loud as he could, hoping to distract her. Still, she was about to launch her attack on the petrified boy. Jim lifted his rifle and aimed at a boulder inches from the bear's nose. He was reluctant to kill the bear and orphan the cubs, so he squeezed the trigger, sending a slug to ricochet off the rock, whining as it grazed her fur. It had the desired effect. Startled, she jumped backward and ran back down the stream. In a few seconds, her cubs ran after her. He watched for a moment to see the mother and children reunited and bounding across a meadow leading up the mountain.

He turned his attention back to the stream in time to see the boy sink to his knees, wavering as if to fall over any second. Jim hurried across to catch him before he collapsed. "Boy," Jim said, "you're all right now." The boy made no response, staring with blank expressionless eyes, showing no indication that he understood what was being said to him. It occurred to Jim then that his fainting was not all due to fright. Something else was wrong—maybe some kind of sickness. Then he remembered several boys in Two Bulls' village who went into the forest alone, seeking their medicine. They fasted for days, waiting for a dream that would tell them the path they must walk. He looked closely at the boy he was holding up. He was about the same age as the Crow boys. He must have been too long without food and water. What to do with him was now the question. He couldn't take him back to his camp, but he didn't want to leave him unconscious in the woods. Finally, he decided to take him to the edge of the foothills and leave him there. Johnny had said there was a Blackfoot village in the valley beyond the mountains. Maybe he could leave him where they would find him.

He picked the boy up and followed the stream down to the hills below near the valley floor. It was a walk of about a mile before he came to the edge of the trees at the base. Johnny was right—he could see tipis in the distance. "This'll have to do, boy," he said as he laid him gently on the grass and propped him up against a tree trunk. Then he aimed his rifle up in the air and fired it three times in rapid succession. "That oughta get their curiosity up," he said, looking at the boy again, who had registered no more than a quiver when the shots were fired. He waited to see if there was going to be any response from the Blackfoot camp. In a few minutes time, he saw a party of about a dozen riders leaving the village. "All right, boy, here come your folks, so I'd better get the hell outta here."

Moving quickly, he made his way back through the trees and started up a hill, pausing at the top to see if anybody was coming after him. He could see the riders approaching the boy, and he waited just long enough to see them crowd around him. Then he turned and descended the other side of the hill, heading for the ravine he had found when he came down the mountain. As he hurried up the slope at a trot, he wondered what the Indians would make of the rifle shots. As far as he could tell, the boy was still not conscious when he left him. He had to wonder if he had just caused some future trouble for himself by firing the shots. At any rate, he decided it might be best to confine his hunting to the southern end of the chain of mountains for a while.

"Ain't this somethin'?" Johnny remarked to his horse as he rode along the busy main street of Last Chance Gulch. The town was unfolding like a flower opening its petals, spreading out from the creek where four prospectors from Georgia had first found gold. Only this flower was far from beautiful. Already rough buildings were being hastily erected on every piece of land available. There were hundreds of tents and brush shelters crowded among log cabins half finished while their owners were turning every foot of dirt over to shovel into the sluice boxes, looking for the precious metal. The main street followed the windings of the creek as it snaked its way along the gulch, and side streets were already forming with no plan other than to follow the haphazard paths made by the miners on their way to the creek. Johnny nodded to the grim-looking men as he rode slowly past with barely a responding nod, as the rough-clad, bearded miners labored over their sluice boxes. "By God," he muttered, "I ain't ever been to a circus, but I bet it would have to go some to beat this." Seeing one of the miners pause for a moment and lean on his shovel while he spat out his chaw and bit off a fresh one, Johnny reined his horse to a stop. "Say there, neighbor, is there someplace here where a man can trade for some supplies?"

The miner responded with a grin, "Hell, mister, look around you. If you stand in one spot for five minutes, there'll likely be one where you're standin'." He motioned toward a board structure recently under roof a few dozen yards farther up the street with three large freight wagons beside it. "Yonder's one fixin' to open pretty soon. If they ain't ready to trade, you can try that tradin' post back down around the bend of the creek."

"Much obliged," Johnny said, and rode on toward the new building.

Pulling up to the store, he noticed a smaller farm

wagon on the other side that he felt he had seen some-where before, but dismissed the thought when a man walked out of the building to get something from one of the freight wagons. "Mornin'," Johnny greeted him. "You open for business?"

"Good morning," a friendly response came in re-turn. "Well, we won't be officially open for a day or two, till we can get the inside finished, but I never turn down an opportunity to do business. What can I do for you?"

"Well, sir," Johnny started, "I got these furs here...." That was as far as he got before he was startled by the appearance of Harvey McGowan in the doorway. "Well, I'll be go to hell," he exclaimed, and waited for Harvey to recognize him.

Glancing his way, Harvey stopped, obviously sur-prised. "Well, for goodness' sake," he uttered, "Johnny Hawk."

"In the flesh," Johnny replied with a wide grin. "I thought you was in Virginia City."

"I thought you were," Harvey returned, looking be-yond him. "Is Rider with you?"

Johnny shook his head. "Nah, he's back up in the mountains yonder way," he said, motioning with his head. "He ain't likely to come into town." Then he ges-tured toward the store. "Looks like you ain't wastin' no time gettin' started. This your brother you was comin' to see?" He nodded toward Ralph, who was standing by the wagon, marveling over the chance meeting.

"Uncle," Harvey replied. "This is Ralph McGowan. He's the owner of the business. I'll be working for him." Turning to his uncle, he explained, "Ralph, this is Johnny Hawk, one of the scouts I told you about. If it wasn't for Johnny and his partner, I might not be standing here today."

Ralph stepped forward then and offered his hand. "Pleased to meet you, Mr. Hawk," he said. "Step down and have a cup of coffee. We don't have the stove hooked up yet, but the women have a pot on a fire behind the building." He stepped back then after a quick glance at the pack of hides behind Johnny's saddle, knowing that there was no business to be done with him. He had no interest in trading for hides. Gold dust was the currency he operated with. The show of hospitality was only for Johnny's part in helping his nephew on the trip out.

"Why, that'ud be mighty good," Johnny replied to his invitation. "I don't mind if I do." He dismounted then, ignoring Ralph's sudden look of surprise when he discovered Johnny's head was not as tall as his saddle when he got on the ground. He looped his reins around a wagon post and inquired, "You say the ladies are inside?"

"Yes," Ralph replied, "Lucinda's in the front of the store."

"Who?" Johnny asked.

"Lucy," Harvey answered sheepishly. Ralph had begun calling the women by their formal names, feeling a need for more dignity, since they were going to help in the creation of his merchandising empire. He didn't attempt to explain it to this rough-hewn dwarf of a man.

"Oh." Johnny took an extra second to think about that. "How about Tessie? Is she still—"

"Teresa," Harvey replied before Johnny could finish his question.

"Oh," Johnny repeated while he thought that over. Then his smile brightened, putting his lone tooth on prominent display. "You've gone fancy since your wagon train days are over."

"Well, not really," Harvey answered, feeling a bit embarrassed, "although it may look that way to you." Eager to change the subject, he said, "Come on in and say hello to the girls. They'll be glad to see you."

"I wanna see them, too," Johnny replied, and followed Harvey in the door, unaware of Ralph's critical look as he came along behind him.

"My goodness," Tessie replied as she came in from the back room to be startled by the little scout. "Look at what the cat dragged in." Her face lit up with a delighted smile. "Look, Lucy. It's Johnny Hawk."

"Well, so it is," Lucy replied, looking over her shoulder to see if his partner was with him. "What are you doing here?"

"Why, I come to visit you ladies," he replied grandly, and bowed as they both came forward to meet him. Neither thought to give him a welcome hug or even a handshake, but the thought never occurred to him. Morning Flower was the only woman who had ever offered Johnny a hug. "Somebody said somethin' about a cup of coffee."

Tessie was quick to respond and was back in a minute with the coffee while the others exchanged news that had taken place over the more than three weeks since they left Virginia City. "I guess you met Ralph, Harvey's uncle," Lucy said.

"Yes, ma'am. He's the one who offered the coffee."

"Lucinda and I are engaged to be married," Ralph interjected after seeing that Lucy was not going to mention it.

Startled, Johnny was rendered speechless for a long moment, a condition rarely encountered in his life. He almost spilled his coffee. Glancing at once at Lucy, he detected a slight flush of embarrassment, and he guessed that she had not planned to announce it. Glancing then at Harvey and Tessie, he saw similar expressions on their faces. After another moment, he found his voice. "Well, congratulations," he said. "I reckon that'll make her your aunt Lucy, won't it, Harvey?" Still in the discomfort that Ralph's announcement had seemed to settle upon Harvey and the two women, Johnny could not resist the urge to say, "I know Rider will be tickled to hear the news."

"You never said what really brought you to town," Lucy said, eager to change the subject.

"Me and Rider are runnin' a little low on coffee beans and flour, so I brought some pelts in to see if I could trade for some. They ain't really prime, but they're worth more than that." He looked at Ralph then to gauge his reaction. It was as he had already surmised. Ralph's expression said as much.

In his best business manner, Ralph attempted to explain. "I'm sure I don't have to tell you that the fur trade is long gone. I won't be dealing with any hides because I have no market for them. Our business will be mostly in hardware and tools, some feed stock maybe, but we won't be selling food staples like coffee and flour." Johnny nodded his understanding without replying, and drained the last of his coffee while Ralph continued. "There's an old fellow who runs a trading post about a mile up the gulch. He's probably the man you're looking for."

"It may not always be that way," Lucy was quick to interject. "I plan to make the lower section of the store a place where women can shop without coming in through the hardware store. They'll be able to buy just about anything they need for the kitchen and the house." Johnny nodded his head thoughtfully, and Lucy went on. "Later on, we'll build onto the other end of the building and put a saloon in there. When we finish, folks will just have to go to one place to get everything they need."

"That sure does sound grand," Johnny said. He was beginning to get a clear picture of the attraction between the engaged couple and he recalled Lucy's oft-quoted declaration, "I didn't come west to be poor." *She stumbled upon a grubstake and she's gonna marry it*, he thought. *It won't be long after the wedding before he'll know who's the boss*. "I'd best be on my way," he announced, "see if I can find that tradin' post you're talkin' about. Good to see you all again. Good luck with your store." This last, he aimed squarely at Lucy. "And thank you for the coffee." He placed the cup carefully down on an unfinished counter and with a wave of his hand, took his leave.

Tessie walked after him to stand in the door, watching him as he rode up the gulch. He said something as he left, but she was not sure what it was. "What did he say?" Harvey asked, standing behind her.

"I don't know," Tessie replied. "It sounded like he said *jaybird* or something similar to that."

Grover Bramble ran the little trading post on the lower end of the gulch, and he agreed to trade with Johnny for the pelts. He had coffee beans and a small quantity of salt and sugar, but no flour. "Everythin's scarce as hen's teeth," Grover remarked, "but flour's been the scarcest of all. Feller last month brought in a wagonload of flour and put it up for sale at a hundred dollars a barrel for a hundred-pound barrel. He sold part of the load before folks got so mad at the price that they got up a committee to go after him to lower the price on his flour." He shook his head for emphasis. "Damn cold day in hell before I'd pay that price." Then he chuckled and said, "So, no, I ain't got no flour to sell."

"Well, I reckon me and my partner will do without it," Johnny said. "It ain't like we ain't been doin' without it all along." He stuffed his purchases in his "possibles bag" and tied it on his saddle, then said farewell to Grover Bramble.

"Come this winter," Grover called after him, "if you get some prime pelts, bring 'em on in, and I'll give you a little better trade."

"I'll do that," Johnny said, and waved as he kicked his horse into a comfortable pace.

It was late in the evening when he returned to their camp in the mountains. "We ain't rich enough to afford flour in that town," he said when he saw Jim, "but I got some coffee beans. That's the most important thing."

"I reckon," Jim allowed.

Johnny took care of his horse before returning to the campfire to recount the happenings of the day. He was anxious to see Jim's reactions when he informed him of Lucy's upcoming marriage to Harvey's uncle, but he was also a little hesitant about inflicting damage to a healing sore. He knew it was news that he would be unable to keep, so he came out with it. "I ran into Harvey McGowan and the girls in town," he finally blurted. "They're settin' up a new store with Harvey's uncle." The announcement caught Jim's attention right away, but did not invoke the familiar screen that descended over his friend's face whenever that subject was broached. "That ain't the best part," Johnny went on. "Lucy's gonna marry Harvey's uncle." There, it was out, and Johnny paused to watch his friend intently as Jim's expression never changed. *He ain't showing a sign*, he thought, *but it's got to feel like I just drove a knife through his gut.*

Johnny was only partially right, for Jim was struck by the news that Lucy had so quickly taken a husband. But his heart had been hardened by the scar tissue over his wounded soul, and the impact of the words could be felt against the shield he had built around his emotions, but they could not penetrate. Consequently, he had trained himself never to be wounded by attacks upon his heart again. The fact that Lucy would marry so quickly seemed to slam the final door on his young life, the life he knew as Jim Moran. He no longer wanted to remember anything about that life, and he no longer wanted to be called by that name. His name was Rider Twelve Horses. Jim Moran was dead.

Chapter 7

"You were too many days without food and water," Black Horn told his son. "Maybe the time was not right and you should have waited a while and then tried again."

"I think it took a long time to see my dream," the boy answered, "because it was a powerful message, too big to carry in a single dream. When it came to me, I was weak and sick, but I could feel the spirit who came to help me. He came first as a fierce grizzly bear, but I did not run, so he called down the thunder and sent the bear away. I was lifted from the ground, then, as if I was flying, yet I could sense the presence of his strong arms carrying me to a place of safety."

The more Black Horn thought about his son's story, the more he began to believe that it was a medicine dream, especially when told about the spirit pointing to the sky and calling down the thunder to tell Black Horn to come for him. Everyone in the village had heard the thunder, once, and then three times more. Black Horn and a group of other warriors rode out to the hills to see what had caused the thunder, for it sounded like gunshots. However, there was no one to be seen near the place where they found the boy. The rest of the warriors scouted the forest all around the foothills while Black Horn took his son home. When the scouting party returned, they reported that there was no one there, so Black Horn was convinced that his son had been given his medicine dream and he should take the name of Spirit Bear. The incident might have been forgotten, had not the people of the Blackfoot village all heard the sharp cracks of thunder that sounded like gunshots.

The story of Spirit Bear's dream was soon spread among the people, and they took it as a sign that a powerful spirit lived in the mountains nearby, and many of the young warriors went into the mountains in hopes of seeing this powerful being, thinking it would strengthen their medicine. Rider Twelve Horses had no idea that he had become a Blackfoot legend, and that the mere sighting of him would give a young warrior cause to boast of it in the village. He did notice the occasional sighting of a Blackfoot hunter near the center of the mountains where he had seen none before. He had always been fortunate before to see them before they saw him, but on one occasion, while hunting, he had climbed out on a high rock precipice to scan the valley floor. It was one of his favorite spots, for the valley stretched out before him as far as the eye could see. As his eyes scanned up the slope below him, he suddenly caught sight of a solitary Indian hunter standing in a small clearing about halfway up. From the way the Indian was staring at him, there was no doubt that he had been discovered. There was no sign of aggression, or in truth, of action of any kind. He just continued to stand and stare until Rider backed out of his view.

When he mentioned it to Johnny, it surprised the little man. "He didn't try to shoot at you or nothin'? A Blackfoot ain't usually that peaceful. You'd better mind you don't bring one of 'em back here to our camp."

"I expect I'll start huntin' more in the lower part of the mountains," Rider said. He had already planned to do that, after happening upon the Blackfoot boy, but he had thought he could be careful enough to avoid the Indian hunters.

"Maybe so," Johnny replied as he studied his friend's face, and wondered how much longer it would be before this chain of mountains would no longer satisfy him. He already knew practically every foot of the Big Belt Mountains, and never seemed to tire of scouting them. But winter was coming on, and Johnny was not enthusiastic about spending another winter in this secret camp. Unlike Rider, Johnny craved the enjoyment of a saloon once in a while, as well as contact with other folks, especially of the female persuasion. In the beginning of their camp here in the mountains, he was of the opinion that his young friend would soon heal his wounds and satisfy his desire for the solitude a man finds in the high country. Then, hopefully, he would develop the itch for bawdy houses and strong drink like any normal man, but the longer they remained there, the more ingrained Rider's need for solitude became.

One thing that Johnny had not foreseen was Rider's potential for supplying hides. He had taken to the bow like an Indian, and it had become his weapon of choice—not only for the saving of cartridges for the Henry rifle, but for its silence—allowing him to kill more than one animal in a group and not scare the others away. Of course, the bow also would not alert any Blackfoot hunter that might chance to be close by. Rider's proficiency with a bow was cause for a comment from Grover Bramble on one of Johnny's trips to the trading post.

"Where are you findin' all these hides?" Bramble asked as he rubbed the fur on a bear hide that Johnny brought to trade. "This pelt is almost prime and we ain't but a little way toward a hard winter yet."

Johnny smiled. "Back in them mountains over yonder, there's plenty of game if you know how to find it."

"You still campin' over in the Big Belt range?" Grover asked. When Johnny nodded, Grover continued. "You better be careful you don't run into that spirit that roams them mountains."

"That what?" Johnny asked, puzzled by the comment.

Grover laughed. "I reckon you ain't seen him yet. There's a half-breed feller named Sam Brightwater comes in here to trade, maybe two, three times a year. His mama lives in that Blackfoot village on the other side of those mountains you're campin' in. He was in here about three weeks ago, and he said all the people in the village are talkin' about some spirit that wanders over those hills. Several of their hunters claimed they've seen him, standing on top of a cliff or somewhere, lookin' down at 'em." He paused to allow himself a chuckle over the tale. "Thought maybe you've seen him."

"I've seen him, all right," Johnny replied at once. "I even know his name—Rider, his name's Rider." Seeing the surprise in Grover's face, Johnny was about to explain the sightings when he hesitated to give it some thought. It might be wise to let the Blackfeet believe Rider was a spirit. It could be a lot safer for his friend if they thought he was one. It couldn't hurt, anyway, he decided.

Grover looked at him expectantly, thinking there was more to the story. "Rider?" he questioned. "How do you know that?"

Becoming evasive then, Johnny shrugged and said, "I just know it, that's all."

"Huh," Grover huffed, not satisfied with the answer. "Sounds like somebody's made up a tale."

"Maybe," Johnny replied, and shrugged again, "but that's his name."

Grover might not have believed Johnny's story whole cloth, but the next time Sam Brightwater came to trade at his store, he passed the information forward, and within a few weeks' time, the people in the Blackfoot village had a name for their spirit. On his ride back to the mountains, after a brief stop to visit McGowan's, which was now operating full steam, Johnny broke out with a chuckle every time he thought about it. "Wait'll I tell Rider the Injuns think he's a spirit," he said aloud.

Rider was not particularly amused by Johnny's ruse with Grover Bramble, but there was nothing he could do to explode the myth unless he made it a point to go into town with Johnny to confirm to the owner of the trading post that he was flesh and blood. And as always, he did not want to go into town. When Johnny recounted his visit to the new store, Rider listened to him, for there was no longer any pain from that quarter. He had healed. He listened with interest when Johnny told him how hard Harvey was working in the store while Tessie was setting up housekeeping in a cabin some distance behind it. Lucy, however, was very much in the thick of the new construction, leaving Ralph to take responsibility for providing a home for them. "There ain't no doubt about that woman's ambition," Johnny remarked. "She'll be runnin' that whole damn store in a couple of years—if it takes even that long."

Rider thought about the picture Johnny painted of the first and only woman he had ever loved, and he shook his head in amazement that he had let her rejection of him hurt him so much, when it seemed so unimportant now. "Are they married yet?" he asked.

"Oh, yeah, they're married," Johnny replied with a snort. "Lucy—I mean Lucinda—insisted on gettin' hitched by the justice of the peace." He chuckled. "Ralph wanted to have a church weddin'—plan a big affair—and he's old enough to be her daddy." He paused to express his opinion of that, then said, "Jaybird," and continued. "That poor man ain't got sense enough to know that Lucy just wanted to get that *Mrs.* in front of her name, so she could grab hold of the reins of the marriage." He paused to stroke his beard thoughtfully. "Hell, I don't know. Maybe he is smart enough to know, and he thinks it's worth it to get to sleep next to that warm young body." Forming that particular image in his mind *was* enough to cause Rider a little tinge of pain in spite of his resolve.

The first light snow fell on the mountains and valleys early in the fall, and it seemed to bring a sense of longing over Johnny Hawk. Each new dusting of snow seemed to dampen the spirits of the typically carefree little man. His lack of enthusiasm in preparing for the hard winter finally caused Rider to seek the cause. In a frank confession, Johnny told him that he guessed he missed Morning Flower more than he thought he would. When they had left Fort Laramie, he didn't plan to return to see her until spring. "But I guess I'm gettin' old enough that I get to missin' a warm body to keep my joints from freezin' up on cold winter nights," he said.

Rider studied his friend's face for a moment, thinking how difficult it must have been for one so confident and independent to confess that he needed the company of another. After a few more moments, Rider smiled and said, "Well, you're sure as hell not gonna cuddle up to this warm body. I reckon the only way to cure your hurtin' is to pack up and head on back to Two Bulls' village." He saw an immediate flicker of excitement in Johnny's eyes, much like that seen in a child at Christmastime.

"To tell you the truth," Johnny said, "I've been thinkin' 'bout headin' back down there before real bad weather sets in and closes off these mountains. I figured I'd be goin' alone, though. I didn't figure anything could pull you down where there's people. Hell, you've already gone half wild, roamin' around up here by yourself." He paused to give his friend a suspicious eye. "You ain't got to believin' them tales the Injuns has been spreadin', have you?"

The question brought a smile to Rider's usually solemn face. "Maybe you're startin' to believe it, and that's why you wanna split up with me—afraid I'll turn into a grizzly some night when you're sleepin'."

"That might be it," Johnny said, chuckling.

Pleased to see a hint of renewal of the old sparkle in his partner's eyes, Rider went on. "There's nothin' to hold us here. We've got meat laid back and plenty of hides we can trade at Fort Laramie. Everything else we can cache, and it'll still be here when we come back." He was thinking that it might be a good thing to sleep in Morning Flower's warm lodge and visit with Deer Foot and White Fox and his other Crow friends. The thought surprised him, for as recently as a week before, he still had no desire to see civilized man. Maybe he really was healed, although his first reaction to Johnny's intention to return to Fort Laramie alone was concern for his safety. On his routine visits to the trading post Johnny had heard that the Sioux and Cheyenne were actively raiding any parties attempting to travel the Bozeman Trail in protest to the forts under construction by Colonel Carrington's expedition. Grover Bramble said he'd heard that all civilian wagon trains were being denied permission to continue past Fort Laramie because the army could not guarantee protection. "The two of us, with Henry repeatin' rifles, can hold off a pretty good-sized war party," he said. "If we keep our eyes sharp, maybe we can avoid a big party."

"That's a fact," Johnny replied, his old enthusiasm

returning rapidly. "They might jump us, but it'd be like a man tryin' to grab a yeller jacket—he might catch him, but it'd pain him too much to hold on to him." Then he got serious for a moment. "I know why you're really goin', partner, and I 'preciate it." His simple thank-you did not express the full appreciation he felt for Rider's support. He was too vain to admit it, even to Rider, but during the past couple of months he had realized that things in the distance were becoming difficult to see clearly. This was especially so in poor light, and he was afraid that he might need spectacles, something he swore to himself he would never do, even if he knew where to get them. So there was no measuring the relief he felt when Rider volunteered to accompany him home to see his wife.

Two days later, they left their camp early on a chilly morning after carefully checking every access to the place to make sure they had left no clue of its existence. Heading on a trail to the southeast, they planned to strike the Yellowstone at the great bend where the river turned from north to east. It was an easy uneventful two-day ride without pushing the horses too hard. Arriving at the Yellowstone, they made their camp in the bluffs of the river, and set out the next morning, heading east, holding the horses to a spirited pace. It was not until reaching Clark's Fork of the Yellowstone, about forty miles from Fort C. F. Smith, that they caught sight of an Indian war party. They hid the horses in the willows along the side and watched the Indians from the bank of the stream. The hostiles had apparently not spotted the two white men hiding in the brush as they passed at a distance of a little over a hundred yards. "We're all right," Rider said as he held his rifle before him, his hand clamped over the brass receiver plate to make sure there was no reflection from the sun. "They ain't even looked this way." He glanced at Johnny then. The little man's face was all scrunched up as he strained to see the warriors more clearly. "Sioux," Rider said. "Look like Sioux to me."

"Yeah," Johnny replied, "they look like Sioux, all right. Wonder where they're headin'. It's a day's ride from here to Fort Smith. How many do you see?"

Rider paused while he counted. "Twenty-one is what I count," he said.

"Yeah, that's what I get," Johnny lied. "Must be a village back south. The way they're headin', they ain't goin' to Fort Smith."

After the Sioux warriors had disappeared over the hills toward the Bear Tooth Mountains, they decided that it was too late to continue that day, so they set up their camp there at Clark's Fork. The night was passed without any visitors, and they were in the saddle again under a leaden sky promising snow before noon. They were within five miles of the fort when they sighted the war party again. "Yonder," Rider said, pointing to the south. "Looks like that same bunch we saw yesterday."

"Damn, they musta doubled back on us. Maybe they ain't seen us," Johnny said.

"They've seen us," Rider replied. "We'd better see if we can beat 'em to the fort. Come on!" He kicked the buckskin sharply and the race was on. It was Rider's guess that the Sioux had spotted Johnny and him some distance back and were now angling across in hopes of intercepting them before they could reach the safety of the fort.

Over the rough terrain their horses raced, oblivious of the possibility of a headlong tumble in the snow-frosted grass, side by side, until the broad-chested buckskin gradually began to pull away from the spotted gray carrying Johnny. The race soon went to the Sioux, however, owing to the fatigue of the white men's packhorses. "No good!" Johnny shouted when they were within sight of the fort. "They're gonna cut us off. Look for a place."

"There!" Rider shouted, and pointed to a shallow ravine that was just deep enough to provide cover. He jerked his reins over and the buckskin veered off toward the ravine with Johnny right behind, the packhorses bumping together as all four horses entered the narrow defile at once. The hostiles responded immediately, wheeling their ponies toward them, knowing they had succeeded in cutting them off from the fort. The first shots rang out while the two scouts were still pulling their horses to the deepest part of the ravine for cover.

"If we can keep these boys occupied for a few minutes, maybe the army will send out some help," Johnny said as he and Rider scrambled to positions on either side of the ravine.

The fact that they were within a mile of the fort was not lost on the Sioux war party, so they wasted no time in charging upon the two white men, hoping to overwhelm them quickly and retreat before soldiers were sent out to rescue them. It was to be, however, that they were destined to experience the firepower of two marksmen with repeating rifles. With hostile fire kicking up dirt all along the edge of the ravine, the two scouts took steady aim and one by one began a deadly toll on the advancing Sioux. In a matter of minutes, seven of their number had fallen, causing the others to wheel away to scatter in retreat. "By God!" Johnny shouted. "That'll give 'em somethin' to think about." He rose on one knee to get a better look. "They're bunching up again to talk it over and decide if they want some more." The decision was made for them, however, in the form of a cavalry detachment charging from the fort at full speed.

As the hostiles fled, Johnny and Rider led their horses up from the ravine to meet their reinforcements. "That's a pretty sight, ain't it, partner? Johnny remarked while reloading his rifle. "The cavalry ridin' to the rescue."

Rider didn't answer. His eyes sharper than his older partner's, he was looking at the lieutenant leading the column. When he was positive, he spat and muttered, "Carrington." Why, he wondered, did it seem that he was destined to run into the troublesome lieutenant no matter where he went?

Carrington was equally surprised when he realized who the two white men were. Pulling up before them, he hesitated before deciding whether or not to chase after the war party. "Hawk," he finally blurted, but his focus was on the mysterious scout called Rider, "what are you doing back here? I thought you two had gone to Virginia City." Before Johnny had time to answer, a corporal interrupted to ask the lieutenant if they were going to chase after the hostiles. "No," Carrington replied, "let them go."

The corporal looked around at the bodies of the slain Indians and remarked, "Looks to me like you two didn't need no help. We shoulda waited a few minutes and you woulda cleaned up the whole war party."

"We're just as glad you didn't," Johnny said. "Cartridges are expensive."

Carrington continued to study the quiet scout, although he directed his question to Johnny. The more he puzzled over the resemblance to the boy Jim Moran, the more convinced he became that they were one and the same, but he couldn't prove it. So he held his thoughts on the matter until he could find proof, even though it was especially galling to think that they might be playing him for a fool. "So, what are you doing here at Fort Smith?" he asked Johnny again.

"Just passin' through on our way back to Fort Laramie," Johnny replied. "Thought maybe we'd visit with the army here tonight, then head on in the mornin'." He climbed back on his horse. "What's the Injun talk between here and Bridger's Ferry? Much trouble since the weather's gettin' cold?"

"We're still getting attacks on our woodcutting details and any small patrols," Carrington replied. "The word we get from Fort Phil Kearney is that they're seeing fewer attacks. We haven't gotten any reports of major attacks, and of course all civilian traffic has been halted since the end of the summer." He raised an eyebrow and remarked, "I guess a couple of former army scouts can risk it if they want to."

"I expect we will," Johnny said. "It's a good week's ride from here to Fort Laramie, providin' the weather don't go bad on us." He nudged the spotted gray to follow along behind Rider and the soldiers, who had already started back to the fort.

Carrington fell in beside him and they rode in silence for a few minutes until the lieutenant said, "Well, you and your silent partner up there can eat with the company tonight."

"Much obliged, Lieutenant," Johnny said.

Carrington raised his voice and called out, "That would be all right, wouldn't it, Moran?" When there was no response from the broad-shouldered man riding the buckskin before him, he called out again, "Moran, Jim Moran!"

Again there was no response from the silent scout ahead, and no indication that he had even heard the lieutenant. Johnny, however, reacted with an expression of contrived puzzlement, looking ahead as if expecting one of the troopers to respond. *He must think Rider's dumb as a stump*, he thought.

Although he made not even a slight hitch when the lieutenant called, Rider heard it, all right, and he could not help feeling a tightening in the pit of his stomach. It appeared that Carrington had decided never to forget Jim Moran and just let the issue die with the end of the war.

"Who'd you call?" Johnny asked, looking ahead again.

"Nobody," Carrington answered, and quickly changed the subject. "Why are you going back to Fort Laramie?"

Johnny grinned sheepishly. "I got a little woman back there in Two Bulls' camp that's waitin' to keep me warm this winter. Course Rider's a member of that village, and he's just goin' home to wait the winter out and visit his old friends. Then I expect we'll be back up Helena way come spring if we don't run into somethin' more interestin' somewhere else."

It was difficult for Carrington to take his mind off the broad-shouldered man in buckskins ahead of him, and he was bound to express it. "There's an uncanny resemblance between your friend Rider and that boy Jim Moran," he blurted, "don't you think?"

"You think so?" Johnny replied. "I hadn't really noticed it, myself. There's a helluva difference between Rider Twelve Horses and that young boy you captured back on the Solomon."

"Yeah, I suppose," Carrington said, but he was still not convinced. Since there was nothing he could do about it now, he decided to let the matter rest for the time being. *But don't think I'll quit until I find out the truth of this thing,* he silently promised. He had to admit that he had become obsessed with solving this mystery if only for his own satisfaction. He had even persuaded his uncle to order Wanted posters printed for information on the whereabouts of Jim Moran. Maybe, if this Rider person didn't remind him so much of the boy he had let escape, he could put it aside for good. Letting it go for the moment, he remarked to Johnny, "There's a dispatch detail going to Fort Phil Kearney in the morning. You and your friend might want to ride with them."

"That'd be good," Johnny said. "Always nice to have extra folks with guns to ride along with you through the Powder River country."

Later, he and Rider accepted Carrington's invitation to join his company for supper, but only in order to save their own supply of coffee. As Johnny noted, the coffee was the only thing that was fit to eat, so he and Rider passed up the moldy hard bread and bacon for some dried deer jerky they had brought with them. The following morning, they rode out of the fort with a detail of fifteen troopers, bound for Fort Phil Kearney. From that post, they left once more on their own, bypassing Fort Reno and heading straight for Fort Laramie, a trip of almost five days, making their ride from the Big Belt Mountains to Fort Laramie a total of thirteen days. It was good time, considering the weather.

"By God, what they say about a bad penny always showin' up must be true," William Bullock sang out when Johnny and Rider walked into the sutler's store.

"Hello, Bullock," Johnny replied. "How come Seth ain't fired you yet?"

Laughing, they shook hands and pounded each other on the shoulder. Bullock graced Johnny's solemn companion with a friendly smile and acknowledged, "Rider." Something about the silent man reminded him of a great cat about to strike, and he seemed hardly likely to participate in the friendly joshing that his partner thrived on. Rider nodded in response to his greeting. Turning back to Johnny, Bullock asked, "What brings you back to Laramie? You lookin' for Two Bulls' camp?"

"Yep," Johnny replied, "that's a fact. You know where he set up his winter camp?"

"Yeah, I do," Bullock said. "There was a soldier in

here last week that said his patrol had run across Two Bulls' camp on the North Laramie, east of the mountains, just before the river makes that big turn back to the north."

Johnny thought that over for a moment, tracing the route in his mind. Then he turned to Rider and said, "That's close to two days' ride, and damned if we ain't runnin' short of supplies." Turning back to Bullock, he said, "Are you in a tradin' mood? 'Cause we need a few things, and we've got a couple of prime bearskins and some fine-lookin' deer hides we might could let go if the price was right."

"You know I'll always give you a fair price," Bullock said, "but hides ain't bringin' what they once did—bearskins are always good, but every other pelt is down."

"Damn, Bullock, you say that every time I come in here."

"Well, you know I'm just bein' honest with you," Bullock said. "I ain't the one sets the price."

Johnny shook his head and sighed. "I know it. Just do the best you can."

When the trading was done, Bullock walked outside with them and stood by while they loaded their purchases on the packhorses. When they were finished, Bullock asked, "You boys headin' up the river right away?"

Johnny glanced up at the sky before answering. "I expect so. We ain't gonna get very far before dark, though."

"I've never known you to ride out without takin' a

turn at a saloon for a drink of liquor," Bullock said with
a grin. "You might run into some old friends of yours
that lit here a few days ago."

Curious, Johnny asked, "Who might that be?"

"Big ol' feller said he used to scout with you and
Rider here. Bodine, I think he said his name was—
couple of other fellows with him. I don't recall their
names." He chuckled then when he saw the sour expression the news brought to the little man's face.
"Maybe they ain't close friends of your'n after all."

"I expect Billy Hyde was one of 'em," Johnny said,
"a kinda scrawny half-breed?"

"I believe that does sound like one of 'em," Bullock
replied.

"I don't know who the other'n might be," Johnny
said. He grabbed the saddle horn and pulled himself
up on his horse. "But I thought somethin' smelled bad
around here when we rode in. Now I know what it
was."

Bullock laughed, then said, "Quincy, that was the
other fellow's name." He stepped back to the door
then and gave them a little wave as they turned their
horses away.

There were few occasions when the somber expression ever changed on Rider's face, but Johnny had
lived with the serious young man long enough to de-
tect changes no matter how slight. And he had noticed
the slight reaction in his friend's face when the name
Quincy was dropped. When they had ridden a few
yards away from the sutler's, he asked, "You know this
feller Quincy?"

"I know *a* Quincy," Rider replied. "A man named

Quincy rode with Henry Butcher's gang. He was on the raid on that farm where I got shot. He was one of the ones that got away."

Johnny nodded solemnly. "Maybe this ain't the same Quincy."

"Maybe," Rider replied, "but if he's ridin' with Bodine and Hyde, it doesn't make much difference if he's the same one or not. He's up to no good."

"Well, we ain't likely to run into the bastards, anyway. Let's get on outta here and head toward Two Bulls' camp."

They rode out of Fort Laramie and picked up a well-traveled trail along the bank of the North Laramie River. They would make only a little over six miles before darkness threatened, so they made camp there by the river. Rider took care of the horses while Johnny built a fire and used some of the coffee beans they had just bought. Rider could not help noticing the lifting of the stumpy little man's spirits, and he recalled the first time the two of them had gone in search of Two Bulls' village, and the eagerness he exhibited on that occasion—like a child anticipating a birthday party. He was tempted to tease him. "What are you gonna do if Morning Flower has decided to take up with another buck after you left her all summer?"

"Never happen," Johnny replied confidently. "She knows I'm comin' back." He grinned real big then. "She'll wait for ol' Little Thunder 'cause she knows I ain't short all over."

Rider had to laugh. "I expect the biggest thing about you is your talk."

*   *   *

Another day and a half brought them to the bend in the river and they spotted the Crow horse herd just shy of it, pawing and scratching the light covering of snow to get to the grass. Beyond the herd, back in the shelter of the hills, they could see the smoke trails from the tipis snaking up through the cold gray sky. Accustomed to a big arrival whenever he approached the village after a long absence, Johnny drew his revolver and fired several shots in the air to let everybody know he was coming. His announcement got the results he desired and he turned to flash Rider a quick grin as the people poured out of their tipis.

The greeting was certainly equal to the first one Rider had experienced with Johnny, and maybe even greater, for Rider Twelve Horses was welcomed as warmly as Little Thunder, with one exception. Giggling like a small child, Morning Flower ran out to meet them and caught Johnny in her arms as he dismounted. Caught in her powerful embrace, the little man barely reached the ground with his tiptoes, causing the people to laugh delightedly. As they crowded around the two, everyone wanted to touch them and welcome them. Deer Foot and White Fox pounded Rider on the shoulders, all smiles as they expressed their pleasure in seeing him again. This time it was a genuine homecoming for the quiet man, and he felt that he was truly a member of the village. Appropriately, Two Bulls called for a dance to celebrate the return of the two white Crows.

The dance went on until the wee hours of the morning. Rider tried to remain awake till the end, but sleep overtook him shortly before dawn and he lay down close to one of the fires with only his saddle blanket for a bed. Little Thunder, on the other hand, not only stayed awake, but participated in the dancing, delighting the people with his comical kicks and bounds. Gradually the crowd retired to their lodges until finally there was no one left to dance. Exhausted to the point of staggering, Johnny and Morning Flower paused before the sleeping form of Rider Twelve Horses. Johnny studied the situation for a few seconds before deciding to leave him where he was. "If he can sleep like that, might as well leave him be," he said. "He's too big to carry, anyway." They wandered off to bed and left him huddled up like a baby on the saddle blanket. A little while later, when the camp was quiet, a slight young girl came from one of the lodges and spread a blanket over him, put some more wood on the fire, then paused to watch him for a few moments before slipping back to her tipi.

He awoke with the sun shining directly in his face. Unable to remember at once where he was, he sat up and looked around him before recalling how he happened to be in the center of the Crow village. Feeling a little foolish, he quickly got to his feet, just then noticing the blanket that he had been sleeping under. He had no idea how it got there, but he folded it carefully while looking around for the best place to empty his bladder. When he decided upon a likely place in a thick stand of pines near the base of the hill, he placed the blanket on his saddle and went to take care of his morning business. He had seen no sign of anyone else up and about, and he had no desire to wake everyone in Morning Flower's tipi, so he decided he'd build up the smoldering fire and try to revive himself without coffee. He returned from his morning call in time to glimpse a slender Crow girl as she picked up the blanket and hurried toward the circle of tipis. He thought to thank her, but she was already too far for him to call out to her, so he took his time walking back to the fire. There were plenty of half-burned sticks of wood left around the ashes of the large fire that the dancers had circled, so he built up his smaller fire using these. When he had a strong flame going, he sat down on the saddle blanket, warming himself and wishing that he had his coffeepot and coffee beans from the packs in Morning Flower's lodge.

He had not sat there long when he saw the slender girl again, coming toward him, carrying a parfleche. When he was sure she was coming to him, he got to his feet to greet her. Using the sign language he had learned when living with her people before, he thanked her for the blanket.

She smiled at him and said, "I afraid you get cold."

"You speak English," he said, surprised.

"Little bit," she replied. "I bring you food." She opened the parfleche she was carrying and offered it to him. Inside, he found cakes of pemmican, a food staple of almost all Indian tribes. He had learned to like it when he spent the previous winter with the Crows. It was an excellent way to preserve meat to have when fresh game was not available. Sun-dried buffalo or deer pounded fine with a maul was mixed with melted fat and sometimes marrow. To give it flavor, a paste of crushed wild cherries was added. The result was a surprisingly pleasant tasting cake that provided nourishment as well, and they couldn't have come at a better time. He was hungry.

"That's a lot of pemmican," he said.

"You big man. I don't know how much you eat."

He smiled at her and said, "I don't eat that much." He took what he wanted and closed the parfleche. "Here, you take the rest back to your tipi—and thank you." She smiled and took it from him, her eyes averted to avoid his gaze. "And thank you for bringin' that blanket."

"Deer Foot tell me to bring blanket," she said.

"Deer Foot? Are you Deer Foot's wife?"

She placed her hand over her mouth to hide her giggle. "No wife," she said, then paused while she sought to remember the English word she searched for.

"Sister? Are you Deer Foot's sister?"

She nodded vigorously, still laughing. "Yes," she said, "sister."

"Well, it's plain to see who got all the looks in the family," he said, causing her to look puzzled, and he realized that she didn't understand what he meant. So he told her in words she could understand. "You are a very pretty girl," he said, then told her again in sign language, to be sure she got it. She did, for she blushed and promptly turned on her heel and fled back to her lodge. "Well, what in the hell got into her?" he questioned aloud.

Later, when the camp came fully alive again, Johnny came looking for him. Beaming openly, he apologized for leaving him lying by the fire all night. "You was sleepin' so peaceful-like I didn't wanna roust you out. Besides, I had some urgent business I had to tend to."

He winked mischievously. "Come on back to Morning Flower's lodge. I know you. I bet you'd give a big toe for a cup of fresh coffee, wouldn't you?"

"As a matter of fact," Rider replied, "I reckon I'da starved to death if Deer Foot's little sister hadn't brought me a sack of pemmican this mornin' while you were still snorin'."

This captured Johnny's attention right away. "What? Deer Foot's sister brought you food?"

"Yeah, and she covered me with a blanket last night," Rider replied.

"Hot damn!" Johnny exclaimed. "Sounds to me like that little Injun gal is takin' a shine to you."

Rider had to give that some thought. He had assumed that the girl's actions were no more than a show of kindness to welcome him back to the village and nothing more. He expressed as much to Johnny. "It was Deer Foot's doin'," he said. "She said he sent her with the blanket."

"I swear," Johnny replied, perplexed by the naïveté of his young friend. "Ain't you learned nothin' about Injuns? Course Deer Foot sent her. It'd be an honor to him to have you in the family." He grinned at his astonished partner. "It might not be the last little gal that gets paraded by you. Might be a good time to take a wife."

"You're crazy," Rider said good-naturedly. "She ain't much more'n a child."

"Well, I don't know about that," Johnny replied. "I ain't got a look at her yet, but she was a sight more'n a child when we was here last winter. You sure you took a good look?"

In fact, he hadn't. Thoughts of women and prospective wives had never entered his mind since his unpleasant experience with Lucy Taylor. That episode had all but closed that door in his brain. Deer Foot's sister might have caused it to drift ajar.

Chapter 8

Life had meaning again for Rider Twelve Horses—beyond the solitary need he had felt the winter before when he had known a sickness that only the lonely peaks of the mountains could cure. He hunted for deer and antelope with his two Crow friends, Deer Foot and White Fox, in the Laramie Mountains and the mountains beyond—ranging often as far south as the Medicine Bow and north along the Lightning River, where they happened upon a small herd of buffalo. Rider's prowess as a hunter only grew—and he did take notice of Yellow Bird, Deer Foot's sister, although he did not mention it to anyone. Most of all, he denied it to Little Thunder, who would have ridden him mercilessly if he knew the lithesome maiden had captured Rider's eye. Gone entirely were the troubling thoughts of Lucy Taylor McGowan, just as Johnny Hawk had predicted during his darker days.

All in all, it was a happy time for Johnny and Rider. There was some regret, however, for Johnny's eyesight was failing rapidly, so much so that he was forced to admit it to Rider, but he was well taken care of by his ever-faithful Morning Flower, who was happy that he didn't take to the mountains to hunt with his friend.

The peace was not to last, however, for there was no Eden in this savage land west of the Missouri. It came in the form of three white miscreants and two pack-horses loaded with four barrels of rye whiskey. The Union Pacific Railroad's track reached Cheyenne, Wyoming, on November thirteenth. And on the first train to reach that town were four barrels to be picked up by Frank Wooley to be delivered by mule to a saloon five miles outside the post area at Fort Laramie. On his way to Fort Laramie, Frank Wooley had the misfortune to meet up with three road agents who were waiting to rob the stagecoach from Cheyenne to the army post.

"Somebody's comin'," Billy Hyde called back to the others, "but it ain't the stage."

"Lemme see," Bodine said as he moved up beside him and peered over the bank of the creek. After a minute or two, he asked, "What the hell is that? Reckon what he's totin'? Looks like barrels on them two mules."

"That's what it is, all right," Quincy said, having moved up behind them to have a look for himself. "And I'm bettin' those barrels are full of whiskey." Being somewhat more of a thinker than his two companions, he knew right away that, if he was right, and it was whiskey the lone rider was transporting, it was probably of more value than what they might have gotten from the stage.

"Whiskey!" Billy exclaimed. "That'ud be enough to last us for a month."

"Hell, you damn fool," Quincy said, "it don't make no sense to drink it all up when we could sell it and make some good money on it."

"Quincy's right," Bodine said. "We can sell it to the Injuns—sell it to the soldiers cheaper'n they can get it at the saloon."

"All right, then," Quincy said, "let's get ready for him when he crosses the creek."

They had picked this particular place to waylay the stage where the trail led to a natural ford of the shallow creek. From the old tracks around the banks, it appeared that the stage usually stopped there to water their horses before moving on. It would work equally well for a whiskey peddler. With their horses out of sight in the trees, the three outlaws took positions on either side of the trail and waited. In about fifteen minutes, Frank Wooley reached the south bank of the creek and guided his horse down into the water. Just as the stagecoach drivers did, he stopped in the middle to let his animals drink. When they finished, he nudged his horse and started up the other side, only to rein back suddenly when the formidable form of Bodine stepped out of the brush beside the trail. Almost immediately, the startled peddler was confronted by the other two. It was too late to run, for Bodine took hold of his horse's bridle.

"Afternoon, neighbor," Quincy greeted Wooley, who already feared for his safety. "Where you headed?"

"Fort Laramie," Frank answered, his voice trembling. "I got a shipment of molasses for the soldiers' mess," he lied.

"Molasses, huh?" Quincy replied. He looked at

Bodine and smiled. "How long has it been since you had a good drink of molasses?"

Always one to enjoy a game of intimidation, Bodine responded with a wide grin. "It's been a spell. I could use one right now. How 'bout it, mister? Reckon you could spare a little taste of that molasses?"

Frank figured that he was already a dead man, but he tried to talk his way out of it. "Honest to God, fellers, if this stuff belonged to me, I'd be the first to offer you fellers some. But the army said it had to be delivered with the wire on the taps and the taps unopened."

"Is that a fact?" Quincy replied. "We wouldn't wanna get you in any trouble with the army, so I guess we won't get no molasses, boys." He jerked his head back around to face Frank again. "You ain't japing us, are you? That is molasses in them barrels?"

"Oh, yes, sir," Frank said, "I swear it ain't nothin' but molasses."

Tired of the game Quincy and Bodine were amusing themselves with, Billy suddenly drew his .44 and fired at one of the barrels. Frank's horse bucked, tossing him from the saddle, and the mules tried to rear back. Bodine's firm hand on the bridle saved the three animals from bolting. "Damn you, Billy," Quincy yelled. "What's the matter with you?"

Billy paid him no mind. He and Bodine were both watching the steady stream of whiskey spurting from the bullet hole in the barrel, but only for a second before Billy holstered his pistol and cupped his hands to catch some of the whiskey. "Goddam, that's good molasses!" he exclaimed, catching as much as he could in his hands and downing it.

"We're losin' it, you damn fool," Quincy roared. "Cut a piece offa that cottonwood switch and plug that hole." When neither of his partners responded, both more intent upon tasting the free-flowing whiskey, he grabbed a branch off the ground, pulled out his knife, and quickly whittled it to a peg, which he jammed in the hole. "That'll hold till we make a better one," he declared. Then he turned to Frank Wooley, who had gotten up on his knees after being thrown. "You lied to us, mister. You know what happens to liars? They go to hell. That's where you're fixin' to go right now."

To Bodine's delight, Frank began to beg for his life. "Please don't kill me, fellers. Take the whiskey and I'll turn around and head right back the way I came. I won't say nothin' to nobody, I swear."

Quincy smirked as he drew his pistol and Bodine and Billy drew theirs; then the three came to stand over the cowering man. "Oh, dear God," he whined, "don't kill me."

"Damn, lookee yonder," Billy said, laughing as he pointed to a rapidly spreading wet stain on Frank's trousers. The three revolvers fired at almost the same instant, putting the terrified man out of his shame.

Lame Pony got to his feet and looked out across the river to watch the riders approaching. They seemed to be following the river. As they came closer, he could identify them as white men, three of them, and they were leading two packhorses loaded with what appeared to be barrels. Curious, he called to Kills With Hand and pointed to the strangers. Kills With Hand stood up and, after following the direction pointed out by Lame Pony with his eyes, came to stand by him. There was no cause for alarm, for the Crows were friends of the white man and the army. They left the pony herd and walked down to the riverbank to meet the white men, who had now spotted them and guided their horses in their direction.

"Howdy, friends," Bodine called out, and gave a peace sign just in case the two Crows didn't understand English. When they returned his signal, the white men forded the river, pulled up in front of them, and dismounted. "Speak English?" Bodine asked. When both Indians nodded, he favored them with a wide grin, then turned to wink at his two companions. "Whose village is that?" he asked, pointing beyond the pony herd toward the tipis in the trees.

"Two Bulls," Lame Pony answered.

"Good," Bodine said. "We've heard of Two Bulls. The great white father in Washington says Two Bulls is his friend, and he sent us to bring his people a gift of firewater." He turned and pointed to the barrels. "You like to try some firewater?"

Lame Pony looked at Kills With Hand, undecided as to what he should answer. He knew about the white man's firewater, although he had never tasted it. Two Bulls had counseled his people to let the white man have his firewater; it was not for his people to drink. Yet Lame Pony knew that Little Thunder seemed to need the strange water that appeared to make him happy.

When he saw the Indians' indecision, Quincy dismounted and stepped over to one of the mules. Drawing a cupful from the bullet hole, he walked over to

Lame Pony, took a long swallow of the whiskey, then extended the cup toward the young Crow, smacking his lips as he did so. "This stuff burns real good," he said, smiling. "Did ol' Two Bulls tell you not to drink fire-water?" When both Indians nodded at the same time, Quincy laughed. "You know why? It's because drinking firewater makes you happy and smarter, and the chief don't want you to be smarter than him." When the two were still hesitant, Quincy said, "You can just try a little bit, and ol' Two Bulls won't never know about it."

While Quincy was busy persuading the Indians to give in to the temptation, Bodine and Billy made a show of helping themselves to some of the whiskey and obviously enjoying it. Finally Kills With Hand said, "I try." Quincy was quick to oblige, handing the coffee cup, still almost full, to him. Kills With Hand took a big gulp of the fiery liquid and quickly swallowed it. Then he shook his head violently like a dog trying to swallow a yellow jacket.

They all laughed at his antics as he tried to cool his burning throat. "Good!" Bodine chortled. "Make you strong." He took another drink to show how he could handle the firewater. "The more you drink, the stronger you get."

Kills With Hand wasn't sure about that. He held the cup out to Lame Pony, motioning for him to try it. Lame Pony hesitated for only a moment before succumbing, but his reluctance to let Kills With Hand be the only one to experience the white man's firewater was the deciding factor. His first drink produced similar results to those of his friend. Quincy was very persuasive, and before long, they were all drinking and enjoying themselves. At least it seemed that way to the two Indians, and they giggled foolishly at each other when they could no longer walk without staggering. It was not long after that when both of them lay down on the riverbank and went to sleep.

Looking at the two sleeping Indians, Billy Hyde commented, "Well, now what are we gonna do? These two bastards is passed out on us. How we gonna trade anythin' with 'em?"

"The trouble with you," Quincy answered, "is you ain't got the patience to make money. We get these heathens hooked on whiskey and they'll trade everythin' they got to get some more."

"Well, why don't we just ride on in to the village and put it up for sale?" Billy wanted to know.

"'Cause Two Bulls is liable to run us outta there before we sell a cupful," Quincy replied. "These boys here are gonna feel like hell when they wake up, so we gotta give 'em some hair of the dog that bit 'em. They'll feel better again and think it's big medicine. They'll want more. Then we'll just set up shop right here and let them bring our customers to us. This stuff makes Injuns crazy."

Quincy's predictions worked almost to the letter. After the two Crows were recovered from their first drunk and feeling happy again, he told them that he wanted to trade for horses and hides, and sent them back to their village to bring more of their friends to trade for the magic firewater. They traded on into the night without any of the village's elders aware of the chicanery. It took another white man to discover the evil influence that had descended the village's young men.

Little Thunder walked out of the tipi, facing the sun, and stretched his stiff back. Something had poked him in the back during the night, or he had slept on something under his bed that shouldn't have been there—he didn't know which—or maybe it was nothing but the fact that his bones were getting old. Anyway, a cup of hot coffee would fix it up. He had started to turn around and go back inside when his eye caught sight of a body lying on the ground near the back of a tipi several dozen yards away. He immediately looked all around him, alert for a sneak attack of some sort, but all seemed peaceful in the camp.

He hurried over to investigate. It was Lame Deer, lying facedown in the frozen snow, and by the smell of alcohol, Johnny knew at once that he was dead drunk. Knowing he would likely freeze to death if he didn't get him up, he rolled him over and shook his head in disgust when he saw the frozen contents of the young man's stomach crusted all over his shirt. "Damned if you ain't tied a good one on," he said as he tried to wake him, pulling him up to a sitting position and gently slapping his face back and forth. The rude procedure finally resulted in bringing Lame Deer back to reality—unfortunately a reality that he cared little for, because he was sick again with a throbbing head and queasy stomach. "Come on, boy, we got to get you up and get you some coffee. You're gonna feel like hell for a while."

He walked Lame Deer back to Morning Flower's

tipi and called for his wife. "Morning Flower, bring me some coffee out here." It took a little while before they were able to bring the young man back to life; then gradually the story of where he obtained the alcohol unfolded. "Those sons of bitches," Johnny swore when told of the three white men with the whiskey barrels. He went at once to inform Two Bulls of the trouble; then they, with a party of mostly elders, went to see if the white whiskey peddlers were still by the river. Rider, with most of the warriors, was gone to hunt a herd of buffalo reported to have been seen near the South Platte, but they shouldn't be needed to rout three white men.

They were still there, evidently hoping to continue trading with the Indians. Johnny and Two Bulls had no trouble finding their camp, for a good portion of the camp's horse herd was picketed on several ropes tied in the trees on the riverbank. The three men were seated around their campfire, and it was not until they discovered the delegation approaching and got to their feet that Johnny recognized two of them. "Bodine and Hyde," he said, the words dropping from his lips like something foul and evil-tasting.

"You know these men?" Two Bulls asked.

"I do," Johnny responded, "at least two of 'em, and they are no-good trash."

"Uh-oh, here comes trouble," Bodine uttered when he saw the stumpy little scout leading the party of Indians.

"You know the little half-pint?" Quincy asked.

"Yeah," Bodine answered, "I know the little son of a bitch, and if he didn't have all his Injun friends backin' him up, I'd shoot the bastard where he stands." He waited then until the party from the village came up to face them. "Well, well, if it ain't my old friend, Johnny Hawk, come down to say hello. Where's your sidekick, Rider?"

Johnny waited for the chief to speak. Two Bulls held up his hand and pointed across the river. "Go from our village. You are not welcome here with your firewater that is already burning the insides of many of our young men."

"We came in peace," Quincy said, "to trade with your people."

"You have nothing to trade with us," Two Bulls replied. "Get on your horses and leave us."

"All right, we don't want no trouble. We'll take our horses and leave." He turned to Billy and said, "Go take up them picket lines and we'll herd our ponies across the river with what whiskey we got left."

"No," Two Bulls said, slowly shaking his head. "The ponies stay here. You will take the horses you rode."

"I'll be damned!" Bodine flared up. "We traded fair and square for them horses. They're ours now. Them young bucks of your'n drank up half our whiskey."

Silent to this point, since he felt it was the chief's place to speak for his village, Johnny could hold his tongue no longer. "You heard what he said, Bodine. You ain't give them Injuns nothin' for their ponies but a headache and a sick stomach, so get on your horse and get the hell outta here before Two Bulls decides to shoot you. Where'd you steal that whiskey, anyway? I know damn well you ain't come by it honestly."

"You sawed-off little bastard," Bodine fumed,

"where I got it ain't none of your business, and I'll trade it with whoever the hell I want."

His patience gone, Johnny pulled his rifle up and pumped three rounds apiece in each of the barrels, tearing gaping holes that released the whiskey to spurt out on the ground. His sudden action caused all parties to come to an immediate state of alertness. Bodine started to react, but the sight of the party of Crows bringing their weapons up ready to fire was enough to discourage him.

"Hold steady now," Quincy warned his two partners. "There's too many of 'em. We'll just back away and get our horses."

They backed slowly to their horses and climbed into the saddles. Wheeling his horse to cross back over the river, Bodine uttered a threat, "I'll be seein' you, runt."

"Kiss my ass," Johnny replied.

They had not ridden far before the bickering began. Quincy was the first to complain. "By God, that was a fine piece of work. I told you last night that we shoulda left there as soon as it started gettin' dark. It cost us twenty-nine horses and the two barrels of whiskey we had left to wait around here till mornin'. Maybe next time you'll listen to me."

"I don't remember you cryin' about leavin' last night," Bodine said, "so just keep your trap shut about it." He was in no mood to take a scolding from anyone. Once again he had come out on the losing end of a confrontation with Johnny Hawk, and it was eating away at him something fierce. As if to remind him of the first time, he could feel an irritating itch beside his ear where there was still a scarred patch left by the burning of a flaming limb. True, it was not Johnny Hawk who laid him out with two blows of the limb, but it was the little man who caused his tall friend to do it. "That little bastard," he muttered, "I'll get to him one of these times when he ain't got no help with him, and when I do, I'm gonna take my knife and carve him up proper."

"What did you say?" Billy Hyde asked, unable to understand the huge man's mumbling.

"Nothin'," Bodine snapped. They rode about a mile farther while he was thinking about the incident just behind them, his mind working on his lust for revenge. "I'm goin' back," he suddenly announced. "That little bastard has crossed my trail too many times."

All three pulled up to a stop. "What the hell are you talkin' about?" Quincy wanted to know. He was as frustrated and angry as Bodine over losing all they had gained by murdering Frank Wooley, but he wasn't ready to go to war against a whole village of Crow warriors. "You think you can walk right in that Crow camp and kill him and won't nobody lift a finger to stop you?"

"I'll pick me a spot to watch that camp," Bodine said, making his plan as he talked. "There's gotta be some time when he's by hisself, and when that time comes, I'll be waitin' for him. You two just go on ahead. I don't need no help."

"I'll go with you," Billy piped up. He had been following Bodine's lead for so long that he wouldn't know what to do on his own. And they hadn't been riding with Quincy long enough to trust him.

"You're both loco," Quincy said. "You ain't likely to ever catch him by himself." He was tempted to leave them then, but until he hooked up with somebody better, he needed the two of them. It was a hard decision to make because of the danger that could be involved if Bodine went off half-cocked. "Ah, shit," he finally said. "I'll go with you, but if you start thinkin' about takin' some crazy chances, I'm cuttin' out."

It took a while in the gathering darkness to find a spot that all three found suitable, but they decided on a small hill from which they could see the edge of the river and the backside of the camp. There was a clear escape route down a ravine into a canyon if they had to make a hasty retreat. They tied the horses there and left them saddled. Then they waited, with Quincy reminding the other two periodically that it was a damn fool thing to do, and Bodine telling him he could leave at any time.

"When Rider Twelve Horses come back?" Morning Flower asked.

"Well, that's hard to say," Johnny answered. "Depends on whether or not that tale about seein' buffalo is true or not, and if they find buffalo, I don't expect they'll be back for a week or more."

The big woman nodded. "I make him new shirt," she said, holding her hands apart to indicate. "Bigger." Then her expression turned serious. "Who is bad white man? Why he come here?"

"Bodine's his name," Johnny said. "It was just bad luck he came to our village. If he'da knowed I was here, he might not'a come," he boasted. He reached over and stroked her hair. "I expect one of these days I'll have to settle Bodine's hash. If he shows up here again, I just might do it."

She shook her head as if perplexed. She was accustomed to his bluster. "I go to fill water skins now," she said.

"Hell, I'll go with you," he said. "I'm gettin' tired of lyin' around here. I shoulda gone huntin' with Rider, I reckon." He got up and followed her out the flap of the tipi.

"We been lyin' around on this damn hill all day," Quincy complained. "You ain't gonna see that son of a bitch by himself. I think we've waited here long enough. I'm headin' to Fort Laramie."

He started toward his horse, when Bodine suddenly stopped him. "Wait! There he is! Yonder by the river. I told you!"

Billy and Quincy both crowded up behind Bodine to get a look. "Damned if it ain't," Billy said, "and with the biggest Injun squaw I've ever seen, but he's pretty far away to get a decent shot."

Bodine didn't answer right away while he studied the terrain between the hill they were on and the bank of the river. "There's plenty of cover between here and the river if they'll come a little bit farther down this way," he said. "That's right, that's right," he coaxed. "Come on, you little son of a bitch."

Puzzled by the vengeful brute's hesitancy, Quincy asked, "What are you waitin' for? Follow that ravine down to the bottom and you're plenty close enough for a good shot." He pointed to a spot that would put him close to one hundred yards from the little man and the big Crow woman.

Bodine was more ambitious than that. He was busy figuring out a route beyond the bottom of the ravine Quincy pointed to, a route that would allow him to get closer to Johnny, one that would permit him to enjoy the satisfaction of using his knife. When he got it mapped out in his head, he told his partners what he intended to do. "I'll lead my horse down that ravine and leave him there. Then I'll work my way around them bushes along the bluff, and I won't be no more'n a couple dozen yards from him."

Quincy shook his head, not convinced that Bodine's plan was a good one. "You're gonna put yourself mighty damn close to that Crow camp. One shot and they'll come pourin' outta there like a hive of bees."

Bodine could not be swayed. His lust for vengeance was too great to consider risks. He turned to cast a contemptuous look at Quincy. "Quit your whinin'. I'll have my horse down in that ravine. I'll have plenty of time to skedaddle before them Injuns know what happened. You two can hightail it and I'll catch up."

"It's your neck," Quincy said with an indifferent shrug.

"It damn sure is," Bodine shot back, and started toward the ravine.

Down at the bottom, he tied his horse to a gooseberry bush and, running in a crouch, made his way along a low rise toward the bluffs. When he reached the point where the rise leveled out, and no longer offered adequate cover, he was forced to stop and con-

sider his next move. Watching from the hill, Billy said,
"He's gonna get hisself killed."

"That's as close as he's gonna get," Quincy said.
"Take the shot, you damn fool. Hell, it can't be over
fifty yards."

But Bodine was determined to finish Johnny Hawk
with his knife, close and personal. His dilemma, however, was the open space between him and the river
bluffs. Bodine was a big man, and not fleet of foot. He
knew that if he tried to sprint across the open area between them, he would be seen and probably get shot.
"Dammit!" he swore as he watched the Indian woman
fill her water skins with Johnny standing by, watching
her. The skins filled, Morning Flower turned and they
started back toward the village. Bodine panicked. His
only option to stop them was to shoot. He didn't hesitate. Raising his rifle, he took aim and fired.

Hit in the back, Johnny went down immediately
and Morning Flower dropped the bags filled with
water and dropped on her knees beside him. Seeing
Johnny go down, Bodine saw it as his opportunity to
complete the execution the way he wanted. Screaming
in horror, Morning Flower tried to take Johnny in her
arms as he tried desperately to draw his revolver to defend himself against the hulking man charging toward
them. "Bodine," Johnny spat weakly, unable to clear
the pistol from his holster. Shrieking her rage, Morning
Flower grabbed the pistol, pulled it free, and got off
one wild shot with the single-action revolver, but she
was still trying to cock it when she was knocked sense-
less by a blow from Bodine's rifle butt.

Knowing there was little time left before the village responded to the shots, Bodine nevertheless took a few seconds to gloat over his dastardly act of murder. "Now, you sawed-off little son of a bitch, you're gonna get what's comin' to ya," he taunted, holding his skinning knife up for Johnny to see. Hearing loud voices coming from the village, he knew he'd better get his evil business done. With a quick thrust, he sank his knife deep into Johnny's side as the little man grunted with the pain and struggled to get his hands on Bodine's neck. The big man swept them aside with ease. "Die, you little bastard," he commanded.

"Go to hell," Johnny spat back at him.

Knowing his victim had little time left before he died, Bodine withdrew the knife, intent upon scalping him while he still had life enough to feel it. "How you like bein' scalped, like them Injuns you been livin' with?" With that, he grabbed a handful of Johnny's thinning gray hair and drew his knife across the little man's forehead. He didn't have the opportunity to complete the job, for he was interrupted when Morning Flower recovered her senses enough to reach for Johnny's pistol again. Having to react quickly, he kicked the pistol out of her reach in time to hear a mob of Indians pouring out of the village. There was no time left. He turned for just a second to take a quick shot at Morning Flower, then retreated as fast as he could run to the cover of the rise. Breathing heavily from his exertion, he still found satisfaction in finishing off the little man who had been such a pain in his side.

Back beside the river, the people of Two Bulls' village had found the victims of the cruel attack, and warriors were running to find the raiders, but Bodine had too great a lead to be caught by men on foot. After a search of the area around the bluffs, they discovered the place where he had tied his horse, but they were too late to catch him. Because of Bodine's need to hurry his shot, Morning Flower was only wounded in the shoulder, but Little Thunder appeared to be near death. He was covered with blood from the bullet wound and the knife wound with blood streaming over his face from the scalp wound. Crying, and still in a state of profound shock, Morning Flower kept repeating the name she had heard Johnny utter, *Bodine*, over and over.

They carried the injured couple back to Morning Flower's tipi, where the women worked with the village's medicine man to tend the wounds as best they could. Morning Flower was recovering well enough since at that close range, Bodine's rifle slug had passed all the way through. Little Thunder, however, was in grave trouble. He was alive, although barely, having already slid into a state of unconsciousness, and it looked as if he would not make it through the night.

A war party rode out to track the murderers, and they picked up their trail down a long ravine into a shallow valley. They followed the trail north before losing it just before dark in the Laramie Mountains. Discouraged, they returned to a village in mourning for a beloved little white man who would probably not make it through the night. As soon as her wounds were bandaged, Morning Flower was at Johnny's side, bathing his bloody scalp wound and singing softly for his recovery, while the medicine man administered every ritual he knew. The prognosis did not look good.

Much to everyone's surprise, Little Thunder was

still among the living the next morning. Always a stubborn man, he wouldn't improve and he wouldn't die, it seemed, and yet he wasn't there mentally. For Morning Flower would talk to him constantly, hoping for some response, but there was none. This was the condition Rider found him in when the hunting party returned.

He noticed a rather strange welcome when the hunting party rode into the village with packhorses loaded with deer meat. They had been unable to find the reported buffalo, but they were fortunate to have run up on a small herd of deer, and ordinarily any successful hunt in winter was met with a warm welcome. They soon discovered the reason for their lukewarm homecoming, and Rider went at once to Morning Flower's tipi when he was told of the tragic attack on his friend.

As soon as he entered the lodge, Morning Flower got up to meet him. "Little Thunder sleeps," she cried. "No wake up."

At first, he thought she meant Johnny was dead, but she then explained his friend's condition. Looking down at the man who had risked his life to free him from federal custody, and taken him in practically as a father might adopt a son, he was overcome by a wave of emotion the likes of which he had never experienced. Then he felt his fists tighten as Morning Flower related the details of the attack, ending with the word she kept repeating so as not to forget. "Bodine," she said. "Little Thunder say *Bodine* when white man shoot him." Rider pictured the bully in his mind as he started to scalp Johnny, and the anger in him seemed to race red-hot through his veins. *I will find you and I will kill you*, he vowed to himself. But his first concern was what he could do for Johnny. Bodine would have to wait until after Johnny was taken care of.

"How long has he been like this?" Rider asked as he watched the medicine man chanting over Johnny's bed, shaking a rattle made from a gourd. When told it had been two days now, he decided what he must do. He did not wish to offend the medicine man, but there was little doubt in his mind that Johnny's condition was well beyond his chanting and herbs. "Get him wrapped up in warm blankets," he said. "I'm takin' him to the surgeon at Fort Laramie." The medicine man insisted that his medicine was the only thing keeping Johnny alive, so in terms as politely as possible Rider told him it would not be his fault if Little Thunder died. He then went to cut poles for a travois to transport him.

While he trimmed the poles for his travois, he was approached by Yellow Bird, who came up so quietly behind him that he almost knocked her over when he suddenly turned to pick up his hatchet again. He just managed to catch her by her shoulders to keep her from falling. She smiled sweetly as he apologized for his clumsiness. "I am sorry for Little Thunder," she said, and he nodded in response. "I am sorry for your hurt," she added. "If you need me, I will help you."

"Thank you," he said, then paused to study her face. He remembered how Johnny had teased him before about Deer Foot's sister. His initial impression had been that she was just a girl, not really old enough to even consider Johnny's speculations. There were too many other things to occupy his mind at the present, dire, lethal thoughts to consume his thinking. Yet he could not at the moment help noticing the soul of a woman in the dark eyes that seemed to look so deeply into his and the full lips that spoke so softly. He quickly reminded himself that there were other things to think about now. "Thank you for your offer," he said, "but Morning Flower is goin' with me to take care of Little Thunder."

She nodded and said, "I will watch for your return." She smiled then, turned, and left him to finish his travois.

"It'll be a while," he said, and picked up his hatchet.

She turned and replied, "No matter, I will wait for you."

His mind was too preoccupied with worry for Johnny at that moment to think about other things. It would come to puzzle him at a later time when he would wonder about the young woman's attention toward him.

Chapter 9

With Johnny loaded as comfortably as they could make him with layers of blankets, they left Two Bulls' camp early the next morning. Rider led the horse pulling the travois while Morning Flower rode behind, her arm in a makeshift sling, leading a packhorse with all their supplies. Yellow Bird watched them leave, standing apart from the crowd of well-wishers so that he would see her. On a trip that took Rider and Johnny less than two days when they had come in search of Two Bulls' camp, they took three full days going back, because of the travois and the frequent stops to make sure Johnny was all right. At night, when they made camp, Morning Flower insisted on doing her usual work, taking the sling off and using both hands. Rider tried to help, but was roughly rebuked for his efforts and told to keep out of her way.

They arrived at Fort Laramie late in the afternoon and Rider pulled the travois straight to the post hospital. The surgeon was in, and seemed reluctant at first to examine Johnny, but consented to admit the patient when told that he was a scout for the army, hired by Jim Bridger. Rider declined to tell him that they had left the service of the army at Fort Reno. The surgeon was a man dedicated to his profession and he undertook the treatment of Johnny's various wounds, but he could not in all honesty give Rider any hope for the patient's recovery from the apparent coma. His frank diagnosis to Rider was that he simply didn't know. "He hasn't had anything to eat for about five days, according to what you tell me," the doctor said. "And to be honest with you, I think you've been hauling a dead man around, or at least he might as well be. I don't see how he's made it this long without nourishment of some kind. All I can tell you is that if he doesn't come out of that coma pretty damn soon, there's nothing more we can do for him."

"I 'preciate it, Doctor," Rider said. "I'm gonna take this woman over to the Crow camp. Then I'll be back to sit with Johnny."

"Suit yourself," the surgeon said.

Morning Flower was reluctant to leave Johnny, but Rider explained that she couldn't stay in the hospital. She argued that she could make a bed for herself beside the building, but he finally convinced her that the army wouldn't allow it. She finally gave in after he promised that she could come back first thing in the morning. Then he took her to a Crow village a couple of miles up the North Platte, where she was warmly welcomed. Rider was welcomed as well, but he thanked them graciously and returned to camp by Johnny's bed. There were many thoughts on his mind throughout the long night, most of them concerning the possible whereabouts of Bodine and his partners.

It was just as well that Rider wasn't aware that the men he sought were closer than he thought, for had he known they were on their way to Helena, and only a couple of days ahead of him, it might have caused him a great deal of anguish as whether or not to leave Johnny. Seated Indian-style on the floor beside Johnny's bed with his back against the wall, he had fallen asleep sometime in the wee hours of the morning. He was jerked awake by a gentle tapping on his shoulder, opening his eyes to see Morning Flower's beaming face. Still groggy from lack of sleep, he got up when she pointed to the bed, to discover Johnny's eyes open and seemingly staring straight at the ceiling. They were the unblinking eyes of a dead man, he feared, and wondered why Morning Flower's expression was one of joy. Then Johnny's eyes blinked and he saw a weak attempt to display the lone tooth in a smile.

Dehydrated to the point of approaching death, Johnny was immediately given water by the orderly on duty, and Rider went in search of the doctor. Scarcely believing what he was told, that Johnny had come out of his sleep, the surgeon went to examine the patient. "It's a damn miracle," he pronounced. "I don't mind telling you I didn't expect him to make it through another night." Although apparently alive, the patient had not spoken a word up to that point. "We'll change those bandages and clean him up a little," the doctor said, "but first I want to get a little food in him." He had to pause then to again comment, "I swear, this man oughta be dead."

"He always was stubborn," a relieved Rider replied with a wide smile on his face.

"I ain't ready to go yet," Johnny said, startling the three standing over him, his words barely audible.

"Doctor fix. I take care of you," Morning Flower gushed gleefully, causing Rider to smile. It was obvious that the big woman was finding it difficult to restrain from snatching him up from the bed to hug him.

When the doctor agreed to permit the Crow woman to stay by Johnny's bedside, Rider felt it was time to attend to the vengeful business that had now returned to the forefront of his mind. With assurance that his friend was going to live, he did not want to delay any further the quest he had promised himself. "I've got to take care of some unfinished business," he told Johnny. "Morning Flower will take care of you." He directed his next comment to the Indian woman. "When they say he's well enough to get out of here, take him to the Crow village. I don't know how long I'll be gone, maybe a long time, 'cause I won't be back till I take care of business." Directing his comments to the frail-looking little man in the hospital bed, he said, "Don't give them any hard time, and I'll expect you to be on your feet the next time I see you." That said, he took his leave, heading first to the sutler's store to trade what pelts he had left for a few staples.

William Bullock was surprised to hear that Johnny Hawk was in the post hospital, and when told that the man who caused him to be there was the oversized brute called Bodine, he was quick to inform Rider of some important news. "That big bastard was just in here two days ago, him and his two cutthroat friends. They were trying to weasel me down on the price of .44 cartridges, but I told 'em the price was what it was, no more, no less. They didn't seem too happy about it. And to think they'd just come from tryin' to murder Johnny Hawk." He paused to shake his head in disbelief.

"They didn't say where they were headin', did they?" Rider asked.

"Well, no. That is, they didn't tell me, but they got into an argument among themselves about what they were fixin' to do. I couldn't help overhearin' what they were arguin' about. I didn't hear them mention the exact place, but if I had to guess, I'd say they were plannin' to ride up to Last Chance Gulch, Helena way, 'cause that's the hot diggin's right now. And that's what they were arguin' about—talkin' about doin' some gold minin'." He gave Rider a knowing look then. "And that threesome ain't likely to go to the work of puttin' a pick in the ground or a pan in the stream, if you know what I mean."

"I reckon," Rider replied. He could well agree with Bullock's speculation. It made sense to him that Bodine and his two partners would seek to put some distance between them and Fort Laramie. And where else would they head except someplace where they might rob and murder some innocent souls who were working to pull the wealth out of the ground? "I'm much obliged for the information," Rider said. "I expect I'd best get on my way." He gathered up the few staples his furs would buy and turned to leave. Before he reached the door, Bullock stopped him.

"You goin' after those three?" he asked.

"I expect so," Rider replied.

"Well, hold on a minute." He reached under the counter and pulled out a box of cartridges. "Here, take these. You might need extra cartridges."

Surprised, Rider's initial response was to refuse them. "Ten dollars a box. I can't afford extra cartridges right now," he said.

"Take 'em," Bullock insisted. "You can settle up with me later if you want."

"I'm obliged. I can sure use 'em," Rider said. "I'll pay you back when I get the hides."

"I ain't worried about it. You just watch your back and good huntin'."

He left Fort Laramie, guiding the buckskin north, once again following the old Bozeman Trail through Powder River country, hoping to cut down some of the two-day lead Bodine had.

There was no way he could know, but the outlaws were not wasting any time on the trail, so he was not really gaining on them. Even though he rode long days, they were doing the same, anxious to put places and people where they were known behind them. It was a three-day ride to Fort Reno, and when he reached that post and asked about the three, he was told that they had stopped there briefly two days before and continued on after a stop only long enough to rest their horses. Planning to do the same, he was delayed when he had to take a longer route, following the Powder River instead of heading more westerly to strike Crazy Woman Creek, because of the reported presence of a large band of Sioux camped on the Crazy Woman near the Bozeman crossing. He was more cautious about avoiding hostile war parties, unwilling to take any chances that might endanger or hinder his mission. When he reached the confluence of the Crazy Woman with the Powder, well above the usual Bozeman crossing, he guided the buckskin directly west toward Fort C. F. Smith. He was disappointed, but not surprised, to learn that he had lost ground to the three killers. He continued on his way as soon as his horse was rested.

"My ass is gettin' damn tired of settin' in that saddle," Bodine complained as he rubbed his backside.

"Huh," Quincy snorted. "Think how sore that horse of yours must be from totin' your big ass all the way from Fort Laramie." His remark caused Billy to giggle, but the remark was more fact than jest. They had pushed their horses hard over the last week in snow over a foot deep in some places, and they were constantly on the lookout for an opportunity to trade for fresh mounts. So far, none had been encountered.

"My ass is about to freeze off," Billy said. "If it keeps snowin' like this, the damn trail is gonna be hard to find."

"All we gotta do is follow the river, you dummy," Quincy said.

"We ought'n to have more'n three, four days to Helena," Bodine said, "and I'm damn glad of it." He got up to move closer to the fire.

"I hope we strike it rich pretty quick," Billy said. "I

need to hit a saloon before I perish of thirst." He helped himself to another cup of coffee. "You reckon there'll be any fuss about that business back at that Crow camp? I mean, them Crows is pretty tight with the soldiers. They mighta told them troops over at Laramie."

"What are they gonna tell 'em?" Bodine replied. "The only one knows our names is Johnny Hawk and he's dead, and that's a fact. Besides, we ain't told nobody we're headin' to Helena, even if they was to look for us."

They were within a hard day's ride from reaching their destination before finding an opportunity to switch to fresh horses. Approaching Sixteen Mile Creek, a mile or so east of its confluence with the Missouri, they came upon a ranch house built hard up against the south side of a low hill. A couple of hundred yards from the house, a small herd of about twenty-five horses were pawing around in the snow by the creek, looking for the grass underneath. "There we go, boys," Quincy sang out, "fresh horses."

"Let's go look 'em over," Bodine said, and turned his horse toward the creek.

"Go ahead if you want to," Quincy said, "but I think I'll go talk to the owner there in that cabin. That bunch of horses is in easy rifle range of the cabin, and he might not be real generous with anybody cuttin' out his stock."

"Quincy's right," Billy said, looking at the smoke curling up from the chimney. "Besides, I wouldn't mind warmin' my feet by that fire in the house there." That thought appealed to all three of the cold, weary riders, so they headed directly to the cabin.

As they suspected, they had been spotted as soon as they had topped a rise about six hundred yards south of the cabin. Pulling up in front of the door, Quincy called out. "Hello the house. Anybody home?" In a moment, the door opened ajar, far enough to see a man standing there with one hand holding a shotgun by the barrel. "Howdy, neighbor," Quincy said. "You've got nothin' to fear from us. We're U.S. Marshals on our way to Helena and our horses is about wore out. We was wonderin' if you're interested in tradin' us some fresh horses. We've got government cash money to pay to boot, if you're willin'."

His interest sharpened by the mention of cash money, the man opened the door a bit wider to get a better look at the horses they rode. It was just wide enough to provide a better target as well and he doubled up and fell back inside when Quincy's pistol shot ripped into his stomach. "Yee-haw!" Billy shouted as he fired through the open door a split second behind Quincy, and all three quickly dismounted and stormed through the door, their revolvers ready to shoot anything inside that moved.

"Check behind that quilt!" Quincy ordered as he quickly surveyed the room, looking for anyone else that might be hiding in ambush.

Bodine snatched the quilt aside that served to divide the bedroom from the rest of the cabin. "Well, lookee here," he chortled. "Look what's hidin' behind the bedpost. Come on out here, darlin', and let me have a look at you." The woman tried to cower farther between the bed and the wall, bringing a chuckle of amusement from Bodine. The big man grabbed the side rail of the bed and flipped it upside down to land out of the way. "There, now," he said. "That'll make it a lot easier to get outta there."

With fearful eyes darting back and forth between the three intruders eyeing her, she got slowly to her feet and stood before them. Bodine took a long look at the haggard old woman, her hair in long dirty strings, framing a face, wrinkled and lean with hollow eyes from too many harsh winters. "Damn," Bodine muttered, then turned to his partners. "She's all yours, boys," he said, preferring to wait to satisfy his primal urges with one of the prostitutes in Helena.

Interest in the woman as a sexual object was also lacking with Billy and Quincy, and their attention immediately shifted from their groins to their bellies. "Get in there and rustle us up somethin' to eat," Quincy ordered.

Relieved to see that she was not to be assaulted by the three, she asked, "Can I see to Lonnie first?"

"Lemme see," Bodine replied, and went back by the door to take a look at the wounded man still doubled up on the floor, grasping his stomach and painfully gasping for breath. Bodine pulled his pistol again and put a bullet in the suffering man's forehead. "Lonnie's all right," he said with a chuckle. "He's feelin' a lot better." He holstered his pistol, grabbed the man by his heels, and dragged him outside to lie on the porch. "Now get to that stove and get busy," he said as he came back in the door. "I'm hungry."

"I swear, Bodine," Billy Hyde said. "You sure got a way with women."

Quincy watched the woman's face during the execution of her husband, and he was compelled to remark, "You sure don't look too broke up over ol' Lonnie's death." There was not a tear in her eye, and he would have expected a hysterical eruption from most any woman in like circumstances. She didn't respond to his comment, but went directly to the kitchen stove as she had been directed.

There were no tears left in Luella Perkins after a hard unrewarding life with Lonnie Trabert. She had shed the last of them when she had reluctantly followed him down the Yellowstone and up to this wilderness where he was set on building a working ranch. By that time, she had little choice, for her youth was gone, and he had not possessed the decency to marry her, often expressing more concern for the horses he had managed to accumulate than he had for her. Lonnie's death seemed no more surprising than anything else that happened in this harsh country, and she could not bring it upon herself to weep for him. Without spending a moment's thought on what was to become of her, she placed her skillet on the stove and plopped a dollop of lard in it, preparing to fry some potatoes.

"I'd say this was a real piece of good fortune," Quincy commented to Bodine and Billy after satisfying his hunger. He stirred a heaping teaspoon of sugar into his coffee, took a sip, and smacked his lips to express his pleasure. "It's been a helluva long time since I've had any sugar." He jerked his head around to focus on the woman. "What's your name, old woman?" When she answered, he repeated it after her. "Luella, huh? Well, Luella, I just might take you with us to do the cookin'. Whaddaya say 'bout that?"

She paused to think the suggestion over for a few moments before answering. Already having witnessed Bodine and Billy ransacking the cabin and pulling out every useful food staple they could find, she could imagine that there was going to be very little left after they'd gone. Maybe, she thought, she could go with them and look for a chance to escape when they were close to Helena. That was evidently where they were heading, according to their conversation as they sat around the table, drinking their coffee. Considering the alternative, she knew she would likely perish if she stayed here alone. "It's all right with me," she answered then.

"How 'bout that, boys?" Quincy exclaimed. "Luella's joinin' the gang." He tapped his cup on the table. "Bring that coffeepot over here, Luella."

She went over to the table and poured more coffee in all three cups, oblivious to Bodine's hand on her weary backside. "I swear, Luella," he said, "if you were a few years younger—hell, if you was just one year younger . . ." The three men all enjoyed a good laugh over his remark. She returned the pot to the stove and sat down on a stool in the corner.

They enjoyed a leisurely morning in the cabin, but eventually decided it was time to move on. Once again in possession of something they could sell, they planned to drive Lonnie's herd of horses into Helena. There were only a couple dozen to drive, easily handled by the three of them. They packed all the provisions they could find from the cabin on a couple of packhorses, and they were ready to ride. After putting a saddle he found in the barn on one of the horses, Quincy went back inside the cabin, where he found Luella gathering up her clothes to put in a cotton bag. "Looks like you're gettin' ready to go," Quincy said. She did not reply as she struggled into a heavy coat. "You ain't gonna need that," he said. She turned around to find his revolver in her face and carried her tired, overworked expression into the next world as the gun exploded.

He walked outside to find both Billy and Bodine staring at the cabin door with guns drawn. "What the hell was that?" Bodine asked.

"Luella decided she ain't goin' after all," was Quincy's casual reply.

"Damn, Quincy," Billy whined, "you shot our cook."

Quincy cast a condescending eye toward Billy and replied, "Have you got one single brain in that thick head of yours? We can't take a witness to town to run off and tell the sheriff what happened here." He shook his head in disgust for Billy's ignorance.

"Well, what did you throw a saddle on that horse for?"

"Because it's worth a little money," Quincy answered impatiently. "Now let's get movin'."

They drove their herd of horses to within a few miles of the busy town of Helena, and Bodine and Billy stayed to watch them while Quincy went in search of a buyer, promising that he would bring a bottle of whiskey back with him. After making the rounds of the larger mining outfits with no prospects, Quincy wished they had stolen mules instead of horses. There seemed to be no market for horses, and they wanted to get the animals off their hands as quickly as possible, so he had no alternative but to keep trying. On his third attempt, luck finally came his way. Talking to a stable owner in town, he was told that an army officer had been in his stable the day before looking for replacement horses for a detachment of troops sent all the way from Fort C. F. Smith to escort a gold shipment back. The lieutenant had said that his troop's horses were in poor condition and he had been authorized to buy replacements. "Well, I've got the horses he's lookin' for," Quincy said. "Is he still around town?"

"I expect so," the owner of the stables said. "He said the shipment he was sent to escort ain't ready yet, so he'll be around for a few days, maybe a week."

"Reckon where I can find him?" Quincy asked.

"Well, his men are camped east of town, but you might see the officer in town. I've seen him a couple of times on the street. There ain't that many soldiers at Last Chance Gulch, so if he's here, it oughta be easy to spot him. I wish I'd had the horses. The army don't haggle much on price. You just tell 'em the price and they wire the money."

The officer Quincy was hoping to find was at that moment in Helena's newest dry goods store, talking to the wife of the owner. "Is the army thinking of building a fort near Helena?" Lucy McGowan asked. The prospect of the increased business that might bring her way was intriguing.

"Not that I know of, ma'am," the lieutenant replied, "but then I wouldn't know what the army's plans might be for the future. It seems like you folks might need the presence of the military, since you're now the capital city of Montana."

"Yes, that would be nice," Lucy said. "What was your name, sir?"

"Carrington, ma'am, Lieutenant Jared Carrington."

"Any relation to Colonel Henry Carrington?" she asked.

Carrington smiled. "I get asked that question a lot since I was reassigned to the Wyoming district. And yes, ma'am, Colonel Carrington is my uncle. Do you know the colonel?"

"Not really, but I do know of him. I met him at Fort Reno on my way out here with my sister and her husband. We left there and continued on with a wagon train led by Jack Grainger."

"That is interesting," Carrington said. "You no doubt remember an odd pair of civilian scouts named Johnny Hawk and Rider somebody, or somebody Rider. I don't know which."

Lucy raised her eyebrows in surprise. "I certainly do. We still see Johnny Hawk occasionally, but his partner, Rider . . ." She paused then. "His name is actually Jim Moran . . . Seems to spend all his time in the mountains."

If she had hit him with a pickax, the blow to his senses could not have staggered him more. He was right! He had known it all along! This simple confirmation of what he had known to be true caused his heart to pound with the excitement of justification when others had advised him to forget about his suspicions of the fraud perpetrated right under his nose. He thought of Johnny Hawk's implication in the hoax and was convinced now that it was the little scout who had actually helped Moran escape. Knowing that he now had what he needed to bring Jim Moran to justice, he fairly beamed at Lucy, his strange reaction to her innocent comment having left her astonished. In a moment, when he could speak again, he asked, "Would you know where in the mountains Jim Moran—this Rider character—is hiding?"

"Why, no, I don't have any idea," she replied. After witnessing the lieutenant's exaggerated reaction to her comment, she sensed that she might have unintentionally brought trouble to Jim, which was never what she had in mind. It also occurred to her that he had asked where Jim was *hiding*, not where he had a camp.

"What about Johnny Hawk?" he asked, his mind racing with possibilities. "Have you seen him recently? Do you know where he is?"

"No," Lucy stated firmly, "I don't know where he is, and I haven't seen him in quite a while." Fully realizing that she might have caused trouble for two people she would not wish any harm, she resolved not to give the lieutenant any more information than she already had.

It didn't make any difference to Carrington. He had the information he needed, and neither Hawk nor Moran could know that he did. *If I don't find Moran while I'm here, I'll run into him somewhere*. He took his leave of Mrs. McGowan, thanking her graciously for her conversation, and went directly to the telegraph office to request permission to extent his stay in Montana Territory to look for the escaped prisoner. He could not wait to tell his uncle that he had been correct in his suspicions about the mysterious Mr. Rider.

*   *   *

Some of the troopers in his command knew Johnny Hawk and the man called Rider. The two had ridden scout with his uncle's command as far as Fort Reno, so Carrington could count on a positive identification from these men. He divided his detachment into four scouting parties, making sure that every party had at least one man who knew the two on sight. He then sent them out to scour the town of Helena, up and down Last Chance Gulch, hoping to get lucky enough to catch Johnny Hawk on one of the visits to town Lucy McGowan had spoken of.

Because of the existing network of telegraph wires and the necessity to relay signals, the lieutenant did not receive a reply to his request to extend his mission until later the next day. In effect, his orders were to delay his return no longer than that already necessary to prepare the shipment he had been sent to escort. That didn't leave much time, but it no longer mattered because the wire also told him that Johnny Hawk was in the hospital at Fort Laramie, and Rider had brought him there. Had Carrington known that Rider was on his way to Helena, he might have been tempted to disobey his orders and wait for a chance to arrest him. Not knowing that, he bought replacement horses from two former scouts for his uncle and prepared to return to C. F. Smith, confident now that he would eventually bring Jim Moran to justice. The following day brought changes to everyone's plans in the form of a heavy winter storm that dropped two feet of snow on top of close to a foot that was already on the ground—and it continued to fall throughout the day. Miners, businessmen, freighters, and everyone else—including soldiers—had no choice but to settle in to wait it out.

Pete Bender, owner of the Pay Dirt Saloon, paused in his efforts to clear the snow away from his front door to watch three riders plowing their way toward his establishment. Their horses, almost belly-deep in the snow, could make their way only by lunging, so that they appeared to be bobbing up and down in the sea of white. *They must want a drink awful bad,* Pete thought, when it was apparent they were not going to pass him by. It was early, but he knew these three wouldn't be his only customers. When the weather hit the way it had over the last night and today, it was always good business for him. He always kept a good supply of firewood and his whiskey stores were more than ample. He might well be the only businessman—he and the other saloon operators—who welcomed the storm.

He shoveled the last of the snow from the board walkway, leaned his shovel against the wall beside the door, and stood waiting to greet his customers as they dismounted from the steaming horses. "Howdy, boys," Pete said. "Come on inside and thaw out." He stood aside and held the door while the three filed in. Looking again at the horses, emitting clouds of steam to rise in the cold air, he was prompted to say, "There's a stable right up the street if you wanna get those horses under cover."

"They'll be all right where they are," Bodine said, "but I need a drink of whiskey."

"Well, you came to the right place," Pete said, and hurried over behind the bar. If they weren't concerned about their horses, then neither was he. He set three glasses on the bar and poured three shots.

"Leave the bottle," Quincy said, and when Pete placed it on the bar, Quincy picked it up and carried it over to a table nearest the stove. Bodine and Billy followed and the three sat down to warm their outsides while the whiskey took care of the insides.

After a few minutes, Pete came over to pass the time of day with them. "Don't recall seeing you fellows in here before. You new to the gulch?"

"Yep," Quincy replied, "we thought we'd ride up here to see what all the fuss was about."

"If you're interested in the gold minin'," Pete said, "there's still some folks pullin' pay dirt outta the ground. Some folks say the most of it is about done, but I think it's the big mines that are complainin'. I know for a fact that some of my customers working small claims are still findin' it, and in worthwhile yield." When there was not much reaction from any of the three, he asked, "Are you fellows thinkin' about strikin' it rich?"

Quincy snorted, amused. "I doubt there's a piece of this gulch that ain't already been turned over two or three times. We're more in the buyin' and sellin' business—horses, things like that. We just sold some horses to the army." That was welcome news to Pete after seeing how fast the contents of the whiskey bottle were disappearing. "What we need right now is a good place to make camp."

Pete slowly shook his head. "Well, if you're talkin' about someplace where there's shelter, you can see for yourself that there ain't much around that ain't been took. But there are some shacks that folks have already left and gone on somewhere else. You might find one of them that would do till you find somethin' better. And like I said, the stables are right at the end of the street to take care of your horses."

"Thanks for the advice," Quincy said. "We'll look into it, and I expect we'd better do it right now if we don't wanna sleep in the snow tonight." He got nods from his two partners, and they all pushed back from the table. Quincy paid for the whiskey, saying to Pete, "I expect we'll be back to see you."

"Good," Pete replied. "Glad to have you boys in town."

"I'd like to take that stove with me," Billy commented on his way out the door and into the cold again.

Outside, they took a few minutes to study the situation. The main street followed the gulch, and on both sides they could see buildings in various stages of construction. Looking away from the main street, up the slope, they could see dozens of small shacks like those mentioned by Pete Bender. They all looked vacant, even though almost all of them were not. Off by itself, however, there was a more substantial shack with smoke drifting out of a hole in the back. "That looks more like it," Quincy said. "Let's go tell the owner he's movin'."

"Hello the shack," Quincy called out when they had made their way up the slope.

In a minute, a head poked out of a canvas flap that served as a door. Looking the three strangers over, the owner inquired, "What can I do for you fellers?"

They dismounted and Quincy said, "We're from the sheriff's office. We've come to serve your eviction notice."

"Our what?" The question came from a voice inside the hut. "What the hell are they talkin' about, Lige?"

The man with his head outside relayed the question. "What the hell are you fellers talkin' about?"

"Your eviction notice," Quincy answered impatiently. "How many more's inside there?"

"Just my partner," Lige answered.

"Well, we need to see you both out here so we can officially serve you both," Quincy said, "and we ain't got all day."

Lige came outside, followed shortly by his partner, and the two of them stood staring, puzzling over the impromptu visit by the three strangers. "Mister," he said, "I ain't never heard of no eviction notice. You must be lookin' for somebody else."

"No," Quincy said, "you're the ones we're lookin' for. Bodine, show 'em the eviction notice."

"Right," Bodine replied enthusiastically. This was the part he enjoyed. He stepped up close to tower over Lige. "Here it is." He brought his hand up quickly with his skinning knife in it. Lige shrieked in pain as the long blade plunged up to the hilt just beneath his breastbone. Lige's partner tried to dive into the hut, but Billy threw an arm around his neck and jerked him backward to land in the snow, where he and Quincy quickly finished him with their knives.

With both men dead, Quincy stood up again and looked around him, scanning the hillside for any sign of anyone else about. "Nice and clean, nice and quiet," he pronounced. "Let's dig the boys a place in that snowbank yonder, and they'll keep till we get a thaw."

They carried the bodies to their crypt in the snowbank and filled it in again, then went back to the hut to inventory their new abode. "Them two fellers fixed theirselves a right cozy little hut," Billy commented as he paused by the stove to warm his hands while Bodine dumped the contents of their knapsacks on the floor. The bags yielded very little that could be useful to them, but there was a generous supply of canned food and some dried apples stacked against one wall of the hut. Lige and his partner had laid in a good stack of firewood just outside the doorway, so the three outlaws were satisfied that they had everything they needed for their comfort. There was only one thing more that would have made their choice of shacks perfect, and Quincy was the first to mention it.

"Them two fellers must have some gold dust hid around here somewhere. It don't make no sense that they were holed up in this hut for their health," he said. "They had to be payin' for all this stuff with somethin' and I'm thinkin' they must have struck it rich in the diggin's."

His observation was enough to cause his partners to join him in searching the entire hut from top to bottom, front to back, and side to side, looking for a stone to turn over, a loose board in the wall, any place where pouches of dust could be hidden. They were about to give up when Bodine tripped over a bucket filled with water, knocking it over. "Dammit, Bodine," Quincy growled as he jumped backward to keep from getting his boots soaked.

"That bucket looked like it was plum up to the top," Billy said, surprised to see there was not nearly that much water spilled over the floor. "I reckon I must be seein' things."

Quincy was quick to see the significance of the small amount of water. He immediately grabbed the bucket and began beating it against the wall. Thinking he had gone loco, Billy stepped back in case he started banging the bucket against somebody's head, but in a moment he saw the purpose of Quincy's madness. The bucket's false bottom finally gave way under Quincy's assault and he pulled it up to reveal two equally weighted pouches. They had struck their pay dirt. Quincy held up the two identical pouches to the whooping and hollering of his partners. Eager to see how rich they were, they weighed their treasure on the balance they found among the tools along the back wall. "I thought that bucket was awful damn heavy when it was empty," Quincy said. "I don't know what the price of gold is, but there's enough here to keep us in whiskey for a while."

"I reckon we could afford to keep our horses at the stables," Billy said, "now that we got a little to add to the money we got from the soldiers."

"I expect we'd best keep our horses right here where we can get to 'em in a hurry. But if ever'thin' goes right, I'd say we're in a pretty good fix to wait out this weather," Quincy said. "When it lets up a little, we can get around and see what else we can dig up."

"This minin' business pays off pretty damn good," Billy commented. "Let's get the horses took care of and go back to have a drink."

For the next couple of days, they became regular customers of Pete Bender's, drinking and playing cards. On the third day, the sun appeared again to light up the broad valley with glare as it was reflected off the snow, bringing the inhabitants of Last Chance Gulch out of their holes, as well as a traveler from the south.

The man known to the Indians as Rider Twelve Horses guided a weary buckskin horse toward the buildings of Helena. Although he was well-known by the Blackfeet as well as the Crows in the surrounding mountains—and some white men in the town—it was his first visit to the sprawling town of Helena. Approaching the town from the lower end of the gulch, he headed for the first stable he came to. After crunching through the snow leading into the stable, he dismounted onto the dry floor of the long wooden building. His legs cold and stiff from hours in the saddle, he tried to stomp some feeling into them as the attendant came from the tack room to greet him. "It's right nippy out there, ain't it?" Arthur Tice remarked.

"I reckon," Rider replied as Tice took a moment to look the formidable stranger over. "I need to put my horse up for a day or two while I look around town. He could use some oats. There ain't been much food for him to find the last few days."

"I expect not," Tice said. "Bad weather for traveling. You come a long way?"

"A piece," Rider answered.

When it was obvious that the tall, broad-shouldered stranger was not going to elaborate, Arthur continued to talk. "My name's Arthur Tice," he said, and offered his hand, which Rider accepted silently. "I'm the owner of this establishment."

Rider nodded in response, then turned to take his rifle from the saddle scabbard while Tice recited his prices for boarding and feed—and after another look at the wild figure his customer appeared to be—the extra fee if he chose to sleep in the stall with his horse. After the contract was agreed upon, Tice returned to his casual conversation. "You ain't the only lost soul roaming around in the snow this week. Couple of days ago, three fellows came in from Bozeman City."

Rider's head immediately turned to face him. It was the closest thing to a reaction of any kind from the quiet stranger, enough to cause Tice to pause and ask, "Friends of yours?"

"Maybe," Rider replied. "Are their horses here?"

"No, they didn't board 'em here. I think they found themselves someplace to camp, and I reckon they're keepin' their horses there."

"They say where they're stayin'?" Rider asked.

"I didn't talk to them," Tice answered. "Pete Bender told me about them." He was a little uncertain whether or not the information he was supplying might prove to be detrimental to the three men, and this stranger asking all the questions might or might not be a friend of theirs. "Somewhere up on the hill, I s'pose."

Rider took a few moments to make sure the buckskin and his packhorse were all right. "Maybe I'll bump into them somewhere around town." He looked back at Tice then and asked, "Are there any saloons near here?"

"There's five right here on this end of town," Tice

replied. He could have mentioned that Pete Bender owned the Pay Dirt, but he was already concerned that he might have volunteered too much information. And whatever business the stranger had with the other three was none of his.

"Much obliged," Rider said, and turned to leave.

Standing to watch the stranger depart, Tice could not help thinking, *There goes a heap of trouble for somebody.*

Outside, Rider paused to look down the street where people were beginning to emerge and shop owners were shoveling their walkways. The main street was not yet churned into a black slushy thoroughfare, but he guessed it soon would be, for he saw the first freight wagon crawling up the middle of the road, its sixteen-mule team plowing through the new-fallen snow. It was not difficult to identify the saloons, even swamped in snow, so he wasted no time in visiting each one. They all seemed to be doing a spirited business for that time of day. One by one, he looked over the crowded rooms, filled with men waiting for the weather. They were so crowded, in fact, that he was not able to clearly see all who were seated at the tables, owing to others standing around them, so he would approach the bar and ask if they knew a man named Bodine. With no luck in the beginning, he approached the last one.

Pete Bender, owner and bartender of the Pay Dirt Saloon, looked up from the bar to see why the light through the open doorway had suddenly dimmed. The entrance to his rustic drinking parlor boasted a door only three feet wide, and the shoulders on the man standing there nearly touched both sides of the frame as he surveyed the smoke-filled, dimly lit room. Ducking his head slightly, he stepped into the saloon, a panther on the hunt. Pete knew him instantly, although he had never seen the man before. From the broad buckskin-covered shoulders to the trim waist, to the beaded knee-length moccasins, he could only be one man. He was known by the one name, *Rider*. No one knew if it was a first or last name. And because no one had ever seen him in the settlement, some believed he was just a myth made up by the Indians. But John Red Feather had told Pete that the Blackfeet knew him and had seen him on occasion when hunting deep in the Bitterroots or Cabinet Mountains. They said he had a camp somewhere in the Big Belt Range as well, but nobody had ever found it. Red Feather claimed that he was known by Blackfeet and Crow, even though they were enemies. Whether or not he could be claimed as a friend of either tribe was not certain, but he was left alone by both tribes just as the grizzlies and the mountain lions were left alone.

The deafening noise of the crowded barroom went silent like a great wave rolling from the front of the room to the back as those nearest the door turned to see him, until there was no sound save that of a chair scraping on the floor as someone pushed back to see what had silenced every tongue. A path was instantly cleared for him when he walked toward the bar to confront the suddenly speechless bartender. One word was all he said. "Bodine." Without hesitation, Pete turned and pointed to a big man seated at a table in the corner, relieved that it was not his name this messenger of death had called out.

Bodine, having heard his name in the silent barroom, instinctively reached under the table and pulled his revolver from his holster when he recognized the tall scout. When Rider approached him, he brought the pistol up, aimed and cocked, ready to shoot. Ignoring the weapon threatening him, Rider walked up to stand over the table. With only the shifting of his eyes, he glanced quickly from side to side, looking for Quincy and Billy, as Bodine's drinking companions moved away from the table, but Quincy and Billy were not there. Obviously having the upper hand with his pistol already drawn and aimed, Bodine grinned. "Well, look who's here. What the hell do you want?"

"Johnny Hawk says hello," Rider pronounced, his voice low and lethal. The events that followed in the next split second came faster than Bodine could blink his eye, and held the crowd of spectators paralyzed. Rider grabbed the edge of the table and turned it upside down on Bodine, sending him and his chair crashing to the floor. By the time he pulled the trigger, his pistol was aimed straight up at the ceiling. Before he could pull it again, his wrist was pinned against the floor by Rider's foot. Desperate to free his gun hand, he clawed at Rider's leg with his other hand. His eyes wild with fright, he looked into the cold dark eyes of his executioner for a brief moment before he suddenly grunted with the impact of the long skinning knife as it was thrust deep into his abdomen. Their eyes remained locked until gradually Bodine's gaze began to fade as death came to claim him.

Not a soul stirred as the big man withdrew his knife from Bodine's body. In the next moment, the crowd was frozen in horror as Rider took Bodine's scalp. His bloody execution completed, he carefully wiped the blood from his knife on Bodine's coat. He turned then to survey the crowd of horrified bystanders, searching again for Billy Hyde and Quincy. They were not in the room. His business finished there, he walked out the door, leaving Pete Bender's patrons to recover from their shock.

It was no more than forty-five minutes after the incident in the saloon when Billy and Quincy returned to the Pay Dirt to join Bodine. As soon as they walked in the door, Pete Bender ran to meet them and told them what had happened there. "Big wild-lookin' feller," Pete exclaimed, his voice higher in his excitement. "He walked right up to your friend and killed him with a knife, and then he scalped him, just like an Injun."

"Rider!" Billy said as he instinctively looked around him cautiously. "Couldn't be nobody else. He musta got the jump on poor ol' Bodine."

"That's who I figured it was. Your friend had a gun on him," Pete insisted, "but he walked right up to face him and turned your friend upside down before he knew whether his ass was up or down." He turned then to gesture toward a gruff-looking man in a heavy wool coat, holding a shotgun in one hand. "Sheriff Tate, there, just got here. He'll be lookin' for the killer, and he said he wanted to talk to you fellers."

Just the word *sheriff* was enough to cause both outlaws to become nervous. "What are we gonna do?" Billy asked Quincy. "I don't wanna talk to no damn sheriff. That damn Rider will be comin' after us next—sure as hell. That man's crazy."

"I expect we'd best get him first, before he has a chance to get us," Quincy said impassively. Seeing the fearful look in Billy's eyes, he took a quick look around him, as Billy had done, half expecting this mystery man to appear at any second. He could see that Billy's inclination was simply to run, but he was of the opinion that there was no one man that he feared so much that he would hightail it rather than deal with him.

"Why don't we just let the sheriff take care of it?" Billy asked.

Pete Bender was an intrigued spectator at this point, and he was prone to offer any information he had on the subject of Rider. "The Injuns think he ain't a man," he interjected. "They say he's a spirit that lives in those mountains east of this valley."

"Horseshit," Quincy responded. "If I get my sights on him, I'll make a spirit out of him."

"I know him," Billy said, still excited. "He ain't no spirit, but he's crazy as hell—been livin' with the Injuns too long to be civilized."

Impatient with their talk of spirits and Indian legends, Quincy knew the best way to deal with a dangerous man was to simply eliminate him. "Did anybody see where he went when he left here?" he asked Pete. The bartender's answer that no one had noticed further disgusted Quincy. Evidently everyone in the saloon was so frightened by the brutal execution that took place that they were all frozen motionless until they were sure Rider was gone. "Dammit, he ain't but one man," he fumed at Billy. "He's most likely out lookin' for you and me. So come on, we'd better make sure we find him before he finds us."

They started to leave, but were not quick enough to escape the sheriff's eye. "Hold on, there, you two," Tate ordered. "I need to talk to you." He walked over to them followed by a young man Quincy assumed was a deputy. "I'm told that this fellow layin' on the floor over there is a friend of yours. Maybe you'd like to tell me why this Rider fellow killed him."

Quick to answer before Billy blurted something incriminating, Quincy spoke up immediately. "We ain't got no idea why he murdered Bodine. Maybe he just didn't like his looks. He didn't have no quarrel with us that I know of. Bodine was a peace-lovin' man—never did no harm to anybody."

"I hear you fellows just hit town a day or two ago. What brings you to Helena?" Tate asked.

"We was just in town to sell some horses, wasn't plannin' on staying, but when the weather turned, we decided to stay till it improved a little." He shook his head slowly in mock distress. "Poor ol' Bodine, if the snow hadn't come, he'd be on his way home right now."

"Poor ol' Bodine," Billy echoed, trying hard to assume a mournful expression.

"Well, I expect it'd be a good idea for you boys to stay around a while till we can run this fellow to ground," Tate said. He didn't buy the peace-loving story about the dead man, or his two friends, for that matter, and he suspected there was a good reason why Rider killed Bodine. The question before him now was to determine if the killing was an isolated execution, or if there was going to be more involving these two. "You stayin' in the hotel?" he asked.

"No, sir," Quincy replied. "We're staying with a couple of friends in a little shack up on the hill. We'll be right here if you need us."

"I expect, since he was your friend, you'll take care of his burial."

"Hell no—" Billy started, but Quincy cut him off.

"Of course we'll take care of it," he said. "He was a good friend, and I know his family will be mournin' his loss."

"I'm sure the undertaker will be contacting you," Tate said. Then he looked at his young deputy and said, "We'd better get goin', see if we can find this feller. From the description we got, he shouldn't be hard to spot, if he's still in town."

In the sparse cover of a dwarf cedar, Rider knelt, oblivious to the cold snow about him, watching the activity at the Pay Dirt Saloon. It had not been a wise plan, even though he had eliminated one of the three murderers. He knew he should have waited to catch all three together, but he had let his emotions take control of his common sense, and now he had to look for an opportunity to finish his business with Billy and the other one. Witnessing the uproar his act of vengeance had spawned, he knew that he had to get out of town. Two men arriving at the saloon looked to be lawmen, judging by the way the others made way for them. He told himself that it was time to get back to the stable and get his horses before the sheriff found them. He had started to get up from his position behind the cedars when he suddenly knelt back down, stopped by the sight of two more arrivals. *Billy Hyde,* he thought, and peered hard at the man with him. There was something familiar about him, but at that distance he couldn't be sure, and then it struck him—*Quincy!* His mind shot back to that day on the Solomon. Quincy was one of those who had escaped the ambush at the farmhouse, and he was the first one to take a shot at him when he made his run to warn the Thompson family. His emotions running wild again, he labored to keep a calm head. His common sense told him that he still had to run before he was caught by sheriff's deputies, but the urge was almost overpowering to settle the debt right then, out in the open. The only thing that kept him from giving in to his anger was the thought of being locked away in a prison.

Chapter 10

Word of the murder in Pete Bender's saloon spread rapidly around the town of Helena. Accustomed as the residents of the town were to an occasional shooting between two drunken miners, Bodine's murder was especially disturbing because of the brutal nature of it. Sheriff Tate was anxious to find the killer before he was able to kill again, and he had a suspicion that as long as the deceased's two friends were in town, there was a definite possibility of another murder. So he put all his deputies out to scour the town, unaware of a similar search initiated by the cavalry detachment in town under the command of Lieutenant Jared Carrington. His search was narrowed almost immediately, however, when stable owner Arthur Tice tracked him down to tell him that the man he searched for had his horses in his barn at that very moment. Tate called his four deputies in and headed for the stables.

All too aware that he might well have delayed his escape from Helena much too long, Rider hurriedly threw his saddle on the buckskin. He hesitated to consider whether he should take the time to load up the packs on his other horse, or leave them and the horse. He decided that he couldn't spare the time, so he reluctantly left them. Thinking back on this day in the future, he chose to blame the weather for his capture. For when he charged out of the barn, the sheriff's posse was just approaching. Had there been no snow on the ground, he felt certain he would have escaped, for the buckskin would have quickly carried him out of harm's way. As conditions were, however, when his horse raced out of the barn, he was forced to almost stop when he hit a snowdrift outside the stable door, momentarily presenting a near stationary target for the posse. In the bevy of shots fired, two found home, one in the leg, and one high in the back, knocking him out of the saddle.

More angry than hurt, although there was considerable bleeding, he lay in the snow, knowing that to try to get up and run would result only in his death. He had no desire to shoot back, for he did not wish to harm honest lawmen, so he offered no resistance to his arrest, lying in the snow, watching while deputies caught his horse and returned it to the stable. Ordered to his feet, he struggled to get up, roughly helped by two of the deputies. Then he was paraded through town to the jail, where he was shoved into a cell. There was no offer of medical attention to his wounds as he was left to fall on a cot and told by Tate that common murderers were not treated lightly in his town.

Once again the news was quickly passed along concerning the violent killing in the saloon—this time it was the welcome report that the killer was safely incarcerated in Sheriff Tate's jail. One, whose interest was more than casual, was the officer commanding the cavalry detachment temporarily camped outside the town. When Carrington heard that the man called Rider had been arrested, he went straight to the sheriff's office in hopes of negotiating a transfer to military custody.

"What difference does it make to the army whether we try him and hang him here, or you try him and hang him somewhere else?" Sheriff Tate asked.

"It's a matter of principal and prior rights," Carrington replied, affecting his best official-sounding voice in hopes of influencing the sheriff. "This man you know as Rider is actually a fugitive named Jim Moran who escaped military custody almost two years ago. The army has been looking for him ever since. I followed him to your town and was preparing to arrest him when you intervened." This last statement was an outright lie, but Carrington felt certain Tate had no choice but to take his word. "For these reasons, I think he should be released into my custody, and I assure you he will be dealt with to your satisfaction." When Tate appeared hesitant, Carrington said, "I think this matter is rightfully within military jurisdiction."

The sheriff was reluctant to turn his prisoner over. He had committed a heinous murder in his town, and Tate wanted to make sure he was properly hanged. "I guess it doesn't make much difference where his neck gets stretched," he finally conceded, but not entirely. "I ain't so sure I can just hand him over to you without some written authorization from somebody higher up, so we'll leave it up to Judge Corley to decide. If he says it's all right, then the prisoner's yours and welcome to him."

After a disappointed cavalry lieutenant left his office, Tate walked back to the cells to take a look at his prisoner. He found him standing at the tiny window, gazing at the mountains in the distance, like a trapped animal. Holding on to the bars to keep his wounded leg from collapsing under him, he seemed oblivious to the fresh blood oozing from the wound in his back.

"Don't you think you should have the doctor come and look at his wounds?"

The voice came from behind Tate and startled the sheriff. He turned to face the woman standing in the open door to his office. "Mrs. McGowan," he exclaimed, surprised to find a woman in his jail. He considered what she had said for a moment before conceding. "I reckon maybe you're right. I'll send somebody to fetch Dr. Blake as soon as one of my deputies comes back." He took her arm to guide her back to his office. "What can I do for you, ma'am?"

Lucy resisted his effort to direct her. "I want to talk to the prisoner," she said.

"Oh, no, ma'am," Tate quickly replied. "You don't wanna talk to that man. He's as wild as any Injun out in those hills."

"He's an old friend of mine," Lucy insisted. "I just want to talk to him. I don't see any reason why I shouldn't be allowed to."

"Why, no, ma'am," Tate sputtered, "I guess there ain't." He scratched his head while he decided. "You go ahead and talk to him if you wanna, but we'll keep this door open and I'll be right outside in case you need me."

"Thank you, Sheriff," Lucy replied.

An astonished witness to the conversation between Lucy and the sheriff, Rider sat down on his cot, watching as the sheriff left the room and Lucy came up to the cell door. She looked different, dressed in a very businesslike jacket and matching skirt, far more ladylike than the last time he had seen her when she rejected his bumbling, boyish proposal. He could not deny a slight ache in his heart that had nothing to do with his wounds, but it was of a minor nature, more closely related to regrets for decisions he had made in the past that had no influence on the present.

Not quite sure how she was going to be received by him after their last meeting, she didn't speak for a few moments while they gazed at each other awkwardly. She had to consider the common talk about this Indian legend. Maybe he was the wild being reported to be haunting the mountains surrounding the valley. Maybe he hated her intensely for the way she had rejected him. Maybe he knew it was she who had told the lieutenant his real name. She was relieved, however, when he spoke.

"How've you been, Lucy?" he said softly.

"You know me." She smiled. "Full speed ahead."

"I reckon I oughta thank you."

"For what?" she asked.

"Tellin' the sheriff to send for the doctor," he said. "I don't feel like I'm hurt that bad. If the shot hadn't knocked me off my horse, I mighta got away. But I can't stop bleedin', so I'm glad they're gonna get the doctor." He tried to show her a smile. "I'm kinda surprised to see you, though."

"I had to come see you, Rider. I owe you that. I'm the one who told Lieutenant Carrington that your real name is Jim Moran. It was accidental. I had no idea that man was after you." She threw her hands up, flustered. "If I had known, I would never have told him. I thought you scouted for the army. Why are they after you?"

"I don't think the army is," he said. "It's more like that one man is after me. He's been doggin' me everywhere I go." He went on to explain Carrington's obsession with him for escaping with Johnny Hawk, and the circumstances that led up to his arrest in the first place.

"So you were trying to warn those people at that farmhouse," she repeated, feeling no reason to doubt his word.

"That's a fact," he replied, "but Carrington insists I was leadin' the raid."

"Why did you kill that man in the saloon?" she asked, abruptly changing to a new subject.

"Bodine," he said. "I killed him because he carved up Johnny Hawk and left him for dead. I just did the same for him."

Lucy jerked her head back in alarm. "Is Johnny dead?"

"He was alive when I left him in the hospital at Fort Laramie, but I ain't sure he's gonna make it. He looked pretty bad. Bodine gutted him and started to scalp him, but he didn't have time to finish the job."

She understood the savagery of his attack on Bodine

then, and the report that he had actually taken the man's scalp.

"I wish I could do something to help you. Maybe they won't release you to the army and give you a trial here. Then I can testify for you." She was interrupted then when Sheriff Tate came in to say the doctor had arrived. "I'll come see you again," she said. "Maybe Tessie and Harvey will come with me."

"I 'preciate it, Lucy, but don't worry about me. I'll be all right."

She nodded and went through the door to the office as Dr. Blake stepped back to let her pass. He might have said he'd be all right, she thought, but she remembered the sight of him hanging on to the bars and gazing longingly out the window at the mountains. *It's a sin against God to cage a wild spirit like that*, she thought.

Lucy's hopes that Rider would remain in Helena for trial by civilian court were not to be realized. Lieutenant Carrington pled his case to Judge Corley, and the judge had no objection to his request, influenced no small amount by the fact that it was approaching Christmastime when Corley had planned to keep his docket clean. It was like a Christmas present to Carrington, however, whose obsession with punishing the man who embarrassed him with his escape, had reached insane proportions. He was unwilling to wait the extra couple of days that the judge insisted upon for treatment of Rider's wounds, but he had little choice. To further complicate Carrington's life, the gold shipment that had been the sole reason for his presence in Helena was now complete. As added irritation to him was the fact that his men had become rather lax in their military conduct, brought on by the extended camp in the snowy valley with the primary objective in their view being to keep from freezing to death.

During the extra two days of his confinement in the Helena jail, Rider had two faithful visitors, Lucy and Carrington. The lieutenant's visits were to assure himself that his prisoner was secure and to assure Rider that he would not lose him a second time. Lucy, true to her word, brought Tessie and Harvey with her one day for a very brief visit that proved awkward for them. With the deputy's permission, Lucy took the heavy coat that Rider had worn when captured with her to repair the bullet hole. On the third day after Lucy's first visit, Dr. Blake pronounced Rider fit to ride, so Tate released his prisoner to an extremely satisfied lieutenant.

A sizable crowd of spectators gathered to watch the transfer of the prisoner to the army patrol, most of them to get a glimpse of the savage killer known only as Rider. There was an audible gasp from the onlookers as Rider was led out of the jail. Taller by almost a head than the two troopers who stepped up to escort him to his horse, he looked every bit the part of the legend the Blackfeet had created. "Look there," a voice in the crowd whispered. "You can see where they shot him the back, and he don't look like it even slowed him down."

"He's a big'un, all right," another replied. "Grover Bramble said the Blackfeet think he's a spirit and you can't kill him."

"Huh," Billy Hyde grunted, standing close enough to have heard the comment. He grinned at Quincy standing next to him and whispered, "He sure as hell ain't no damn spirit. You can kill him, all right. Ain't gonna have to worry 'bout Mr. Rider no more. The soldier boys are gonna stretch his neck. Save us the trouble of killin' him." Quincy didn't answer. His mind was concentrating on the tall man in the animal skins. There was something familiar about him, and he couldn't quite place him, but there was little about him that would have made him recall the gangly boy who rode with Quantrill's raiders.

Somewhat surprised that he was of such interest to the citizens of the town, Rider was at least gratified to see that the soldiers had brought his own horse. The problem at the moment, however, was how to climb into the saddle with his hands tied behind his back. Carrington, when told of the problem by one of the troopers, reluctantly ordered them to tie his hands in front of him so he could get on his horse without help. While he waited for his binds to be retied, he glanced up to see Lucy making her way through the crowd, carrying his coat. It was a welcome sight on this frigid morning, and he nodded his appreciation as she started to approach him.

"You'd better not get too close, ma'am," one of the soldiers said, and stepped in front of her.

"Nonsense," she responded. "He's not going to hurt me. We're old friends and I want to give him his coat before you let him freeze to death." The soldier reached out to take the coat, but she abruptly ignored his hand and pushed by him. "I'll put it on him," she declared.

Surprised, and even a little amused by her typical aggression, he smiled at her as she stepped up and held the coat for him to slip into. "I'm much obliged," he said as she stood before him to tie the belt that Morning Flower had attached. It was not until she pulled it tight that he felt the heavy object in the pocket of the coat, and realized what she had done at a terrible risk to herself. "Thank you, Lucy," he said softly as she backed away a couple of steps.

"I owe you that," she said before turning to the guards. "Now you can tie his hands." She promptly turned away then and made her way back through the crowd.

With the prisoner now in the saddle, Lieutenant Carrington glanced at the departing woman with sardonic amusement for her act of compassion. He had more important things to think about than Jim Moran's comfort, the foremost at the moment the acceptance of a gold shipment to be escorted to Fort C. F. Smith, where it would then be relayed to Fort Laramie. There was still the weather to be concerned with. The storm that had dumped over two feet of fresh snow was past, but the trails were still difficult to travel, and he was long overdue to return. Morale among his men was at a low point already and he feared the possibility of desertion by some if he didn't remove them from the temptations of the wide-open mining town. With these problems in mind, he decided that they would have to make the long cold march, thinking it better than spending another night in Helena. So he ordered his detail to move out and proceed to the Dempsey Mine, where the shipment was even then being transferred from the originally planned freight wagon onto mules. The thinking was that the wagons could easily become bogged down in the snow.

The completion of the loading brought only partial relief of Carrington's problems, for now he had half of his detachment of twenty troopers trying to drive a mule train, a task for which they were poorly trained. Nevertheless, he ordered the march to begin, although it was already well past noon when the mules were loaded. Leaving Helena, they started south, making their way slowly through the snow. The first day's march saw only about eleven miles before darkness approached, and the troop was forced to stop and make camp while there was still enough light to clear away spaces for tents and find enough firewood to keep the fires going through the long cold night. Their choice for a campsite was in a cedar grove in hopes of gaining some protection from the wind and cold.

Throughout the long day, Rider sat stiffly in the saddle, his bones aching from the cold, wondering if there would be an opportunity for escape, for his mind had thought about little else from the time he was led from the jail. His only consolation was that his guards were as miserable as he, and were rapidly turning into a detachment of malcontents. When the troop finally went into camp, his hands were freed so that he could clear snow away for his place to sleep, although no canvas was provided for him to use as a tent. The horses were unsaddled and he was told that he would have to make do with his saddle and blanket to devise what comfort he could. With his hands free, it was his first opportunity to feel the object Lucy had slipped into his coat. It turned out to be a heavy knife, and under the lax supervision of his two guards, he deftly stuffed it under his saddle when he made his bed, thinking that when they retied his hands, he might not be able to get it out of his coat.

With several fires blazing, the soldiers prepared their supper. On orders from Carrington, the prisoner was given one cup of coffee and two pieces of hard bread. Carrington, himself, came to gloat over his captive and make sure he was secured for the night with his hands tied together and then bound by a rope to a cedar limb. "There's no one to help you escape this time," Carrington said. "Johnny Hawk's not here. As a matter of fact, in the last telegram I got from Fort Smith, I was told that he was in the hospital at Fort Laramie and had taken a turn for the worse. They didn't expect him to survive the night."

This was especially sad news for Rider, for he had left with the feeling that Johnny was going to improve. In fact, it was almost impossible to think that Little Thunder would not always be here. Feeling the lieutenant's eyes searching his for his reaction, he said, "It wasn't Johnny that threw the bolt on that door." It was a lie, but he saw no use in incriminating his friend.

"Who, then?" Carrington demanded, his obsession for a complete version of the incident driving him to know every detail.

"It was one of the boys there," Rider said, making it up as he went along, "the younger one. I don't think he remembered I was locked up in that smokehouse, and your guard was asleep." He figured that was a safe story. He felt pretty sure the army would not file charges on the youngster.

"Damn!" Carrington swore as he re-created the picture in his mind. It never occurred to him that Rider might be lying. "Not that important, anyway," he finally concluded. "Well, it's time to turn in. I trust you'll have an uneventful night. There'll be a guard right here with you, so if you can't sleep, you'll have somebody to talk to." The sarcasm was not lost on Rider. Carrington left him to go to his tent for the night, and Rider settled in as best he could with the first of his guards sitting facing him. None of the soldiers were exempt from pulling at least one two-hour tour of guard duty that night. Because they were carrying a large amount of gold, Carrington had more than doubled the number of pickets ordinarily on duty for a normal camp.

The first two guards pulled their shifts with minimal complaints. After that, however, each new guard that was roused from sleep to go on duty was grouchier than the one before him. Finally, an hour or two before dawn, one of the older privates took over the watch. He freshened up the fire before sitting down opposite Rider, and promptly started fighting against a strong desire to close his eyes. Before very long, he started nodding, closing his eyes for long seconds at a time, but every time Rider would shift his position, or make any movement, the soldier's eyes would pop open immediately—until finally they closed and remained closed, even when Rider softly called out to test him.

This would be his only chance that night because it would be starting to get light in a couple of hours and he desperately needed the darkness in his attempt to escape. Working as quickly as possible, he pulled the knife from under his saddle, then spent valuable frustrating minutes trying to wedge the handle between his feet in a position that would hold it steady enough to allow him to saw away at his ropes. He worked feverishly at the stubborn rope, glancing every few moments at his sleeping guard, afraid he would awaken and catch him in the act. At first, it appeared that his plan was not going to work, for the knife seemed to make very little impression on the rope. He kept after it, however, and eventually the blade began to sink into the stubborn bindings. It seemed like forever before he sawed the last slender fiber and the rope suddenly popped free. Now the dangerous part of his escape attempt was before him. Moving as quietly as he could, he slowly got to his feet and paused to look around him, half expecting to hear an outcry of alarm. But there was none, so he picked up his saddle and blanket and stepped carefully out of the firelight.

Moving only a dozen yards or so at a time, he paused to locate the pickets in their movements around the perimeter of the camp before he proceeded again. He made his way in this fashion, crossing to the other side of the camp where the horses and mules were picketed on a long rope. In a low whisper, he tried to calm the horses, searching for the buckskin as he moved along the line of mounts and pack mules. The buckskin whinnied softly when he approached, and Rider wasted no time in throwing his saddle on the gelding's back. Once he was saddled and Rider was ready to attempt to get by the pickets, he paused to weigh his options. He thought about cutting the rope, then making a lot of noise to try to stampede the horses, but he rejected that idea. At best, he would frighten only a few of the horses, but he would rouse the whole camp in the process. Best just to try to slip by the guards patrolling the perimeter without being seen, he thought, but he was concerned that, because of the gold they transported, the guard posts were too close together to escape discovery by at least one of them. Even as he considered it, he saw one of the guards walk over to borrow tobacco from the man at the next post. He glanced up to cast a worried look at the sky, imagining that it was already showing signs of light. *Not for another hour,* he sternly told himself. Then he decided what he would do.

Walking along the rope, he untied a couple of horses and six of the mules. Gently nudging them toward the edge of the cedars, he led his horse along with them, crouching low so that his silhouette would not be seen above the backs of the animals. As he had hoped, they moved slowly along with him, a couple of the mules drifting off to the side as they neared the picket line. When they were finally spotted, the guards acted just as he had hoped. "Hey, McCauley," one of the guards called to the man next to him, "some of the damn mules is got untied." Since there was no sign of stampede, in fact, the mules and horses were walking casually, the guard who had spoken first called out again. "I'll go see if I can head 'em off and lead 'em back." He propped his carbine against a rock and ran to try to turn the mule in front. Behind him, Rider picked up the carbine and, still hunched low behind his horse, led the buckskin off through the cedars where the guard had been walking his post.

Not until he cleared the last of the trees did he climb into the saddle and point the buckskin's head across the valley, feeling as though he could be seen for miles with his dark form contrasted against the white snow. *So far, so good,* he thought, for there were no shouts of alarm behind him and no shots fired. His one purpose now was to put as much distance as possible between him and the soldiers, for there would be no trouble following his trail in the snow. Guiding his horse toward a line of hills standing out against the dark sky, he planned to strike the river within a few miles. He was confident in the buckskin's ability to stay ahead of the troopers' horses, for no horse was better in circumstances like these where strength and stamina were important, but he wanted to lose his trail completely. The opportunity came when he came to a wide stream, and riding down the center of it, followed it to the river. Spotting another stream that emptied into it from the other side, he urged his horse to enter the water. The buckskin did not hesitate, and Rider clenched his teeth against the bone-chilling water as it rose to his waist. He clung desperately to the saddle horn, afraid if he was swept off the horse, he'd freeze to death before he could swim for the shore. Finding it hard to catch his breath, he managed to guide the buckskin into the stream on the far side. His legs and lower body numb with the cold, he nevertheless was able to hang on when the horse came up out of the water and continued up the stream.

It was difficult to fight the almost overpowering need to build a fire and warm himself immediately, but he feared that all would be lost if he did not make sure he lost his pursuers first. In a stroke of luck, he came upon a bend in the stream where a sizable herd of deer had crossed. From the appearance of the churned-up snow, the animals had pawed around looking for grass before moving on toward the north. It was as good a place as any to leave the stream, so he followed the trail left by the herd with a fair amount of confidence that the tracks of his horse would hardly be discernible in the mix. His concern now was to get far enough in the hills to build a fire to dry his freezing wet clothes, and warm his horse. They had spent too much time in the cold water to continue on until they were both thawed out. A favorable sign was the appearance of the morning sun through the broken clouds overhead. It was going to be a better day.

Back in the cedar grove, the first rays of the morning sun that filtered through the branches of the trees revealed a distressful sight to Private Warren Hatcher as he sat up, rubbed his sleepy eyes, and stared at the empty space before him. He scrambled to his feet at once, looking frantically about him, desperately hoping to see the prisoner, but there was no one. Unable to decide what to do, for he knew he was in terrible trouble, he looked helplessly at the severed rope that had bound the prisoner while the sounds of the camp awaking reached his ears. Falling asleep on guard duty was a serious offense and he had no defense for his negligence. He did not have to wait long for his reprimand, for he turned to see Lieutenant Carrington striding toward him in the next moment.

Carrington didn't say anything at first. Expecting to see his prisoner securely bound, he was startled and confused to find the guard standing wide-eyed in apprehension before the empty space. With no excuse, and unable to think of anything better to report, Private Hatcher said, "I think I fell asleep."

Stunned, scarcely believing his eyes and ears, Carrington was speechless for a long moment before finally finding his voice. Then all his frustration exploded at once, and he shouted for his sergeant, frantically ordering him to get the troop ready to ride immediately. "Put out those fires!" he ordered. "Saddle up and get mounted! The prisoner has escaped." Turning briefly back to Hatcher, he roared, "I'll deal with you later." There was no time for that now. "Find his tracks!" he ordered.

In the frantic pace to break camp, the pieces of the escape puzzle were discovered, fitting together with the incident of the mules somehow getting loose during the early morning hours, and the carbine that one of the guards *lost* in the darkness. Carrington was livid, and when the tracks were discovered leading from the edge of the trees, he ordered the column to immediately pursue. They hustled to load the gold shipment back on the mules as rapidly as they could manage, then started out after the fugitive amid the complaining of the men over having no time for breakfast.

The tracks were easy enough to follow. The time they had been made was uncertain, however. The hoofprints already had ice formed in them, so it was likely that Rider had escaped at the same time the guards were chasing the mules. Heading east across the valley, they followed the trail until it reached the stream where Rider had gone into the water. There was some time wasted there over the possibility that he might have gone upstream in an effort to lose them.

Carrington looked at the mountains in the distance, however, and decided he had to be heading toward them, so they followed the stream until it emptied into the river. "Well, he didn't come outta the stream anywhere," Sergeant McCoy said, "so I reckon he went in the river."

"The question is, which way?" Carrington said. "Upstream or down?" Even though frustrated almost beyond control, he was aware that he was chasing all over Montana with an extremely valuable mule train, the primary purpose of which was to reach Fort C. F. Smith as quickly as he could manage.

Being not afflicted with the obsession that ruled the lieutenant, McCoy was more in tune with common sense. "Coulda gone either way, I expect. That man's at home in these hills. I don't give us much chance of catchin' up with him—if he ain't froze to death from bein' in that river."

Carrington took a few minutes to think about what he should do. He looked back at the string of mules loaded with heavy packs, and considered the risk involved in committing them to the swiftly running water. Though it pained him terribly to admit it, he knew he had no chance at all of catching Jim Moran and a fair chance of losing a valuable shipment. With a taste as bitter as gall in his mouth, he issued the order to turn south and head for Three Forks. Moran had defeated him again.

Chapter 11

He felt confident that he had lost the cavalry patrol for good, so the one thing on his mind was to keep from freezing. On foot, walking and leading his horse, he tried to get the blood circulating in his legs again, and each step delivered a feeling of tiny needles in the soles of his feet and frozen buckskins rubbing against his legs. He was searching for a good spot to build a camp and he trudged through the snow until finding a suitable place in a stand of young pines, hard up against a steep slope, that would effectively block the icy wind that swept the valley. He had been fortunate to find that his saddle and saddlebags had been left intact except for the absence of his rifle, and the things he needed to build a shelter were still there. His first endeavor was to build a fire, so with trembling fingers he got flint and steel from his saddlebag and kindled a small flame in some pine straw. With no regard for the smoke generated by burning pine, he eagerly placed small sticks and limbs on his fire until he could feed the healthy flame with larger limbs. Still shivering, he warmed his hands until he thought he at last had some real feeling in them, enough to fashion a shelter. Then he bent several young pines over together and lashed them with a rawhide rope he carried on his saddle. Taking his hatchet and the knife Lucy had given him, he began to cut pine boughs to place on the framework of trees until he had fashioned a shelter large enough to lead the buckskin inside.

He spent quite some time rubbing his horse down before he was satisfied the big buckskin had suffered no lasting effects from his frigid bath. "Tough as wet rawhide, ain'tcha, son?" he said as he patted the horse's face. When the buckskin seemed content, Rider peeled his wet trousers and underwear off and hung them on some limbs before the fire. Once he began to get warm, he started to feel an aching in his leg where the bullet had entered. Dr. Blake had removed the slug, but his leg had thawed out, and he could now feel the wound. He didn't know if the wound in his back was serious or not, but the bullet was still in it. It seemed to bother him less than the wound in his leg. Dr. Blake had told him he was lucky that the bullet lodged in the muscle and had not hit any of his vital organs, and he felt it was more dangerous to try to remove it than to leave it alone. He was hungry, but too tired to attempt to catch something to eat. Although the back wound had not been serious, he had lost a lot of blood and this, combined with the previous night with no sleep, was enough to cause him to drift off to sleep.

He was awakened the next morning by the pawing of his horse searching for grass inside his pine shelter. Shivering with the cold, for his fire had burned down to a handful of smoldering sticks, he dropped the saddle blanket he had wrapped around him and hurriedly climbed into his underwear and pants, which were now dry. If he had a fortune, he would have been tempted at that moment to give it all away for one cup of steaming hot coffee, and he thought of his supplies and the coffeepot he had left in the stable on his packhorse. He could certainly use those items now, but there were more important things that had been left behind as well—things like ammunition and his bow and beaver skin quiver of arrows. As they came to mind, he began to consider the likelihood that they might still be in Arthur Tice's stable, and the notion that they would become the stable operator's property did not sit well with him. The more he thought about it, the more he realized he needed his packhorse and his belongings, and he now second-guessed his decision to leave them. *It took me a while to accumulate those things,* he thought, *and I don't have the money to replace them.* As far as his Henry rifle was concerned, he figured that was definitely lost to him, for it was in Sheriff Tate's possession. "Damn!" he swore, irritated by the turn of events that had left him wanting. He tried to put his irritation aside while he stoked up his fire, but he was not able to rid his mind of his possessions waiting to be claimed by someone else.

He was not partial to muskrat, but that was the only game he was able to find near the little creek near his shelter. The carbine he had taken from the guard was loaded, and had been converted to rimfire cartridges, but it would be useless to him after the magazine was emptied. For that reason, he would have to be very conservative in deciding when to fire it. His think-ing was to continue to pursue the herd of deer, whose tracks he had followed to this stream, but first he had to find food for his horse. With his hatchet and Lucy's knife, he cut branches from the cottonwood trees by the stream and peeled the bark which the buckskin accepted graciously. Now that his horse was fed, he saddled him and went in search of the herd of deer.

Following the tracks over a low ridge, he spotted them ahead at a distance of approximately five hun-dred yards, too far to chance a shot with the Spen-cer carbine. The herd was not on the move, having stopped to search for young shoots growing along the water's edge of a stream. Looking the situation over, he decided he could work his way along the base of the ridge and possibly circle around to a closer distance. He left his horse there and started out around the ridge on foot and managed to make his way to within about one hundred and fifty yards before his movements were detected by a large buck. The deer jerked his head up, alert, and snorted a warning to the others. In less than a second they bolted, but Rider already had his sights trained on a young doe. His shot was wide, almost missing, but lucky enough to hit the deer in her back leg, causing her to stumble. "Dammit!" he cursed his poor shot, and ran as fast as he could in the snow to get a closer shot before she could get up and run. Knowing now that the weapon had a tendency to miss left, he made allowance for it and delivered a kill shot as the doe was struggling to her feet.

He then went back to get his horse, and when he returned, he found he had competition for his kill. A pack of five wolves had also been following the herd and had already gathered around the carcass by the time he got back. As soon as he approached, they turned in snarling defiance of his interference. Yelling and waving his arms, he advanced toward them, the carbine in one hand and his hatchet in the other, but the wolves refused to retreat. Moving closer, he continued yelling, trying to make them run. It served to only antagonize the beasts, and suddenly a big male attacked, launching his body at the intruder with teeth set to tear into Rider's flesh. Poised and ready for the attack, Rider deftly avoided the teeth and rendered a blow to the wolf's head with his hatchet, causing the animal to shriek with pain and slink away to safety.

"All right," he muttered, "who's next?" And he set himself to repel another attack. The four uninjured wolves all seemed ready to spring, edging toward him with teeth bared. He would have liked to save what little ammunition he had, but he decided it not worth the risk that they might all attack at the same time, which was typical and damn likely. So he leveled the carbine and killed the foremost of the four. The crack of the rifle was enough to cause the other three to bolt for safety. They retreated to form a circle around him and his horse. "If you'll just hold your horses," he said, "there's enough here for everybody." And while he quickly set about skinning the carcass, the wolves sat in the snow, watching his every move. Working as fast as he could, he carved off a haunch and left the rest for the wolves. It would be enough to sustain him for a while, and he didn't have the time to think about smoke-curing the rest for future use, because he had decided that he was going to return to claim his pack-horse and possessions. With that in mind, he knew that the sooner he got back to the stables, the more likely his things would still be there.

With his meat secured on his horse, he paused to address the watching wolves. "All right, boys, the rest is yours." As he stood there, he shrugged his shoulders, just then realizing that the itching he felt was a trickle of blood down his back from the bullet wound. There was nothing he could do about it since there was no way he could reach it, so he decided to ignore it, figuring the only way he could treat it was to build his blood up with the deer meat. Stepping up in the saddle, he returned to his pine shelter to cook his meal, leaving the wolves to their banquet, minus the leader of their pack. *Just means more for everybody else*, Rider thought.

Arthur Tice clamped the padlock tight on the tack room door and placed the bar across the back doors of the stable. He then picked up his lantern and walked to the front of the stable. After one quick look around, holding the lantern up before him, he blew it out and hung it on a nail beside the door. Locking the second padlock on the front doors, he gave it a yank to make sure it was engaged. Then he walked toward the small frame house about fifty yards away, unaware of the figure watching him from the dark shadows of the creek.

Rider waited a while longer after Tice disappeared inside to make sure he was in the house for the night. Then he left the buckskin on the rocky creek bank and moved quickly past the empty corral to the back of the

stable, which faced away from the house. By the light
of a half-moon, he examined the situation confront-
ing him. There was no padlock on the doors, so he assumed there was a bar holding them. He went through
the corral to the front of the building and a quick look
told him that the front doors were secured by a padlock. That left the hayloft, and the door was too high to
reach from the ground. Not to be denied, he went back
to the creek and climbed onto his horse. After another
quick look to make sure no one was around, he guided
the gelding to the front of the stable and stopped him
under the hayloft door. Then by standing up on his
saddle, he could reach the bottom of the door. *Don't
be locked*, he pleaded silently, relieved when the door
moved reluctantly back. With a good grip on the sill,
he pulled himself up far enough to get his shoulders in
and his belly on the sill. After that, it was easy to pull
the rest of himself up.

Moving as quickly as he could in the dark hayloft,
he found the ladder and hurried down to remove the
bar from the back door. Then he ran around to the front
to lead his horse back out of sight behind the stable.
Moving from stall to stall, he could see horses in most
of them, but not well enough to identify his packhorse.
He would have lit Tice's lantern, but he had nothing
but flint and steel to make fire, so he entered a large
stall that held two horses and stood there motionless. After a few seconds, one of the horses came up to
him and thrust her nose against his chest. "Atta girl,"
Rider said softly. "Let's get outta this stall where I can
take a better look at you." He led the mare out in the
alley between the stalls into a patch of moonlight near

the open doors. "I ain't that sure," he muttered, "but you're close enough and I ain't got a lotta time."

He proceeded to the tack room next where his packs had been placed, only to be confronted with a padlock. "Damn!" he swore under his breath, for it was a heavy lock and appeared to be uncompromising. He studied it for a long minute before realizing that the door was not uncompromising. So he hurried to his saddle and got his hatchet. His concern now was for the noise he would make, chopping away at the man's door, so he decided he'd better make each swing of the hatchet an effective one. Selecting the second board in the door, he aimed a powerful blow at a crack in the wood. Then he stopped to listen, afraid the impact had been heard up at the house. There was no sound that would indicate anyone was coming to investigate, and he decided the sound wasn't as loud as he imagined, so he went back to work on the board. After a half-dozen blows with the hand ax, the board split down the middle, giving him room to get a solid hold on part of it. He grabbed that part and wrenched it from the door. He then put his strength behind the other piece and removed the entire board. Then he used the blade of his hatchet to pry the next board until the nails were loosened and backed out of the frame far enough for him to pull the board off. He continued this procedure until he had an opening in the door frame large enough for him to get through.

Even in the dark tack room, he found his packs, only because he remembered where Tice had shown him to stack them. One by one, he passed them through the hole in the door, and in a short time he had his pack harness on the horse and the packs secured. His last act before leading his horses out the back door was to fill a bucket of oats from the bin and dump them into a cotton sack he found on top of it. He paused to pull the doors shut again before climbing in the saddle and pointing the buckskin toward the main street running along the gulch. There was one more task to complete, and he paused to consider the risk involved. He had to feel fortunate to have recovered his packhorse and his belongings, but he needed his Henry rifle. *Hell*, he thought after a moment, *it's my rifle, and they got no right to keep it.*

It was after midnight and no one paid much attention to the solitary figure riding slowly down the slushy street, leading a packhorse. The responsible citizens of Helena were long since home in their beds, leaving the streets to those who frequented the saloons and the bawdy houses. When he approached the sheriff's office, he paused to see if there was anyone there. Inside, he could see just one person, a deputy, he presumed, leaning back in his chair with his feet propped on the desk. Rider dismounted and looped the reins over the hitching post. Drawing the carbine from his saddle scabbard, he stepped up on the walk and moved silently to the door. A slight groan of rusty hinges as he slowly pushed the door open was not enough to arouse the sleeping deputy at the desk.

Rider stood looking at the unsuspecting lawman for a moment before walking around behind him and pulling his revolver from his holster. The slight reduction of weight was sufficient to wake the sleeping deputy, and he abruptly sat straight up and slapped his hand on the empty holster. Still confused, he started to look around on the floor, thinking his weapon had dropped out of his holster. He froze when he felt the cold barrel of the pistol against the back of his head.

"Get up," Rider commanded. When the deputy did as he was told, Rider said, "In there." He pushed him toward the door to the cell room, taking the keys off a hook by the door when he passed through it.

"You're makin' one helluva big mistake, mister," the deputy said.

"Maybe," Rider replied, and prodded him with the rifle barrel again. He marched the lawman up to a cell door and unlocked it. "Get in," he said, and when the deputy balked, he gave him a shove and locked the cell door while the infuriated lawman turned at once to face him.

"You!" the deputy blurted, dumbfounded. "How the hell did you . . . ?" he sputtered, hardly believing his eyes. "Are you crazy—breakin' in the sheriff's office? How'd you get away from the soldiers?"

Rider had no time to answer questions, even had he been inclined to. "I came to get my rifle," he said stoically, "and then I'll be on my way." He turned and walked back into the office, leaving the deputy fuming after him, promising that he would be hunted down and hanged. Seeing a gun rack on one wall, he scanned the weapons locked in it and spotted his Henry right away. He then searched through the desk drawers until he found a ring of keys. One of them fit the lock on the gun rack. After retrieving his rifle, he replaced it with the Spencer carbine, then dutifully locked the rack again and returned the keys. While rummaging through the drawers, he noticed some blank paper, so he took a sheet of it and dipped a pen in the inkwell he found on the desk. He was not practiced at writing, but he remembered some from his childhood, so writing as neatly as he could manage, he left a message.

> *I owe A. Tice for a door I broke and a bucket of oats I took. I will pay him when I get the money. The Henry I took is mine, so I don't owe nuthin for it.*

He paused before signing it, and then wrote *Rider*.

Before leaving, he closed the door to the cells in an effort to muffle some of the deputy's yelling. Then with his Henry rifle in hand, he closed the front door and climbed into the saddle to continue on his way out of town, feeling that he had rectified all accounts.

Sheriff Sam Tate walked out the front door of the hotel and paused on the board walkway to work with a toothpick on some remnants of the bacon he had just eaten in the dining room. Looking up and down the quiet street as he deftly maneuvered his toothpick between his front teeth, he felt satisfied that all seemed peaceful in his town. As he passed a doorway next to the Dry Gulch Saloon, he was surprised to find a miner scrunched up in the fetal position, evidently sleeping off a drunk. He kept a deputy on duty all night to prevent things like that. Jeff Dwyer was on duty last night and he was usually reliable to rid the street of drunks who were unable to find their way home. Tate nudged the drunk several times with the toe of his boot without results, so he administered a firm kick to the man's backside that succeeded in shaking the drunk from his slumber. "Get up from there!" Tate ordered. "You're lucky you ain't froze to death. Get your sorry ass home, wherever that is. I oughta lock you up for drunk and disorderly conduct."

The dazed man took a minute to focus his eyes before realizing it was the sheriff who had awakened him. He staggered to his feet with an assist from the door frame before speaking in his defense. "I ain't drunk, Sheriff. I was drunk last night." He paused while a wave of nausea swept over him. "I'm just sick now."

"Well, get on off the street before you start puking your guts out," Tate scolded.

"Yes, sir, Sheriff," the drunk replied.

Tate watched him as he staggered into the alley beside the saloon and disappeared around behind the building. *He'll probably pass out again behind the saloon,* Tate thought, *but at least he'll be out of sight.* Not inclined to bother with harmless drunks first thing in the morning, he was more concerned about the reason Jeff had failed to dispatch him the night before.

He was surprised to find no one in the office when he walked in the front door. The deputy on duty usually caught a few hours of sleep during the early hours of the morning, but they were always up and in the office when he came in—in an effort to appear they had been awake all night, he suspected. The door to the cell room was closed, which was also unusual for this hour of the day. He opened it and found Jeff Dwyer asleep in one of the cells, having succumbed to fatigue after he had yelled himself hoarse during the wee hours. "Well, if you ain't somethin'," Tate spat in disgust, and yanked on the cell door, realizing at the moment that it was locked and his deputy was confined. "What the hell?" Tate roared, and continued to pull on the locked door, waking Jeff in the process.

The mortified deputy sprang from the cot and exclaimed in a voice so hoarse he could barely be understood, "That Rider, son of a bitch! He got the jump on me! He musta got away from the soldiers!" He went on to excitedly relate the circumstances of the night just passed while Tate unlocked the cell.

Astonished and flustered by the incredulous return of the wild man of the mountains, Tate went back into the office to see if anything was missing. It was then he discovered the rough note on his desk. After reading it, he looked at once to the gun rack, but there was none missing. A closer look revealed the carbine in the slot where the Henry had been. He read the note again, shaking his head in amazement. "He's crazy," he muttered. "He's crazy as hell." He bit his bottom lip in frustration. He had not come in prepared for a hard day, but there was no alternative but to go after Rider. "Round up Fletcher, Giles, and the others," he ordered. "We're gonna have to track the crazy bastard down."

On his way out the door, the deputy almost collided with Arthur Tice, who came to report the break-in at his stable and the missing horse and packs. "He broke up my tack room door," Tice complained, "and them packs and stuff were rightfully mine to pay for his bill." Tate showed him the note left on his desk. After reading it, Tice asked in a huff, "Where the hell is he gonna get the money? He ain't plannin' on comin' back here no time soon."

"Arthur, there ain't nothin' I can do for you," Tate said. "Me and my men are goin' out to see if we can pick up his trail. That's all I can do." It was not enough to satisfy the stable owner, but he understood the sheriff's position.

It was close to midmorning by the time the sheriff's posse was rounded up and prepared to ride. The futility of their quest was evident almost immediately as they rode down the middle of the churned-up quagmire of snow and mud that the recent storms had made of the main street. There were trails in every direction to and from the gulch—the tracks of horses, mules, wagons, even oxen were all mixed together in an impossible stew. The posse wandered almost aimlessly up and down the gulch until one of the deputies, Jake Fletcher, finally asked the question they had all been thinking. "What the hell are we doin'? There ain't no way we can pick up his trail, even if he painted us some road signs to follow."

As frustrated as his deputies, Tate had to agree, but he felt it was his duty to try. "I expect you're right, Jake," he said, while trying to think of what to do. "We know he had a camp somewhere in the mountains east of the valley. We'll ride out a ways and split up. Half of us can ride north, the other half south, and see if we get lucky and cross a trail left by just two horses. When they had ridden about a quarter of a mile from town, they split up. "If you strike a trail that looks right," Tate said, "fire a couple of shots in the air." They divided then and set out on a fruitless hunt, for Rider had been smart enough to follow a well-traveled trail, making it impossible to discern his tracks from those of any others.

As the morning wore on into midday, it became more apparent to all in the posse that they were participants in a pointless exercise. This fact was emphasized by the lone suspicious trail that looked to be a possibility—the only one found with any potential. They followed it a mile and a half to a miner's shack and an astonished miner. Tate could see it in the faces of his men as they sat their weary horses and looked to him to call a halt to the search. "I reckon he's long gone from this valley," he finally admitted. "More'n likely headed out of this part of the country." They all nodded in agreement, all choosing to believe he was gone from the territory, even though they knew he had a camp in the Big Belt Mountains somewhere. No one of them could generate any enthusiasm for a lengthy search in the mountains. "All right, boys," Tate said. "We've done all we can. Let's head for home."

After following a wagon trail to a shallow ford in the river, Rider had crossed over, leaving the wagon trail on the other side to head in a more northerly direction toward the pass that would take him into the heart of the mountains and his camp. Upon finding the camp again, he approached it very cautiously, alert for any signs that might indicate it had been discovered. When he was satisfied that it had not been, he dismounted and led his horses behind the pines and through the rock crevice that served as the entrance to the camp. All was as he had left it. As soon as he had taken care of the horses, and rewarded each with a portion of the oats he had taken from the stable, he went to work setting up his camp. There was plenty of food in the cache he had hidden before leaving for Fort Laramie with Johnny, so after clearing away some of the snow that had gathered in the front of his hut, he built a fire and filled his coffeepot with snow to melt for coffee. He was home.

Chapter 12

For the rest of that winter, no more was seen or heard of the legend the Blackfeet and Crows knew as Rider Twelve Horses. In the early spring, the Blackfeet reported his spirit had returned to the high cliff over the pass where he had first been seen. The sightings were brief and infrequent, but they were sure he had returned. Although several of the young men of the village had ventured into the mountains, hoping to get a glimpse of him before he vanished into the forest, there was never any clue that would lead them to his camp. As for the white people in Helena, Rider was soon forgotten—a brief episode in a violent history of the territory. Sheriff Tate was reminded of him once in a while when he happened to glance at the army carbine in his gun rack. And Arthur Tice would utter a swear word oftentimes when going in or out of the patched-up door to his tack room. For everyone else, Lucy McGowan included, the chapter involving the strange man in the mountains was closed.

Rider knew that he had been seen on several occasions, and with the coming of spring, he decided that it was time to move on to another range of mountains to hunt. For as Johnny Hawk had warned, there would be more young Blackfeet warriors trying to strengthen their medicine with a sighting of Rider Twelve Horses, and somebody might stumble upon his camp. The winter had been long, with many hours spent thinking about his friends in Two Bulls' village, wondering about the fate of Johnny Hawk, for Carrington had said he didn't think Johnny had made it. He often found himself thinking about the girl Yellow Bird. She had said she would wait for his return, but she had no idea he would be gone this long. He would have returned, but it was no longer safe for him to go back to Fort Laramie. There had been a lot to think about during the long nights, but in the daylight, the hunting had been good. Deer, elk, and bear were plentiful in his mountain home and he had a great number of hides to trade. He needed to trade because his supplies were getting low, including .44 cartridges for his rifle. He made it a practice to conserve his cartridges, using his rifle for bear and elk, and occasionally on deer if he couldn't get close enough for his bow. He had made it a practice, however, to use the rifle only when hunting in the southern part of the mountain range, again because of the recent sightings of Indians. Finally he decided that he was going to leave his base camp for a while after he spotted a young Blackfoot warrior venturing close to his mountain, and he started out one sunny morning.

He wished that Johnny was here to take the pelts to the trading post on the lower end of the gulch, for he had no desire to venture that close to Helena. But Johnny had said that the store was a good distance from the town, so Rider decided that if he was careful, he could visit the trading post without risk of running into the sheriff or one of his deputies. Once he had the supplies he needed, he planned to move on up in the mountains west of Helena to look for new hunting grounds. Maybe the Blackfeet curiosity for the spirit of the mountains would die down if he was gone from his camp for a while.

Grover Bramble decided it was time to prop open the board shutters on his front window and let a little spring air inside his store. When he did, it was in time to catch a glimpse of a rider coming up the trail to his door, leading a heavily laden packhorse. At that distance, the rider appeared to be an Indian, but he sat unusually tall in the saddle, and as he came closer, Grover decided it was a white man. He continued to watch his visitor's progress from the window until his horse pulled up before the hitching rail. Then he went to the door and opened it, and stood there waiting to welcome his customer. As soon as the big man was on the ground, it occurred to Grover who he was. He had to be! Tall, wearing clothes made of animal hides, his dark hair almost touching his shoulders, and a Henry rifle cradled in his arms, it was *Rider Twelve Horses*. Excited to meet a legend, he rushed out to welcome him.

"Looks like you got a load of furs there," Grover said in greeting.

"I need some things," Rider replied. "Johnny Hawk said you were a fair man to trade with."

"Well, I try to be," Grover said. "You a friend of Johnny's?" It crossed his mind that it was Johnny Hawk who had told him the Blackfeet's mysterious mountain spirit's name was Rider, although he never claimed to know him personally. "I ain't seen Johnny in quite a spell. I was afraid he mighta run into some trouble back up in the mountains somewhere."

Rider paused to study the man's face for a moment. It had been several months since he had heard English spoken, and it seemed that Grover's questions were coming too rapidly. "I'm a friend of his," he said. "I ain't seen him for a spell, either."

Grover waited for some embellishment on the simple statements, but there was none. Up close, he was taller than he had looked when he first dismounted, and the cold expressionless eyes that looked back at Grover struck him as the eyes of a predator. He decided at once that this man whom the sheriff had arrested for killing the big fellow named Bodine—and scalped him, so he had heard—was not one for idle chatter. So he said, "Let's have a look at them pelts." Rider nodded and went immediately to his packhorse to untie the furs, as Grover continued to watch. The last he had heard, Rider had been escorted off by the army. He was itching to ask how it came to be that he was riding free, but he was too timid to ask. *Probably killed the whole damn patrol*, he thought.

Upon inspecting the pelts, Grover was relieved to find they were of excellent quality. He had harbored some fear that they might be inferior and he would be obliged to tell this lethal-looking hunter they were of little value. But these pelts were filled out with thick winter fur, and he would be able to sell them to be shipped back east. Even so, he still had some concern about giving Rider his price, afraid he might think it was not enough. When his figures were totaled, he handed the paper to Rider and said, "I reckon that's about the best I can do."

Rider spent only a few seconds to look at the number before nodding and saying, "That looks fair."

They carried the pelts inside then and Rider selected his supplies, silently nodding toward one item after another until he had used up most of his credit. Pointing to the balance, he asked, "Do you know Arthur Tice?" Grover said that he surely did, so Rider said, "I owe him for a door. Will you give him this money?"

"I will," Grover replied, and helped him carry his purchases out to pack on the horses. When they had finished, Rider said, "Much obliged," and started to step up in the saddle. He paused when Grover extended his hand.

"If you get more pelts that look as good as these," Grover said, "bring 'em on back here to trade." When he noted a wary glint in Rider's eye, he thought he understood the quiet man's thinking, and added, "I won't say nothin' to nobody 'bout you bein' here." It was a lie because he knew he would have to brag about the transaction to somebody, but he promised himself that somebody wouldn't be the sheriff or his deputies.

Rider's gaze softened and he said, "'Preciate it." Then he shook Grover's hand and climbed into the saddle. Grover stood outside and watched him until he was out of sight, noticing that he didn't go back the way he had come, heading toward the mountains to the west instead.

Satisfied that he had paid his debt to the owner of the stable he had broken into, he rode away from Helena to scout the mountains to the west, where he had never been before. Now that the weather was not quite so harsh, it was easier on his animals, although the mountains he now rode into were much like his home range in the Big Belts. As he climbed away from the broad valley, he came to many streams rushing with melt-off from the peaks above and there was abundant sign of elk and bear. It would appear to be a hunter's paradise. *I wish Johnny could have seen this,* he found himself thinking. Then he remembered his old partner's discontent with recent signs of aging, especially his eyesight, critical to a born hunter.

He spent over three weeks, moving from camp to camp as he gradually moved south, following the game trails, killing what he needed to survive and no more. As he continued south, he was surprised to come across small camps of miners on the streams flowing down some of the higher slopes. He was careful to avoid any contact with them, skirting wide around their camps. Finally, he decided that he must be heading toward another town, so he decided it was time to head back to his secret camp in the Big Belt Range. With that in mind, he made camp, tended his horses, and built a fire, planning to start back in the morning.

"Hello, the camp," Billy Hyde called out.

"Hello, yourself," came the reply as the two miners scrambled to grab their rifles. There had been several attacks on claims on this side of the mountain, and the two partners were not taking any chances with strangers.

"We're miners like yourselves," Quincy called back, "on our way back from Butte—mean you no harm. Saw your fire and just thought we might take a cup of coffee with you."

"That so?" one of the miners replied, still skeptical. "We're kinda low on coffee."

"Well, then it's good we happened along," Quincy said. "We just stocked up on supplies and we've got plenty of coffee beans. We'd be glad to share and it'd save us from havin' to stop right away to build a fire. We got a piece to go tonight before we get back to our camp."

"Whaddaya think, Mose? Sound a little fishy to you?"

"I don't know," his partner replied. "Can't be too careful, but they may be all right."

"Don't blame you for bein' careful," Quincy called out again. "I reckon we can just keep ridin'. Don't wanna cause you no worry." He gave Billy a wink. "Come on, Billy. We'll wait till we make camp later tonight." They turned their horses as if preparing to leave.

"Hold on, fellers," Mose said. "We don't mean to be unfriendly. It's just that there's been some trouble lately." He looked at his partner for confirmation. Receiving a shrug, then a nod, he said, "Come on in."

Billy and Quincy walked their horses into the camp and dismounted. "We could sure use some coffee right about now," Quincy said. "It's a pretty stout ride up from that town back yonder."

"Like I said," Mose commented, "we're runnin' a little low on coffee beans, so if you meant what you said about supplying the beans . . ."

"Oh, hell yeah," Quincy quickly replied, and turned toward Billy Hyde. "Get some of them beans outta the sack, Billy." Turning back to the miners, he asked, "You got your coffee mill handy? Ours is packed somewhere on that packhorse."

After the beans were ground and the coffee on the flame, the two miners and their guests settled into a friendly conversation. "How long you fellers been workin' this sluice here?" Billy asked. When told they had been working the stream since last fall, he asked, "Are you findin' anything?"

"No," came the quick reply from Mose. "We ain't hit no pay dirt yet."

"But you been here since last fall?" Quincy responded. "You musta had some reason to stay with it. Why, I believe I'da moved on."

"I reckon we should have at that," Mose said, and gave his partner a nervous glance.

The glance was noticed by Quincy and he chuckled. "Hell, I don't blame you for playin' it close to the vest. There's been claim robbers hittin' some of these spots. I heard there's two of 'em workin' these mountains."

"Is that a fact?" Mose replied. "Do they have any idea who's doin' it?"

"No," Quincy said with a wide smile forming on his face. "They got a description, though."

"They do?"

"Yessir," Quincy replied, enjoying the game he was playing. "One of 'em looks like Billy, there. The other'n looks like me." Both of the victims grabbed for their rifles again, but they were far too late. Billy and Quincy had their pistols out and cut them down before they could even get a hand on the weapons.

Quincy casually replaced the two cartridges he had spent, then reached for the pot and poured himself another cup of coffee. Billy, on the other hand, was anxious to search for the dust they suspected was hidden somewhere in the camp, and immediately started rummaging through the packs lying outside the primitive shack the miners had been living in. "See if they've got anythin' on 'em," Quincy said, still taking his time with his coffee. "Remember that last feller had a poke tied inside his britches." He was in no hurry to help Billy search the camp. There were no other camps nearby that might have heard the pistol shots. Had it not been for the fact that they had hit quite a few of the claims above the little town of Butte, and might be in danger of inspiring the formation of a vigilante posse, he would have considered using this camp for a few days before moving on north to new pickings.

After turning the shack upside down in their search, they were about to come to the conclusion that Mose and his partner had been telling the truth after all. "Them dumb bastards," Billy swore. "There ain't no gold here." He delivered a kick to the back of one of the corpses to express his frustration. "They ain't even got decent horses," he added, looking at the two mules grazing near the stream. They had been very particular in the horses they kept from their robberies. They had no desire to herd a large number of horses, and in the event they encountered the law or a vigilante committee, they didn't want to be caught with identifiable horses. As a consequence, they led only one extra horse each.

"Let's go have a look around that sluice box," Quincy suggested.

They walked down to the stream, where there was ample evidence of the digging along the banks that bore testimony that the two miners had been there for quite some time. "Don't make any sense," Billy said. "If them fellers hadn'ta been lyin', they'da left this place long ago." To demonstrate his disgust, he raised his foot and shoved the sluice over sideways. The wooden supports offered little resistance and the whole structure went over on its side. "Dumb bastards," he concluded.

But Quincy's eye had been captured by the unstable rock that had served as a base for one of the supports. It had fairly wobbled when the sluice went over, and was reason enough for him to wade into the stream and roll it over. "Here it is!" he announced, grinning in triumph as he pulled up two sodden pokes from a hole in the streambed. "All divided up nice and even." He tossed one of the pouches to Billy, who eagerly untied the strings to look inside. Wading back to the bank with his ill-gained treasure, he said, "These ol' boys was pullin' pay dirt outta here, all right. If I was a man inclined to work for a livin', I might be tempted to stay here a while and see how much more I could pull outta the ground."

"By God, that'ud be the day," Billy said, laughing gleefully as he peered into his poke. "Your hand ain't never felt the handle of a shovel."

"And it never will," Quincy said with a chuckle.

*   *   *

They camped there that night, then moved on in the morning, leaving the bodies where they had dragged them, barely out of the light of the campfire. Satisfied with this final score when the pickings had seemed to be getting leaner, they had decided to head back north, toward Helena, not expecting further opportunities this far from the main strike in Butte. Staying close to the mountains, in lieu of an easier ride in the broad valley to avoid the chance meeting with a posse, they proceeded north through passes between grassy mountaintops and evergreen belts. Dark clouds drifting in from the northwest during the afternoon warned of a possible thunderstorm, but they continued on, hoping to avoid the rain until they had reached a campsite with some shelter as well as water for them and the horses. They were not to be so fortunate, however, for the clouds opened up and dumped a hard rain on the two riders, accompanied by vivid flashes of lightning and pistol-sharp claps of thunder.

Wet and miserable, they plodded on. The rain let up, then finally stopped as darkness approached, still punctuated by occasional flashes of lightning. Their luck changed for the better, however, when a glimpse of light flickered through the trees in a stand of young pines. "You see what I see?" Quincy asked. When Billy strained to see what he was referring to, Quincy said, "Look yonder." He pointed toward the pine stand. "Looks like a campfire in them trees."

Seeing it then, Billy replied, "That's what it looks like, all right. Reckon who it is?" It was hardly likely it could be a miner this far from the diggings. "Might be Injuns," he speculated.

"Maybe so," Quincy replied. "Ain't a very big fire, so if it's Injuns, it don't look like there's many of 'em."

"I hope they got somethin' to eat," Billy said.

Approaching as close as they thought safe, they dismounted and moved closer on foot to get a better look at what they might be riding into. It was hard to tell because of the trees, but they were unable to see anyone near the fire, so they decided to get even closer before announcing their presence. Pulling their pistols from their holsters, they stepped as carefully as possible through the short brush until reaching the edge of a small clearing with the fire in the center. There was still no one in sight, although there was a temporary lean-to beyond the fire with a hide roof to provide shelter from the rain. It was impossible to tell if anyone was inside it. Thinking it not worth the risk of getting shot by some cautious miner or Indian, Quincy announced their presence. "Hello, there in the camp." There was no reply and still no sign that anyone was there. "Well, damn," Quincy cursed after waiting for a reply, "don't seem to be nobody here."

"Maybe he's takin' a dump or somethin'," Billy offered. "Hell, he can't be far."

Moving to the edge of the clearing, pistols drawn, the two outlaws were stopped, by a sudden flash of lightning, following almost immediately by a deafening clap of thunder. The trees were bathed in brilliant light for only a brief moment, but it was long enough to sear the ominous image of the tall powerful hunter onto their brains. Like a messenger of death, he stood at the edge of the forest of pines, gazing at them, his rifle hanging relaxed in one hand, his face dark and menacing under the shadow of his hat.

"Jesus!" Quincy exclaimed involuntarily, and he and Billy fired simultaneously at the spot, now dark, where the image had appeared. Their shots were answered a split second later, the muzzle blasts coming from a spot several yards to the left of where they had aimed. Billy cried out in pain and crumpled to the ground. Quincy did not wait for the next shot; terrified, he turned and ran for his life. He had no thoughts of checking on Billy to see if he was dead or alive. His only thought was to save his hide and to hell with Billy.

Rider walked out into the open when he heard the sound of hoofbeats pounding the wet turf of the mountainside. He paused momentarily to see if Billy was dead. The last flicker of life went out of Billy's eyes as he stared up into his executioner's face. Wide and unblinking, his eyes told of the fear and horror he seemed to see coming to greet him on the other side. Rider hesitated only long enough to make sure Billy was dead before plunging into the trees after Quincy. He was too late to stop him, but he was not discouraged. He assumed that God, or Man Above, was responsible for this chance encounter with the two remaining men involved with the attack on Johnny Hawk. In all this mountain wilderness, He had brought them right to his camp, and that was enough to convince Rider that it was his destiny to kill the one remaining of the three who had caused so much pain and suffering. Making his way quickly then to the trees on the other side of the clearing, he found three horses shuffling about in the low brush. Quincy had been too frightened to spend the time to take any of them with him. Even in the dark, Rider could determine the direction Quincy started in. There were enough broken bushes and limbs to indicate the hurry he had been in, but it would be very difficult to follow his trail after he left the pines. Feeling no sense of impatience, he was not concerned, for he would wait until daylight, track him down, and send him to hell with his partners.

Urging his horse on recklessly, Quincy fled down the mountainside, the image of death, patiently standing in the trees, still in his memory. Near the bottom of the mountain, his horse slid on a patch of shale and tumbled, throwing Quincy from the saddle to land hard on the rocky ground. In a terrified panic, he scrambled to his feet, thinking that Rider had caused the fall and that his horse had been shot. So frightened was he that he wasn't even aware of the high-pitched whine escaping his mouth. Turning around in a circle, looking for his antagonist, he grabbed for his pistol, but found an empty holster. He had lost the weapon in the fall. He was startled again, when he heard a noise off to his left, only to find it was his horse getting to its feet. Almost crying out in relief to see that the horse was apparently all right, he forgot about the pistol and ran to get back in the saddle. Whipping the tiring animal mercilessly, he raced along the valley toward a notch between two mountains ahead.

Morning found him tired and thirsty, walking and

leading his weary horse, pausing frequently to look behind him, afraid he might see the ominous hunter coming on. There was no sign of Rider, however, and the daylight lessened the panic he had suffered all through the night, allowing him to think rationally. One thing he knew for certain was that he was at a distinct disadvantage in the hills and forests. The demon that pursued him seemed to be a creature half Indian, half animal, and all predator. And the wilderness was his domain. So to be safe, Quincy was convinced that he had to go back to Helena, the town where Rider would likely be arrested or shot on sight if he followed him there. *If I can just get to Helena,* he thought, *then the son of a bitch has to fight on my terms.* His courage was immediately lifted and he scolded himself for his prior panic.

Rider reached down and picked up the revolver lying near a wide patch of loose shale. The picture of what had happened there was clear in his mind. There were small traces of blood on some of the sharper edges of the rocky ground to indicate either the horse or the rider had suffered some cuts and bruises—evidently not enough to cause serious injury, for he found the trail leading toward the head of the valley. The length of the stride indicated that the spill had not caused a slowdown in Quincy's flight. He climbed into the saddle and urged the buckskin toward the notch at the head of the narrow valley, his packhorse and one extra horse following. He had picked the best of the horses Quincy and Billy had brought with them, and freed the others.

* * *

Once Quincy reached the town limits of Helena, he began to regain his old confidence almost immediately. His regret now was that he did not stand his ground, for having run, he lost the pouch of gold dust Billy Hyde had carried, and it angered him to think that Rider was now in possession of it. *He's only one man,* he thought. *I ain't never run from one man before. But he had the jump on us. That's the only reason I had to run. Wouldn't have made sense not to. I might have gotten a shot at him when he gunned Billy down, though. If I had it to do over, that's what I would have done.*

He was able to put all the cowardly thoughts out of his mind once he rode down Main Street past all the stores and saloons. He was a high roller again, with gold dust in his pouch. He could put his horse in a stable and himself in a room at the hotel. *Might as well enjoy myself,* he thought, *play a little poker, have a go-round with one or two of the ladies.* Thinking again of the man following him, he thought, *He's a crazy son of a bitch, but he ain't crazy enough to come into Helena looking for me. I'll stay outta the Pay Dirt Saloon, though. That's a bad luck saloon.*

He picked a stable on the other end of the gulch from the Pay Dirt, a few steps down the street from the Montana Hotel. "That horse looks like he's been rode hard," Fred Potts said when Quincy dismounted.

"Well, now, that's a fact," Quincy replied. "And that's why I need to rest him up real good. Give him a double measure of oats, and I might give you a little extra if you take good care of him."

"Yes, sir," Fred said, "I'll take real good care of him."

Feeling his old sense of bravado again, Quincy took his saddlebag and made the short walk to the hotel, where he went in and looked the bar over before deciding to register. *This will do just fine,* he said to himself. There were already several card games in progress at the tables in the back of the bar. Checking in, he requested one of the hotel's bigger rooms on the second floor at the front of the building where he could look out the window and see the street below. Dropping his saddlebags on the chair in the corner, he took a moment to look around at his room. A comfortable bed, a stout door, and a window with no balcony, he felt safe here. *He'd be a damn fool to ride into this town,* he told himself. *He knows he'd likely be shot on sight. But even if he is that crazy, he'd have a hell of a time trying to get to me.* "Let the bastard come," he challenged confidently, and pulled his .44 and spun the cylinder to make sure all chambers were loaded.

In spite of the overwhelming odds against Rider showing his face in town, Quincy could not help taking every extra precaution against being caught by surprise. It took several days before he began to believe that he was actually safe from the grim assassin as long as he was in town where there was a sheriff and four deputies ready to arrest him. After all, the man was instantly recognizable. *He wouldn't get ten feet before somebody saw him and went for the sheriff,* he thought. Still, he pulled a chair up in front of his locked door at night, and stood in the doorway of the bar and the hotel dining room, looking the room over, before entering. Gradually, even those practices were relaxed to the extent that Rider was no longer the constant thought in his mind, and Quincy settled into his assumed life of gambler and big spender. After a couple of weeks of this lifestyle, he realized that he was, indeed, safe in the midst of the town's many people and the well-staffed sheriff's office.

There came a day, however, much sooner than he had expected when the gold dust he kept in the hotel safe started to run out. His luck at the card table took a downhill turn, and he was faced with the realization that his finances were rapidly draining. He was discreetly notified by the hotel manager that he was behind in paying his bill. He reluctantly admitted to himself that it was time to return to his real occupation—robbery and murder—for he had become overly fond of his current existence. Faced with this dilemma, he pushed thoughts of Rider to the back of his mind, replaced by the more pressing need for money. The small prospectors he, along with Bodine and Billy, used to rob were not enough now. He needed a bigger score to continue his high-rolling lifestyle. If Helena had a bank, that would have been his first thought, but so far, the town had not progressed to that point. There were many businesses in town that were prosperous enough to have accumulations of cash and dust. The problem facing him now was his recent status as a well-heeled gambler. Too many men might be able to identify him if he were seen leaving a business after robbing it, even with a sack over his head.

The more thought he gave his problem, the more often the Pay Dirt Saloon came to mind. That unlucky place might, in fact, be the luckiest spot for the job that he needed to pull off. It was at the extreme end of the gulch, a good distance from his new base at the Montana Hotel, and busy as it was, it was operated by only one man—the perfect place, he decided. "And there ain't no reason to wait," he announced to his empty room. "I need the money now."

A bright three-quarter moon shown down on Last Chance Gulch, sharply outlining the dark shadows cast by the lone cottonwood tree left standing near the Pay Dirt Saloon. Impatiently waiting, Quincy watched as Pete Bender escorted the last drunken customer out the front door. Quincy could not see his watch to check the time, but he knew it was somewhere close to three o'clock in the morning. "Goddamned drunks," he complained under his breath, and waited underneath the cottonwood until Pete's patron had made his way unsteadily up the hill. Finally all was quiet in the saloon.

He hurried across the open ground to the front stoop of the building and rapped on the locked door. After a minute, he heard footsteps approaching and then Pete's voice. "Who is it? I'm closed."

"Won't take but a minute," Quincy answered. "I need a bottle of whiskey to take with me for medicinal purposes. Friend of mine's got the shakes real bad. I'll pay you double for it." He listened closely for Pete's response. There was a moment of hesitation; then a sigh was heard on the other side of the door, followed by the sound of the bolt being slid open.

"Come on in, then," Pete said as he swung the door open. As soon as Quincy stepped into the light, Pete recognized him. "You're one of those friends of that feller that got killed in here." He immediately experienced a feeling of foreboding. In the next second, his fears were justified.

"That's a fact," Quincy said as he pulled his pistol, and aimed it at Pete's stomach.

"You son of a bitch," Pete gasped, hardly believing he was being robbed.

Quincy favored him with a malicious grin. "Now, if you behave yourself, and do like I tell you, maybe you won't get hurt. So don't waste my time. I need money and I want it right now." He motioned him back toward the bar with his pistol.

Pete did as he was told, his mind racing as he tried to weigh his chances of getting his hands on his shotgun under the counter. Quincy hadn't even bothered to tie a bandanna around his face, and to Pete, this meant that he wasn't planning to leave a witness. "Mister," he said, "I ain't got enough money in here to make it worth killin' a man for."

"Ha," Quincy retorted. "Who said anythin' about killin' you?" Then the smile was replaced by a scowl. "If you don't get me that money quick, I *am* gonna shoot you."

"It'd be a mistake."

Startled, both men turned toward the door from where the voice had come to discover the grim figure with rifle leveled. In stark terror, Quincy fired at the same time Rider pulled his trigger, while Pete dived for cover behind the counter. Flustered as he was by his fear, Quincy's shot was off, catching Rider in the arm, but Rider's shot tore into Quincy's gut and he dropped his pistol and fell to the floor clutching his stomach. Ignoring the wound in his arm, Rider walked unhurriedly up to his victim and kicked the revolver out of his reach.

His face twisted in agony, Quincy begged for his life. "It wasn't me that shot Johnny Hawk," he gasped painfully. "It was Bodine. I ain't done nothin' to you."

"It's the second time you took a shot at me," Rider said. "The first time was on the Solomon River."

Suddenly Quincy's eyes opened wide as he grimaced with the fire in his gut and it struck him then why this buckskinned avenger looked familiar. "Jim Moran," he uttered.

"That's right, Quincy."

"Wait, wait!" he exclaimed in a panic when Rider took a step back. "Don't kill me, Jim. Hell, we rode together in the war. You don't wanna kill an old comrade. Look, I've got gold dust we can split, partner." He started to reach for his boot. He never made it. Rider's rifle slug split his forehead and he slumped over against the counter. Rider reached down and pulled the derringer out of the top of Quincy's boot.

He stood up then and turned to toss the weapon on the counter, only to confront Pete with a shotgun leveled at him. There was a brief look of uncertainty in Pete's eyes before he lowered the gun and propped it against the counter. "Mister, I don't know nothin' about you except what I've heard—and that wasn't nothin' good. But I got a feelin' you ain't out to do me no harm, and I reckon you just saved my life." He shook his head and frowned. "Now I reckon I'm gonna feel like a damn fool if you rob me and shoot me in the head."

"I'm not a thief," Rider stated simply, then turned and walked out the door.

"No, I reckon you ain't," Pete muttered softly under his breath, still astonished by what had just taken place.

Outside in the moonlight, Rider walked purposely toward his horses tied in the dwarf cedars where he had waited every night, hoping that Quincy would return to the saloon he and the other two had frequented before. Knowing it was too risky to roam the town looking for Quincy, he had been forced to stalk the Pay Dirt, counting on luck. And luck had been with him.

Chapter 13

It was over and done with. He was tired and he hurt, another bullet hole in his body, and those in his leg and back were not even healed yet. But that was not the cause of his melancholy and feelings of emptiness. These were new sensations for him, when the prospects of returning to the solitude of the high mountains did not reach out to salve his wounds, both physical and mental. He thought that maybe he understood Johnny Hawk's longing in his later years for the comfort of other people in his life, especially his Indian wife. He was unable to justify his longings. He was much too young to yearn for the company of other people when there were mountains, whole ranges of mountains, that he had not seen. Thoughts of those places still caused a quickening of his pulse. So why these feelings of melancholy?

He considered the possibility that mental images of a young Crow maiden might have caused him to think about what might have been, had things taken a different path. Then he scolded himself for allowing weak pathetic thoughts to dominate his mind. It was no longer safe for him to live with Two Bulls' village. Johnny Hawk was gone and thanks to Lieutenant Carrington, he was a fugitive and could therefore never return to Fort Laramie and his Crow friends. He was destined to be alone, and that was what he had thought he always wanted, ever since he had made a fool of himself with Lucy Taylor. So he should be happy with the way things turned out. *And so I will be*, he decided at that point. *The only problem I've got is my arm hurts. A few days back in my camp in the Big Belts and I'll be healed up. Then I think I'll head on up in the Rockies.*

The thought was enough to lift his spirits, and he nudged the buckskin gently to increase the big horse's pace as he left the river behind him and set a course toward the foothills before the mountains looming in the distance. "Sorry you ain't gonna be there to see it with me, Johnny," he said. Then something Johnny had said not long after they had joined up came to mind. He said Rider should name the buckskin because Rider treated the horse like family. The memory brought a smile to his lips. "Maybe you're right," he said aloud. "I'll name him Jaybird, after you." It made him laugh.

When he had crossed the foothills, he turned the buckskin toward a narrow pass that led to the first of two mountains that stood like guardians before the rocky mountainside where his camp was hidden. It would be good to get back to his camp. As he climbed the slope toward the top of his mountain, he noticed sign he figured to be that of elk in the broken branches of some smaller bushes. Thinking of the need to replenish his food supply, he felt it was a good omen until his sharp eye spotted the distinct hoofprint that was not elk. He immediately dismounted to examine it more closely. It was the print of an unshod horse. *Indian pony!* he thought. He automatically looked all around him to make sure there was no one watching him. It was no stretch to figure that the Blackfeet had been scouting the mountain. This was closer than they had come to his camp before. He walked a few yards farther, searching the ground, before he found another track. A scouting party, or a war party, it was hard to say which, but it was not a simple hunting party, for they had been too careful, obviously making an effort to hide their tracks.

He tried to estimate how old the tracks were. It was difficult to say, but he was sure they were not as recent as this day, so it was not likely the warriors were watching him now as he approached the rock cliff and the thick stand of pines that concealed the entrance to his camp. When he reached the rocky patch before the pines, he left his packhorse and the extra horse he had picked up when he killed Billy Hyde, thinking to lead the horses in one at a time so as not to disturb the pine limbs and reveal an entrance.

Halfway through the crevice in the cliff, he heard a horse whinny. It was too late to turn around! He pulled his rifle from the saddle sling and dropped to one knee, listening. There was a muffled sound he couldn't identify, followed by the word "Jaybird." His arms grew suddenly weak from the emotion draining his strength, and he almost dropped the nine-and-a-half pound Henry. Taking a moment to recover, he got up and led his horse into the opening where Johnny Hawk was seated by the fire, eating. He barely looked up from his supper. "I swear, this is mighty fine pemmican," he said. "Mornin' Flower! Bring some more food. We got a guest for supper." Then he had to chuckle, enjoying the expression on Rider's face.

In a moment, Morning Flower came from the hut, beaming at him. Almost hidden behind the big woman was the slender figure of Yellow Bird.

Overwhelmed, Rider could only stand there, speechless for a long moment while Johnny got up and followed Morning Flower to hug and pat him on the back. "I figured you were dead," Rider finally managed.

"Well, I ain't," Johnny replied with a great big grin. "Mornin' Flower could tell you that."

The big Crow woman giggled delightedly. Then noticing the dried blood on his sleeve, she frowned and said, "You all the time come back with holes in you. Now I have to make you new shirt."

"No, I make him new shirt." The statement came from Yellow Bird, who had stood back while Johnny and Morning Flower gushed over the tall white warrior. They all turned to look at the lithesome girl when she spoke. Broad smiles lit up Morning Flower's and Johnny's faces. She moved up to stand directly before him then and gazed up into his face. "I will take care of you, Rider Twelve Horses, if you want me."

Flustered, embarrassed, but harboring no doubts, he replied, "I reckon I do" to the delight of Johnny and Morning Flower. Yellow Bird stepped closer then and put her arms around his waist, pressing her head against his chest. He stood there awkwardly for a moment before taking her in his arms and embracing her.

Grinning wide, so that his lone front bottom tooth stood out like a solitary sentinel, Johnny said, "Deer Foot gives you his blessin'. It's his responsibility since her daddy's dead. We already had the ceremony back in Two Bulls' village before we came out here. That was in case you'd got yourself kilt. She wanted to be your wife no matter what. I stood in for you, so if you don't want her, I reckon she'd be mine." He received a solid blow on the shoulder from Morning Flower for his joke.

"I want her," Rider said, suddenly realizing that he had wanted her ever since she had first approached him in Two Bulls' camp. There had been too many other serious things going on in his life at the time that seemed not to allow him to think of happy moments. But that was all behind him now. They would stay here in this mountain home, or push on farther north. It made no difference. He had everything he needed.

Read on for an excerpt from the next exciting
novel by Charles G. West,

Thunder Over Lolo Pass

Available from Signet in April 2011.

"Damn, lookee there, Jug," Cody McCloud exclaimed. "There's a new saloon gone up since we've been back in town." It was one of several new businesses in the settlement, no doubt attracted by the recent establishment of Fort Missoula. Cody, youngest of the three McCloud brothers, and by far the most adventurous, was always ready to follow a new trail. "Whaddaya say we have a look inside? I could use a little drink about now."

Jug, the middle McCloud brother and two years older than Cody, was more interested in getting something to eat. Jug was the largest of the brothers, and his mind was seldom complicated with thoughts more serious than finding the next meal. Gifted with an oversized and powerful body, he was, however, the owner of a peaceful nature, requiring considerable agitation to ignite the fearsome violence he was capable of. "That suits me," he said in answer to Cody's suggestion. "Maybe they've got a little somethin' to eat, too." The gentle giant's real name was Ryan, but everybody had called him Jug ever since he was twelve years old. His eldest brother had pinned the nickname on him after he sneaked a full jug of cider their father had cooling in the spring box and drank more than half of it. Afterward, he had been too ill to refill the jug with water as he had planned. He got the licking his father had promised, but the terrible sick stomach he suffered had been the greater punishment. The nickname had stuck and, in time, replaced his given name.

Having just delivered twenty cattle to the new fort to feed the recently arrived detachment of soldiers, the brothers were in a mood for a mild celebration before riding back up the valley to the M Bar C ranch. Having been already advised of the portion of the money they could spend on food and drink by their father, they were determined to spend the limit, so they tied their horses at the hitching rail alongside a half dozen others and went inside.

Before going directly to the bar, they stopped to look the place over. Generous in size, the new board building featured a long bar across one end of the open room with about a dozen tables filling the rest of the space, except for a small area in between, the purpose of which appeared to be a dance floor. There was a piano up against the wall. About half of the tables were occupied. The thing that caught Cody's eye, however, was the woman sitting with four soldiers at the rearmost table. "Don't even think about it," Jug warned. "Let's just get us a drink and be on our way. We've got a long ride home." From experience, Jug knew the workings of his younger brother's mind, and more times than not, it ended with him in a fight. It never seemed to matter if the woman was young and pretty or seasoned with time. As long as she was not sporting gray hair and a toothless grin, she was worthy of Cody's attention.

Cody flashed a mischievous grin in Jug's direction. "Now, brother, you know it doesn't hurt to look. She don't look all that bad from here. I could tell more if she would stand up."

"Well, she's obviously with those soldier boys," Jug said, "so it don't make no difference to you." He took hold of Cody's arm and started him in the direction of the bar. "Let's get us that drink so we can get started back home."

"I swear. You're gettin' more and more like Cullen every day," Cody complained, but offered no resistance to Jug's prodding. The reference was to their older brother, who was four years senior to Jug and had always employed a quiet authority over the younger two. It was never resented or contested by Jug or Cody. It seemed the natural order of their family. In fact, they were both proud of their older brother. Cody's only concern for him was the fact that he seemed too serious at times, and he wished Cullen would find a woman to lighten his somber moods. On occasions like the present, Cody always preferred to partner with Jug. Even though he complained some, he always went along with whatever Cody wanted to do.

"What can I do for you fellers?" Roy, the bartender, asked.

"A couple of shots of whiskey," Cody replied, greeting the bartender with a friendly smile.

"And a couple of them eggs," Jug added, causing Cody to scrunch his face up in disgust. Jug had been eyeing the large jar of pickled eggs ever since he stood in the doorway.

"You're gonna have to eat both of 'em," Cody said, still making a face.

"I figured," Jug replied with a smile.

After another shot of Roy's whiskey, Cody seemed contented, and he turned around to look the room over again. Someone called out something to Roy, and the bartender went down to the end of the room to a door leading to the rooms in the back. When he came back into the room, he was followed by a thin bald man with heavy gray sideburns. Roy returned to the bar while the bald man shuffled wearily toward the piano and sat down. A few minutes later, the tinny sounds of the old piano ricocheted off the wall in a spirited arrangement of an old hymn. None among Roy's clientele was qualified to identify the tune as a religious selection, especially since it was rendered up-tempo, and after a few seconds, one of the soldiers pulled the woman from her chair and led her to the dance floor.

"She ain't half bad," Cody commented as he watched the woman dance with first one, then a second soldier. He was content to be no more than a spectator since Jug had been persistent in reminding him that they should get started toward home. "One more little drink," he said, "and then we'll go."

"If you didn't buy at least one more"—Roy felt obliged to comment—"I was gonna have to charge ol' biggun there for eatin' all my pickled eggs."

Cody laughed and replied, "I'm fixin' to take him

outta here before he starts gnawin' on the corner of the bar."

Roy laughed with him and was about to offer Jug another egg when a startled cry was heard from the woman, causing them to turn to look toward the dance floor again. A third soldier—a husky brute, almost as big as Jug, wearing corporal's stripes on his sleeve—had cut in to dance with her. It was apparent that his idea of dancing was to physically maul the helpless woman. As they watched, she tried to pull away from his unsolicited advances, a sharp tongue, her only defensive weapon. The more she cursed him, the bolder he became until it appeared the corporal was going to have his way with her right there in the saloon.

"Now, that just ain't right," Cody said. "Even a whore don't deserve to be treated like that." He turned to Roy. "What's her name?"

"Mae," the bartender replied, showing little concern for the woman or the table of soldiers.

"All right, then," Cody said and walked toward the arguing couple. "Hello, Mae," he greeted her cheerfully. "I'm sorry I'm late for our appointment, but I'm here now." Addressing the startled corporal then, he said, "Thanks for entertainin' her till I got here, soldier. You can let her go now." He took her hand and pulled her toward him. The surly corporal was too astonished to hold on to her, and she scurried to safety behind Cody by the time his whiskey-soaked brain realized what had just happened. "Enjoy your drinks, boys," Cody called to the corporal's three companions at the table; they obviously didn't know what to make of the intrusion upon their fun and were slow in deciding if there should be any action on their part.

"Your appointment?" the corporal sneered. "What the hell are you talkin' about, you little asshole? The woman's with us, and I'll bust your head for you if you don't get the hell outta here."

Cody shook his head as if perplexed. "There, now see, you had to go and get rowdy about it when it was all just a simple misunderstandin' between the lady and yourself." He glanced at the woman. "Mae, do you want to go with the soldier or come with me?"

"Hell no, I don't wanna go with the son of a bitch," Mae spat in anger as she examined the abrasions left on her wrists by the corporal's rough hands.

Cody looked back at the corporal and shrugged. "Well, there you go. I reckon that clears everythin' up."

"Why, you little bastard," the corporal cursed, his alcohol-impaired brain just then catching up to the realization that he had been bamboozled.

"Sic him, Jarvis," one of the soldiers still seated at the table goaded.

"Jarvis," Cody responded. "Is that your name?" There was no verbal response to the question, but the corporal's eyes looked capable of igniting a fire, as he appeared to brace himself to launch an attack on the brash young man. Ignoring the threat, Cody continued. "Well, Jarvis, let me give you some advice. I know what you're thinkin', and it's the wrong thing. It's only gonna cause you pain you don't need, so why don't you sit down with your friends there and finish that bottle, and forget about Mae until you sober up a little?"

Knowing full well what was about to follow, Jug unstrapped his gun belt and emitting a tired sigh, handed it to Roy to hold, since it was obvious that the soldiers were not armed. "I shoulda known we had no business stoppin' for a drink," he muttered as he sidled up to the end of the bar. "Ma'am," he offered politely to the still-infuriated woman when she moved past him on her way to sanctuary behind the bar.

Back in the center of the tiny dance floor, Corporal Jarvis was sizing up his opponent after a standoff that had been caused by his astonishment with Cody's emotionless approach. With his anger rising once more, he took a threatening step forward, his fists raised in pugilistic fashion, causing another of his companions to exclaim in enthusiastic anticipation of the contest. "You'd better get on your horse and get your ass on outta here, cowboy, 'cause you just picked a fight with the regimental heavyweight-boxing champion!"

"Is that so?" Cody replied while keeping a steady eye on the formidable figure of a man now slowly moving toward him with nothing save mayhem in his gaze. "Well, if this is gonna be a boxin' match, then I guess we need some rules."

"Rules?" Jarvis bleated, dumbfounded and eager to administer the beating he had in mind.

"Yeah, rules," Cody replied, stepping aside to avoid the bull rush launched at that instant. Drawing his Colt .44, he cracked Jarvis squarely across the bridge of his nose with the barrel as the bully lumbered drunkenly by. "Like none of that," he said. The blow sent the larger man reeling clumsily to keep his feet. "And no kickin' in the balls," Cody said as he brought the toe of his boot sharply up between the corporal's legs. Completely helpless, Jarvis bent over in agony. "And no hittin' behind the head," Cody added as he slammed the pistol barrel down solidly on the back of Jarvis' skull. In that brief space of time, the match was over and Jarvis lay out cold on the floor.

It had happened so fast that the corporal's friends were left still seated, staring in stunned disbelief at their champion lying in a heap on the floor. Finally one of them thought to react. Kicking his chair back, he charged over the table only to be met with Jug McCloud's fist, which stopped his head while his legs ran out from under him, causing him to land on his back, out cold. The third soldier, instantly wiser after seeing his friend finished by one blow from a fist that looked the size of an anvil, scrambled around the table and jumped on Jug's back just as Jug aimed a kick at the fourth soldier, who had sense enough to run for the door. Left then with the one soldier clinging to his back like a parasite, Jug twisted left and right in an effort to get a grip on the desperate man. His antics proved highly amusing to his brother, who stood by enjoying the spectacle of Jug bucking like an unbroken mustang while the soldier hung on for dear life, afraid to let go.

Finally Jug grew tired of the contest. "Get him to hell off my back!" he roared.

Roy, who had been a silent spectator to the whole performance, casually handed Cody a broom and Cody began whipping the soldier across the back with it until he finally released his death hold on Jug and dropped to the floor. As soon as he landed, he started scrambling on his hands and knees across the floor and out the door, the sound of Cody's laughter ringing in his ears. "Well, I swear, that was some fight, wasn't it?" Cody exclaimed, grinning at Jug as his brother picked up the table and set the chairs right side up. "That was downright lively." Turning to Roy, he said, "Don't nothin' appear to be broke."

"I reckon not," Roy replied, "but it might be a good idea for you boys to get on your way. Them other two soldiers might be back here with half their company to get those two." He nodded to the two casualties, who were just beginning to show signs of life.

"I expect you're right," Cody said. "I apologize for runnin' off four of your customers."

"Don't matter," Roy said. "They'd done spent all their money anyway. Besides, I might sell some whiskey to their friends when they come back lookin' for you two."

"What about me?" Mae piped up, having been an astonished spectator up to that point. "You mighta cost me money."

"Oh, yeah," Cody said. In the heat of the action, he had forgotten what started the altercation. "How much do you charge?"

"Three dollars for a straight ride without no extras," she replied.

"Fair enough," Cody said and dug into his pocket. "Here's three dollars and a dollar extra."

She looked surprised. "You want it now?"

"I ain't got time now, lady, but I figure I owe you for one. I'll settle for a kiss." He planted one on the startled prostitute and then sang out, "Let's go, Jug, before the whole damn army shows up." He paused a moment while Jug got his gun belt from Roy and then started for the door after his brother.

Outside, they wasted no time. Stepping up in the saddle, they turned their horses toward the trail to Stevensville. "You gonna tell Pa you gave a whore four dollars of that money we got for the horses?" Jug asked.

"Hell no," Cody answered with a chuckle. "I'm gonna tell him you ate four dollars' worth of pickled eggs. He'll believe that."

Charles G. West

**"RARELY HAS AN AUTHOR PAINTED THE
GREAT AMERICAN WEST IN STROKES SO
BOLD, VIVID AND TRUE."
—RALPH COMPTON**

The Blackfoot Trail

Mountain man Joe Fox reluctantly led a group of
settlers through the Rockies—and inadvertently into
the clutches of Max Starbeau. Max had traveled with
the party until he was able to commit theft and
murder—and kidnap Joe's girl.

Also Available
War Cry
Storm in Paradise Valley
Shoot-out at Broken Bow
Lawless Prairie
Luke's Gold

Available wherever books are sold or at
penguin.com

S805

"A writer in the tradition of Louis L'Amour
and Zane Grey!"

—*Huntsville Times*

National Bestselling Author

RALPH COMPTON

**Available wherever books are sold or at
penguin.com**

No other series packs this much heat!

THE TRAILSMAN

Foll **3 1901 05326 2251** ns at